PRAISE FOR LUANN MCLANE'S CRICKET CREEK NOVELS

Moonlight Kiss

"A sweet love story set in the quaint Southern town of Cricket Creek. Reid makes for a sexy hero who could melt any heart." —*Romantic Times*

"Alluring love scenes begin with the simplicity of a kiss in this romantic southern charmer."

—*Publishers Weekly*

"A very charming story, and I would be more than happy to read the entire series." —The Bookish Babe

"McLane nails the charm, quirks, nosiness, friendliness and sense of community you'd experience in a small Southern town as you walk the streets of Cricket Creek . . . engaging and sweet characters whose chemistry you feel right from the start."

—That's What I'm Talking About

Whisper's Edge

"This latest foray to McLane's rural enclave has all the flavor and charm of a small town where everyone knows everyone else and doesn't mind butting in when the need arises. With a secondary romance between members of the slightly older generation, *Whisper's Edge* offers a comforting read where love does "trump" insecurities, grief, and best-laid plans." —*Library Journal*

"Visiting Cricket Creek, Kentucky, feels like coming home once again." —*Romantic Times*

"A charming Southern romance that will keep you amused with its laugh-out-loud humor!"

—Harlequin Junkie

"Cute, funny, and full of romance."

—Love to Read for Fun

"LuAnn McLane has a rich and unique voice that kept me laughing out loud as I read." —Romance Junkies

Pitch Perfect

"McLane packs secrets, sex, and sparks of gentle humor in an inviting picnic basket of Southern charm."

—*Ft. Myers & Southwest Florida*

"A delightful . . . charming tale." —*Romantic Times*

"Entertaining [and] lighthearted."

—Genre Go Round Reviews

continued . . .

Catch of a Lifetime

"I thoroughly enjoyed this amusing tale of baseball fanatics and a quiet little town that everyone falls in love with. The residents are all amusing and interesting . . . pure entertainment!" —Fresh Fiction

"LuAnn McLane has created a delightful small-town romance that just captivates your heart and has you rooting for these charming characters. . . . I thoroughly enjoyed this romance, and I know that readers will want to spend more time with these handsome baseball players."
—Night Owl Reviews

Playing for Keeps

"A fun tale." —*Midwest Book Review*

"Charming, romantic . . . this new series should be a real hit!" —Fresh Fiction

"McLane's trademark devilish dialogue is in fine form for this series." —*Publishers Weekly*

"No one does Southern love like LuAnn McLane!"
—The Romance Dish

Also by LuAnn McLane

Contemporary Romances

"Mistletoe on Main Street"
in *Christmas on Main Street* anthology
Moonlight Kiss: A Cricket Creek Novel
Whisper's Edge: A Cricket Creek Novel
Pitch Perfect: A Cricket Creek Novel
Catch of a Lifetime: A Cricket Creek Novel
Playing for Keeps: A Cricket Creek Novel
He's No Prince Charming
Redneck Cinderella
A Little Less Talk and a Lot More Action
Trick My Truck but Don't Mess with My Heart
Dancing Shoes and Honky-Tonk Blues
Dark Roots and Cowboy Boots

Erotic Romances

"Hot Whisper" *in Wicked Wonderland* anthology
Driven by Desire
Love, Lust, and Pixie Dust
Hot Summer Nights
Wild Ride
Taking Care of Business

Wildflower Wedding

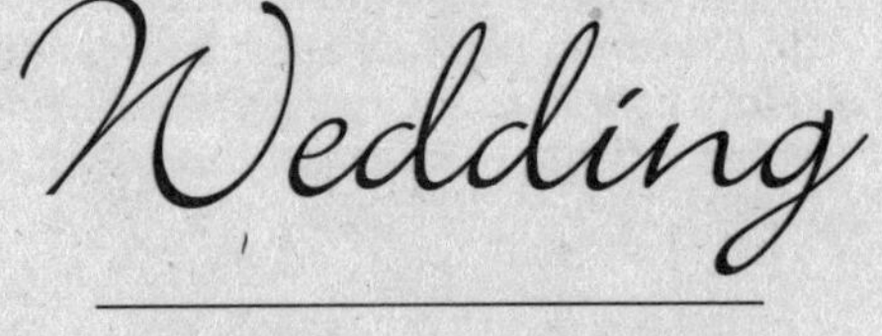

A CRICKET CREEK NOVEL

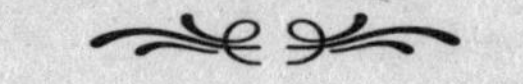

LuAnn McLane

A SIGNET ECLIPSE BOOK

SIGNET ECLIPSE
Published by the Penguin Group
Penguin Group (USA) LLC, 375 Hudson Street,
New York, New York10014

USA | Canada | UK | Ireland | Australia | New Zealand | India | South Africa | China
penguin. com
A Penguin Random House Company

First published by Signet Eclipse, an imprint of New American Library,
a division of Penguin Group (USA) LLC

First Printing, April 2014

ISBN 978-0-451-41559-2

Printed in the United States of America
10 9 8 7 6 5 4 3 2 1

This book is for Stevie
"For Once in My Life"

Acknowledgments

I would like to take this opportunity to thank small-business owners for all of the hard work and the dedication it takes to keep the doors open. I find such joy in strolling down Main Street in a small town, eating at the local diner, trying pastries at the bakery, or shopping in a quaint boutique.

Thank you to the wonderful staff at New American Library. From the gorgeous covers to the detailed copyedits and everything in between, I couldn't ask for a better team in my corner! I want to give a special thanks to my editor, Jesse Feldman. I enjoyed working with you, and I will miss you but wish you the best of luck. A heartfelt thank-you goes to Danielle Perez for making the transition to a new editor seamless. I already love working with you, and I'm looking forward to future Cricket Creek adventures.

As always, thank you so much to my amazing agent, Jenny Bent. We have been working together for over ten years, and I have enjoyed the journey.

Thank you ever so much to my readers. Your support and encouragement mean the world to me and keep my fingers on the keyboard. My wish is to bring a smile to your faces and a happy ending to your hearts.

1

Top Shelf

"JUST WHAT IN THE WORLD WAS I THINKING WHEN I PUT those up there?" Gabby frowned at the neatly stacked spools of ribbon stored up out of her reach. Tapping her cheek, she glanced around her flower shop for her step stool and grinned at the row of garden gnomes staring back at her. "Don't look at me like that. I know I need to be more organized." Gabby walked past potted plants and ducked beneath hanging ferns before pausing to straighten a display of dainty African violets. Sighing, she inhaled a deep breath of floral-scented air, then remembered that she'd taken her step stool upstairs to her apartment. "I need to start carrying the doggone thing around like a backpack," she grumbled. At her five feet three, everything seemed just beyond her reach.

With her hands fisted on her hips, Gabby angled her head at the shelf. Her stomach took the opportunity to growl in protest of missing lunch, but she'd ordered a pepperoni pizza from the new pizza parlor a little while ago, so it should be delivered shortly. She hoped the pizza was good. Cricket Creek was known for some pretty wonderful restaurants but had been sorely lacking in great pizza. Although the dining area of the restaurant wasn't officially open, River Row Pizza had started to offer pickup and delivery on a limited basis. But at this point even so-so pizza would do.

"Maybe I can get it." Biting down on her bottom lip, Gabby stepped forward and reached for the elusive pink ribbon she needed to finish the Get Well Soon flower arrangement she'd been working on for the past half hour. When her middle finger touched the spool, she rose to her tiptoes and stretched forward as far as she could go. Wiggling her fingers, she inched the spool forward until it finally toppled over and bonked her on the head before hitting the floor. "Yes!" Feeling victorious over being vertically challenged, she bent down and picked up the elusive item. "What? Red?"

With a little growl Gabby slapped the red ribbon onto the table and then looked around for something to stand upon. Spotting a wooden crate, she pushed it over beneath the shelf. After putting one foot on the lid, she pressed downward, testing the strength. "Should hold me," Gabby mumbled even though she knew from personal experience those three little words might come back to haunt her, but she decided if she worked fast she'd be okay.

Inhaling a deep breath, Gabby stepped onto the crate. She felt the wooden slats give just a little, so she quickly grabbed the prize, but as she turned to step down the bell dinged over the door, drawing her attention.

Oh my . . .

Gabby's gaze passed over a pizza box and zoomed in on a snug-fitting red T-shirt hugging the contours of a very nice chest. Bulging biceps stretched sleeves that exposed a teasing glimpse of armband tribal tattoos. Her gaze traveled up to a strong jaw shaded by sexy stubble, full lips, a straight nose, and eyes the color of decadent dark chocolate. Nearly black hair fell across Pizza Guy's forehead and brushed the top of his shoulders in a messy but sexy just-out-of-bed way. Hot damn.

"You ordered pizza?"

"Yes." Wait . . . recognition sliced through her ogling. She knew him. "Reese . . . Reese Parker?"

"You guessed right, but I go by Marino now, Mom's maiden name." He grinned slightly and nodded while he walked closer and placed the cardboard box and a white bag onto the counter. "Hi, Gabby. My uncle said you own this place?"

"I . . . I do." Gabby nodded, clutching the ribbon harder.

"Wow." Reese glanced around and his grin widened. "I'm impressed."

"Thank you. Cricket Creek has been growing by leaps and bounds lately. Things are finally looking up."

"I noticed."

Gabby could only manage a nod. Reese had been the hottest guy in high school, oozing edgy, bad-boy danger. Although Gabby and Reese had played together as children, she'd steered clear as a teenager but admired him from afar, a difficult task since they'd grown up in the same trailer park located on the outskirts of town.

"Well, good for you, Gabby."

She cleared her throat, not really ready to explain how she'd come to own the shop. "I ran into your mom up in town a few weeks ago and she said the guy who was opening the pizza parlor was her brother, but she said you were staying in Brooklyn."

"You asked about me?"

"Well . . . of course," Gabby admitted, but felt a bit flustered. She tucked a lock of her short blond hair behind her ear. "So you've moved back?"

Reese nodded. "I had some unfinished business in Brooklyn, but yeah, I'm back." When Reese walked closer her heart did a little tap dance in her chest. "You always did love flowers," he commented with another look around.

Gabby's heart skipped a beat. Really? Reese remembered that about her after all of these years? "Yes," she answered softly, and his gaze came back to land on her face. "It all started with seedlings in milk cartons at school and I was hooked."

He nodded. "Yeah, you helped bring green beans back to life or I would have gotten a big fat F."

Gabby chuckled. "Oh, I remember that now. You overwatered, I think."

"Hey, I'm really sorry about your mother." Reese's dark eyebrows edged closer together and with a tilt of his head he gave her a look of such sympathy that her breath caught.

"How did you know?" Gabby asked, and was a little surprised at his gentle demeanor. The last time she'd seen Reese he was a troubled teenager who was hell-bent on self-destruction.

"My mom told me. Musta been rough." His voice held a hint of Brooklyn, not surprising since he'd been living there for the past eight years.

"Yeah." Gabby swallowed hard. "I sure do miss her."

Reese stepped even closer until he was near enough that she could have reached out and touched him. Because she remained on the box, he had to tilt his head up but just a little bit. "You doin' okay?"

Gabby nodded. "She's been gone over two years. Time heals. Now I can think of Mama and smile instead of cry," she replied, but when she curved her lips to demonstrate, she felt the corners of her mouth tremble. "Most of the time, anyway."

"I remember how much you and your mom loved to garden." Reese shook his head. "I was always amazed how you took that little patch of earth and produced so many flowers and vegetables."

"You remember all that?" Gabby asked, and then felt a blush warm her cheeks.

"I remember a lot about you." Reese gave her a look she couldn't quite read, but it made her pulse continue to race.

"Like what?" Gabby hadn't meant to voice the question, but there it was, hanging between them. She had a habit of blurting things out that she should keep to herself.

"Like how you would sing off-key while pulling weeds."

"I do not sing off-key!" But she had to grin. She still loved to sing or hum while she worked.

"And how you'd always had a streak of dirt on your cheek. Like now."

"I do?" Horrified, she rubbed her cheeks.

"Gotcha." He laughed but then tilted his head. "I'll never forget how you stood up for me," Reese continued but without laughing this time.

Her chin came up. "You were innocent." Her simple statement carried some heat. The Riverbend Trailer Park kids were often blamed for things without any evidence and sometimes called river rats by a few people behind their backs.

"You sure about that?" he asked with a slight twist of his lips, but something flashed in his eyes that told another story.

"You might have been a troublemaker but not a vandal or thief. You didn't steal anything from the concession stand." Gabby shuddered at the memory of Reese being accused and then slammed to the ground by the big old mean sheriff, Bo Mason. She'd been watering plants in the high school greenhouse when she heard the commotion and ran out to see what was going on . . .

"Caught you red-handed, son!" Bo Mason shouted before pressing a knee to Reese's back, so he couldn't get up.

"Doing what?" Reese's voice was muffled from having his face smashed against the concrete.

"Stealing from the concession stand."

"I didn't take anything! Let me up."

"You're a liar and a thief. You ain't goin' nowhere till I git the truth outta ya. Now, where did you stash the cash you stole from the drawer?"

"He didn't do anything!" Gabby shouted as she jogged forward, seeing red when the big sheriff added some weight to his knee planted in the small of Reese's back. "Get off him!"

"And just who are you, missy?"

"I'm Gabby Goodwin. President of the gardening club." She was the only member, but he didn't need to know that. "I was watering tomato plants in the greenhouse and I saw Reese picking up trash in the parking lot. He was nowhere near the concession stand." Gabby pointed in the opposite direction.

"Picking up trash? Ha, Good Samaritan, are ya?" The sheriff looked down at Reese and let out another laugh before looking back at Gabby. "Ya gotta come up with something better to save your boyfriend here."

"Reese had detention," Gabby answered stiffly. "For disrupting class. I know because I was in the classroom when he got in trouble." She tilted her head toward the Dumpster. "Reese just put his plastic bags in there if you want to look."

The sheriff looked unhappy that he was being challenged. "If you didn't take the money, then who did, son?"

"How do I know?" Reese answered, and was rewarded with a harsh tap to his head.

"'Cause of the crowd you run with. Cough up a name."

"I'm going to get Mr. Davenport if you don't let him go right this minute," Gabby said sternly even though her knees were shaking. To her relief the sheriff pushed up to his feet. "You can't harass students like this."

"Yeah, well, I got my eye on you, Reese Parker. Ain't like you haven't been in trouble before," he added before lumbering off toward his cruiser.

"Bo Mason," Gabby muttered at the memory.

"That old coot still the town sheriff?"

"Unfortunately. I don't know who votes for him. It sure isn't me," Gabby assured him hotly. Reese chuckled.

"You were always a quiet little thing until something got you riled up. Then you'd better run and duck for cover."

Gabby shrugged. "My mama taught me to stand up for what you believe in. I believed in your innocence."

Reese dipped his head slightly. "Well, thank you. Not many people did," he said, and then looked as if he wished he hadn't gone down memory lane. But then his cocky grin returned.

"You can come down off your soapbox now." He gestured toward the crate.

"Oh." She wobbled a little bit and was about to step down, but his gaze locked in on her mouth just long enough for Gabby to wonder if he also remembered . . .

The kiss.

The kiss that happened later that same night remained burned into her seventeen-year-old memory, and she unfortunately used her bone-melting response as a measuring stick for all other kisses afterward, all of them coming up short. Maybe it was because she'd fantasized about kissing Reese from the time she'd turned about thirteen. Or perhaps it was because he represented the forbidden bad-boy fruit her mother knew about firsthand and repeatedly warned Gabby against.

Maybe the reaction was something more slid into her brain. She tried to mentally shove the thought away, but it refused to budge. Would kissing Reese feel the same way now that she was beyond teenage hormones and infatuation with the resident leather jacket?

Curiosity coupled with desire had her swallowing hard and the spool of ribbon slipped from her fingers, landing with a thump and rolling away unnoticed by either of them.

As if he'd read her thoughts, Recse's eyes suddenly sparked in silent challenge. Gabby had been one of the few girls who refused to fall at his feet, even after the epic kiss. Well, the sexy bad boy might be back in town, but Gabby was striving hard to make something of herself in the community and she wasn't about to risk her reputation by falling into Reese's arms . . . arms that were suddenly reaching toward her. Oh. Well, maybe just this once . . .

"Can I help up you down?" He angled his head sideways toward the counter. "Your pepperoni with mushrooms and extra cheese is going to get cold."

Great, so she'd been reading Reese all wrong. Wow, he must find her doe-eyed longing quite amusing. With a swift intake of breath, she raised her hands to smack his offer away, but she suddenly heard the sound of splintering wood. When the lid started caving in, Gabby yelped and then lunged at Reese, tipping the box forward. Surprise registered in his eyes, but he caught her.

Gabby flung her arms around Reese's neck, and when he stumbled backward, she went with him, her toes dragging across the floor as if they were suddenly doing a tango dance move. Reese swerved slightly to avoid a colorful display of tulips and then ducked to miss a fat green fern suspended from the ceiling. He clipped a rack of Get Well cards, spinning the display and sending a few fluttering to the floor before it came to a stop between two tall tin pails packed with cheerful sunflowers that seemed to be watching their little dance with amusement.

Reese gave her a lopsided grin. "I always knew you wanted to throw yourself at me."

"I didn't *throw* myself at you!"

Reese raised his eyebrows. "Coulda fooled me."

"I was in . . . peril," she sputtered. Really? Who said peril? Gabby grimaced. "You know, the splintered wood could have . . . hurt me." Okay, probably not since she was wearing jeans.

"Uh-huh." Laughter twinkled in his eyes.

"Let me go!"

"Um, you're the one wrapped around me like kudzu."

"Well, you have your hands on my . . . my *derriere*." Dear God, whose vocabulary was she channeling? Scarlett O'Hara?

"Sorry," Reese said, and although he removed his

hands he didn't appear sorry at all. Instead, his gaze slid to her mouth and for a heart-stopping moment she thought he was going to kiss her. No, she had to be wrong just like before. . . .

Feeling silly, Gabby abruptly released her hands from around his neck. But her traitorous knees felt wobbly and to her horror she did a little backpedal.

"Whoa there." Reese reached out and to her utter surprise scooped her up and after a few long-legged strides deposited her on the counter next to the forgotten pizza box.

"Just what do you think you're doing?" Gabby asked.

"I'm not quite sure. . . ."

Awkward silence followed until the aroma of pepperoni made her stomach rumble.

"How . . . how much do I owe you?"

Reese arched an eyebrow. "For saving you from . . . peril?"

"The pizza," she sputtered.

"It's on the house along with the cannoli . . . and the rescue."

"I didn't order cannoli."

"We're testing desserts. I made it."

"Really?"

"I'm full of surprises," Reese responded dryly. "Be sure to give me some feedback," he added with a crooked smile.

Gabby blinked at him. "Okay, but I don't want you to pay for the pizza, Reese."

His smile faded. "Don't worry about it."

His sudden clipped tone and shuttered expression confused Gabby. She didn't want the cost of her dinner to come out of his pocket. What was so wrong with that? "At least let me give you a tip for the delivery. I mean, I know your uncle owns River Row Pizza, but still . . ."

"Forget about it," Reese insisted. "And listen, I—" he began, but was interrupted by the ding of the bell over the door.

"Drew!" Gabby exclaimed with a warm smile. She scooted forward but then looked at the distance between the floor and her feet, wondering if she could jump without stumbling. Probably not and the status of her legs remained iffy. As if reading her mind, Reese stepped forward and put his hands around her waist, lifting her down as if she weighed next to nothing. When Drew frowned Gabby took a step back, putting much needed distance between her and Reese. "What brings you here?" She tugged at her shirt and smoothed her hair.

"I thought I'd come over and wine and dine you with the hope of enticing you to join the Cricket Creek Beautification Committee. We could use your expertise."

Gabby gestured toward the pizza box. "Oh, I've already ordered dinner."

Drew flicked a glance at the box and shrugged his suit-clad shoulders. "I can do better than pizza. Shove that in the fridge and I'll take you out for real food."

Feeling heat creep into her cheeks at Drew's rather rude comment, she looked over at Reese.

A muscle jumped in his jaw. "I need to go," Reese said. "See you around, Gabby. We should get together and catch up."

"Oh . . . uh, sure."

"You two know each other?" Drew asked.

"Yes, we were childhood . . . *friends*. I'm sorry. I should have introduced you. Drew, this is Reese Parker, I mean Marino. His uncle owns River Row Pizza and Pasta. Reese, Drew Gibbons."

"Mayor of Cricket Creek," Drew announced as he extended his hand.

"Pizza delivery guy," Reese responded with a twist of his lips.

"And maker of cannoli," Gabby added, and lifted the white bag.

"Yeah, can't forget that," Reese said airily, and gave them a little salute. "See you around. Uh, nice to meet you, Mr. Mayor," he said, and then walked out the door.

"So, how about that dinner?"

"Oh!" Gabby hadn't realized she was staring after Reese until Drew spoke up. She'd unintentionally hurt Reese's feelings and she felt the sudden urge to run after him and make whatever she did right. "Drew, I'm sorry but I'm really very busy." She gestured toward her jeans. "And not really dressed for going out."

Drew nodded slowly and then rubbed his clean-shaven chin. Everything about him was neatly groomed and tidy. He wore the dark blue suit well and his shoes were polished to a spit shine. Not one hair on his sandy blond head was out of place. "Well, I could go get a bottle of wine if you don't mind sharing the pizza?" He gave Gabby a pleading smile and took a step closer. The handsome young mayor reigned as Cricket Creek's most eligible bachelor, and even though he was a few years older than her, Gabby had been hoping for him to ask her out. Now that the moment had finally arrived, she was trying to think up a reason to turn him down.

Stupid girl! She smiled back at Drew. "No need. I have a bottle of Chianti upstairs. We can eat at the bistro table in front of the shop if you don't mind?"

"No, I enjoy dining alfresco," he replied.

"Wonderful. I'll run upstairs and get plates and glasses."

"Sounds good but I hope you'll agree to dinner out with me later in the week?"

Gabby smiled. "I'd like that very much. I'll be back in a minute." But as she walked up the steps leading to her loft apartment, she wondered why she wasn't walking on air. She'd been hoping to catch Drew's eye for quite some time. He was everything she wanted in a man and then some. Of course she knew the reason: sexy-as-sin Reese Marino. But the advice of her mother echoed in her head: *"Gabby, honey, don't fall for a sweet-talkin' man like I did. They'll love ya and then leave ya pickin' up the pieces of your broken heart. Find Mr. Strong and Steady. Choose wisely so I know you'll be cherished without me here. Promise me, will you, Gabby?"*

Gabby had made a promise and she intended to keep it. At twenty-nine years old, Drew Gibbons was not only mayor of Cricket Creek but a CPA with his own small but successful accounting firm. Reese, on the other hand, delivered pizza for his uncle. Who knew how long he intended to stay in Cricket Creek, anyway? Enough said.

But then her traitorous brain had to slide back to the memory of being in his arms. And she remembered the compassion in his eyes and the sympathy he expressed about her mother's death. "Stop!" Gabby growled, and then pulled the step stool over to reach the wineglasses on the top shelf. Just like back in high school, Reese needed to remain off-limits. It was just that simple.

Wasn't it?

Besides, maybe a kiss from Drew would cause a heart-pounding, knee-popping reaction, right? Surely it would. Hopefully she'd find out.

2

Sweet Fantasy

Reese stormed into River Row Pizza and pushed through the double doors leading into the kitchen. He made a beeline for the Sub-Zero fridge and snagged a bottle of Budweiser. After a quick twist he tossed the cap into the trash with much more force than necessary and then took a long pull on the beer.

His uncle looked up from where he was stirring a big pot of fragrant sauce. "Whoa there, hoss. Who shoved a burr up your butt? Surely not that cute little flower shop owner you've been daydreamin' about ever since she called in her order."

"I haven't been daydreaming about Gabby." Reese took another swallow of beer. "I don't *daydream,* damn it." His language didn't faze his uncle, who was part father figure but more like an older brother. In fact, with their dark Italian looks and similar build they were often mistaken for siblings. It wasn't until after Uncle Tony's divorce that threads of silver started showing up in his hair.

"Fantasize?"

Reese shot his uncle a glare.

"Hey, man, I was just messin' with ya." Uncle Tony pulled the checkered dish towel from his shoulder and wiped his hands before coming around to lean his hips against a long stainless steel table. Angling his head toward the fridge, he said, "Grab me a beer and let's talk about what's eatin' you."

Reese handed his uncle a bottle. "I'm sorry I was being such a dick."

"Ah, don't worry 'bout it." He gave him a wave of his hand and then tipped back his bottle. "Now, talk ta me," Uncle Tony urged in his typical Brooklyn no-nonsense get-to-the-point way.

Reese lifted one shoulder. "I dunno. I've always had a thing for Gabby and she's always blown me off, at least when we were teenagers. I mean, I get it. Well, I used to get it. I was trouble and she liked to stay out of it. Never got caught drinkin' or smokin', got good grades, you know, the whole nine yards."

"Reese, you turned that corner a long time ago." Uncle Tony swung his arm in an arc. "Does she know you're part owner? Graduated from college with honors?"

"She thinks I'm a pizza delivery dude. Not that there's anything wrong with that."

Tony's eyebrows shot up. "And you didn't set her straight?"

Reese finished the beer and tossed the bottle in the trash. It landed with a *thunk*. "I tried but this douche bag came walking into the flower shop. He's the damn mayor or some such shit and Gabby was falling all over herself trying to impress him."

"Drew Gibbons?"

Reese grabbed another beer from the fridge. "Yeah, him. He wants her on some committee or something. Wanted to take her to some fancy-ass dinner. Thumbed his nose at the pizza."

Tony snorted.

"What? You know him?"

"I know of him."

"Go on."

"Well, apparently there's been a lot of new development in Cricket Creek over the years."

"Damn, tell me about it."

"I've seen even more since I've been here getting the pizza parlor ready for business. Anyway, so . . . back to Drew. I had to go to council meetings to get approval for different stuff, and of course as mayor Drew presided over the boring-ass meetings. Restaurant Row where we're at is the second phase of this shopping mall. The first was Wedding Row where Gabby's Flower Power, the jewelry store, the bridal and tux shop, the bakery, and all of that stuff is located. The recent addition of River Row Pizza and Pasta is just the beginning of phase two." He held up two fingers to demonstrate. "Several other restaurants are slated to open in the next year or so, including a microbrewery and Sully's South, a smaller version of his original honky-tonk bar that will showcase singer-songwriters."

Reese shook his head. "I never would have guessed that this little town would grow so much in the time I was gone. Damn, that baseball stadium sure got things going. Pretty cool that Noah Falcon came back here."

"You got that right. According to your mom, Noah Falcon pretty much saved this town from going under. And now they have that new recording studio down by the river."

"So, go on about Drew the douche."

"Let's just say he likes to take credit where credit *isn't* due. He puts it out there that as mayor he's responsible for a lot of the recent development. Not true. A guy named Mitch Monroe put this mall together. Whisper's Edge, an old retirement community down along the river, is growing like wildfire, but that's because it was bought by Tristan McMillan, a lawyer from Cincinnati."

"Isn't that the guy who bought the trailer park too? Mom was telling me some of this over dinner last night."

"He did. He and his mother are turning it into an affordable subdivision with starter homes. Her real estate office is on the corner. Maggie's a nice lady. She found me the two-family I'm renting down by the river. And get a load of this. Maggie is married to rocker Rick Ruleman. He's the one who built a recording studio not far from where I'm living."

"Seriously?" Reese shook his head. "This little town woke its sleepy ass up big-time." Hc grinned. "Maybe coming back here isn't going to be as boring as I thought."

"But none of the progress is due to Drew. I'm just sayin'. The dude isn't nearly as important as he thinks he is. So, what are you gonna do about it?"

"About what?"

"Him coming on to Gabby."

"Not my business."

"Reese, let Gabby know you're legit."

"Uncle Tony, I'm not what she's lookin' for."

"You just got here a couple days ago. You don't know that."

Reese rolled his head to his shoulders, trying to get rid of the tension. "I represent where she came from, not where she's going. Besides, would ya take a look at me? Tats. A motorcycle. Long-ass hair. I'm the opposite of Drew the dipshit."

"That's a good thing."

"Look, Gabby Goodwin will always think of me as the troublemaker from the trailer park."

"Then change her mind."

Reese shrugged.

"Hey, don't be givin' me that shrug. You used to do that shit when you first came to live with me, remember? Actin' like you don't give a rat's ass when you really do."

"You gonna bust my chops all day?"

"And all night if that's what it takes." He reached over and gave Reese's shoulder a shove. "You still got a thing for this girl?"

"Yeah. I mean, I guess."

"Then go after her. There isn't anybody better than you."

"I'll second that," said Reese's mother as she pushed through the double doors and breezed into the kitchen. "Wow, something sure smells amazing. Tony, what is it?"

"I've been tinkering with the sauce. Tessa, go over and give it a taste."

Tessa dipped a spoon into big pot. "Mmmm." She nodded and licked her lips. "That's some good marinara." She looked at Reese. "I hoped you saved me a cannoli."

"Of course, Mom. I used the old family recipe from Sicily that Uncle Tony found."

"Excellent. By the way, have you seen Gabby yet?"

"Why does everybody care about me seeing Gabby Goodwin?" Reese flicked Uncle Tony a glance. "I delivered a pizza to her."

"She's still cute as a button, isn't she?"

More like sexy as hell. "Yeah."

"You gonna ask her out?"

"Mom! Jeez . . ."

"It was just a question."

"I think she's dating that mayor dude," Reese replied. He waved a hand through the air as if he didn't care.

"No, she's not."

"Mom, how do you know this?"

She tucked a lock of dark curly hair behind her ear. "This is a small town. Trust me, they're not dating."

"Well, he's eating dinner with her right now." Reese couldn't keep from scowling. "So I think that's about to change."

"Beat him to the punch," his mother suggested. "You always were sweet on Gabby."

Reese shook his head. "The two of you need to butt out of my love life."

"Not gonna happen," his mother and uncle responded together.

Reese had to laugh. "Well, at least give me a chance to unpack my suitcases." He loved them both—even if they couldn't keep their noses out of his business.

"Tony, you should go on home and let Digger out,"

Tessa suggested. "You've got circles under your eyes. Get some rest. Reese and I can handle any deliveries that come our way. We'll close up the kitchen and store the sauce."

"Thanks, Tessa. I think I'll take you up on that. I could use a jog and Digger really needs some exercise. I feel rotten that he's been cooped up day after day. Irish setters need to run."

"Then get outta here," Reese insisted. "Mom and I got it covered. Seriously."

"All right already. Feels like you wanna get rid of me. I might develop a complex or somethin'."

"Yeah, right." Reese shook his head.

"Hey, Tessa, the menus arrived. Proofread them and let me know what you think."

"Will do."

"And—"

"Tony! For heaven's sake. Go!" She shooed him with her hands.

Reese laughed when his uncle continued to shout instructions to them as he walked out the door. A minute later a text message came for them to think of a tag line for ads. "He never stops," Reese said with a shake of his head.

"I sure hope this restaurant is a success," his mother said while she stirred the sauce and then turned the flame down. "I knew it was a bit of a gamble telling him to come here, but I also knew he needed to get out of Brooklyn and away from what Gloria did to him."

Reese started slicing some mushrooms. "Mom, closing the Brooklyn pizza shop really tore Uncle Tony up. Losing the family business because you have to hand half of it over to a woman who cheated on you? Yeah, he needed a fresh start."

She smiled. "Well, despite the circumstances I'm glad to have both of you in Cricket Creek. I sure did miss you, Reese. Sending you to Brooklyn to live with Tony was the hardest thing I've ever had to do. I hope you know that."

Reese paused in his slicing. "You might have mentioned it a time or . . . twenty. Mom, I was hell on wheels and heading down the wrong path fast. I didn't like it at the time, but trust me, you did the right thing."

"It's hard not to act out when your father up and leaves you. Rebellion was your way of dealing. Depression was mine. I'm so sorry I was in that dark place, Reese. After he left I should have been there for you."

"Have you filed for divorce?" Reese hated to ask, but his mother needed to find closure and move on with her life.

"No." She concentrated on the sauce as if it had the answers to the universe.

"You can get one based on abandonment. All you have to do is post a notice in the paper and make a reasonable effort to find him, Mom." Reese had done the research. "Come on, we don't even go by Parker anymore. Take that last step."

"That's just it. I'm not so certain I want to find him." She stirred the sauce slowly and then tapped the big spoon against the edge.

"If you ask me, he should have to explain why he left," Reese muttered, but when his mother swallowed hard he decided it was time to drop the subject.

"You're right. Maybe someday I'll muster up the courage to file the petition. For right now I just want to enjoy having you back home." She swiped at a tear and then patted her chest. "Ah, but it made my heart hurt every single day you were gone."

"I shouldn't have put you through all the crap I did back in high school. You needed me to man up instead of adding to your problems. I hope I can make it up to you."

She smiled. "You can."

"How?"

"Grandbabies!" She raised her hands skyward.

"What?" Reese tossed his head back and laughed. "I'm only twenty-six and I need a little thing called a girlfriend to get that whole ball rolling."

"I'm sure you'll find one." She angled her head in the direction of Flower Power.

Reese tossed the mushrooms into a plastic container and sealed the lid. "Like I told Uncle Tony, Gabby will always think of me as trouble, and if you remember she avoided trouble at all costs."

"You're an accomplished young man with a lot to offer. You're not that kid anymore."

"I think in her eyes, I am. And you have to admit that I stick out among all the country boys in Cricket Creek."

"It's pretty simple really. Show her the man you've become."

"I've got nothing to prove," Reese answered firmly. "Those days are done."

"Believe me, I understand." She waved her hand in the air. "Forget about it," she said, and then laughed. "Ohmigosh, I'm starting to sound like Tony and I haven't lived in Brooklyn in years."

Reese grinned back at her. "A Brooklyn accent laced with a Southern drawl. Gotta love it. But hey, let's drop the subject for now too. I just moved back. I've got plenty of time for a love life after we get this restaurant up and running."

"Deal," she said, but there was a slight twinkle in her eye that told a different story.

They talked shop and shared coffee and a cannoli that his mother raved about, but in the back of his mind Reese couldn't forget about Gabby. Plus, it really ticked him off that she assumed he was just a pizza delivery guy barely worthy of an introduction. He was looking forward to seeing her reaction when she found out otherwise.

Reese sighed. The tattoos, the shaggy long hair, the stubble on his face along with his sleek black motorcycle weren't props but an honest representation of finally being comfortable in his own skin. Tony taught him to be proud of his background and where he came from all the way back to his Italian roots. Being a river rat had been tough, no doubt, but he'd survived and was stronger for it. Reese no longer cared what people thought of him, so why did Gabby's dismissal of him hurt so damned much?

Reese knew the reason. Good girl Gabby'd been the one he'd always wanted but never really went after. Except for once.

Reese sighed when he remembered. . . .

"Hey, can I give you a ride?" Reese asked when he spotted Gabby walking out of the side door of Cricket Creek High School. He grinned when she looked over her shoulder as if he must be asking someone else.

"Oh, um, I'm . . . fine. Thanks. I enjoy the walk," she insisted, but she shifted her backpack as if it were too heavy to carry. The damned thing was almost as big as she was.

"Sure you do." Reese walked around her. "Gimme that thing."

"What thing?"

"That monster on your back." Reese grabbed the straps and tugged it off her shoulders. "What in the world do you have in here? Bricks?"

"Books, Reese. We have finals coming up." When Gabby looked at him her long ponytail slipped over her shoulder. He used to tug it when they were little kids, but right now he had the urge to simply reach over and touch it to see if it was as soft as it looked. She gave his truck a wary glance.

"It runs," Reese assured her before opening the door and hefting her backpack inside. "Get in, Gabby. It looks like it's gonna rain."

The rumble of thunder had her nodding. "Okay."

Reese grinned when she had trouble hoisting herself

up onto the seat, but he knew she would freak out if he helped and so he let her deal with it while he walked over to the driver's side. Just after Reese slid behind the wheel, it started pouring, but he was secretly glad because it meant having to go slow and spend more time with Gabby. She seemed nervous, toying with the strap of her backpack.

"So, are you going to the prom?" he asked casually, not even sure why.

She flicked him a glance. "No."

"Why not?"

"I don't have a date." She lifted one shoulder slightly as if it didn't matter, but Reese could tell that it did. He wasn't much on crap like the lame-ass dances, especially the prom, even though his mother had been bugging him about going. But he'd sure bet Gabby would look pretty in a prom dress. . . .

"Go with me," Reese found himself saying. His heart pounded while he waited for her answer.

"Right, me go to the prom with . . . you?" She sounded almost angry, but her eyes were filled with an emotion that Reese didn't understand.

"That's the idea."

"Right," she scoffed, and then shook her head.

Confused and with an emotion bordering on hurt, Reese turned his concentration back to the pouring rain and drove fast enough to have her holding on to the armrest.

Reese inhaled deeply, shaking off the memory. His mother was right. He wasn't that troubled kid any longer, but would Gabby ever truly believe that? Reese had his doubts. Besides, he was back in Cricket Creek to help his uncle make a success of River Row Pizza and to live near his mother. He really didn't need to be thinking about getting involved with someone right now. But when the image of Gabby smiling at Drew slid into his brain, Reese inhaled a sharp breath. He didn't like the guy and he told himself it was just his protective feelings for her surfacing, but deep down he sure as hell knew better. He was jealous.

But the question was: What was he going to do about it?

3

A Little Bit Stronger

TRISH DANIELS PEEKED THROUGH THE RUFFLED CURtains of her kitchen window until Anthony Marino and his dog, Digger, jogged down the road and out of sight. "Oh my . . . my. The man has a butt you could bounce quarters off of," she observed with a sense of wonder. She fanned her face and then inhaled a deep breath. If she timed it right, she'd get to witness his shirtless return from his run down the path through the nearby woods that led to the county park she'd recently discovered. She was a walker, not a jogger, but she suddenly wondered if she shouldn't step up her game.

"Thank you, superhot neighbor," she whispered. Watching her dark-haired, deliciously muscled tenant reignited her pilot light of lust that had been extinguished the moment she caught her now ex-husband banging the front desk receptionist for Daniel's Cadillac. Trish had burst through the door of Steve's office unannounced, mainly because the receptionist was, um, busy. She'd been happily armed with the exciting news that she'd been hired as a food critic for *Cincinnati Fun and Food Magazine*. And, *well*, there they were . . . on top of Steve's desk going to town. You would have thought one of them would have the sense to lock the door.

Steve had begged Trish for forgiveness, blaming Heather Hooter (yes, that was her name) for seducing him and saying he'd caved in a moment of weakness—all while assuring her that it would never happen again. "Ha!" Trish tipped the lemon wedge into her sweet tea and then snorted at the memory. Sure, Heather must have found middle-aged Steve so simply irresistible that she threw her twenty-five-year-old self at him. Her so-called seduction had nothing to do with the fact that Steve owned a car dealership, the voice inside Trish's head railed in a sarcastic tone. No, nothing at all.

Digging deep into a reserve of forgiveness that Steve had managed to deplete over twenty years of marriage, Trish lasted another six months until a repeat performance had her filing for divorce. When Steve realized that no amount of groveling would win her back, he turned mean, telling her she'd pushed him into Heather Hooter's arms because she'd let herself go. Sadly, Trish believed him until her friend Maggie McMillan talked some sense into her.

"That's ridiculous," Maggie had said. "Don't believe a word of it! Trish, I hate to say it but could it be that Steve wanted to hold on to your marriage so he wouldn't have to hand over half of everything, specifically half of the dealership?"

"Probably. I just loathe tossing in the towel after investing twenty years of my life," Trish had tearfully responded. "It sucks so badly."

"I get that." Maggie had given her a long look filled with sympathy but support. "I can't tell you how to live your life or what to do. Only you know what's best." She'd held up her index finger. "But I can tell you this much. After my scare with breast cancer I decided to live life to the fullest and not look back." Placing her hands on the table, she'd said, "Screw looking back, Trish. Do what you want but don't be afraid to move on."

"Oh, Maggie, here I am, whining, when you've gone through so much more than me."

"Trish, I'm not trying to guilt-trip you. But I do know that no matter what you're facing, life is all about attitude." Maggie had lifted one shoulder. "If I were you, I'd let Steve and his little hussy have the house. You should take the two-family I sold you in Cricket Creek. I'm going to move there and help Tristan develop Whisper's Edge, the lovely little retirement community he bought from my not so nice father."

"I love that sweet little town, but what would I do?"

"Write!"

At Maggie's suggestion Trish felt a little flag of freedom waving within her reach. She had a degree in journalism, but Steve had never supported her writing career. Looking back, Trish realized it was all about control. *And I let him control me,* she thought, all the way down to taming her natural blond curls into a sleek, flat-ironed chin-length bob and wearing classic but boring clothing.

"Those days are done!"

With a lift of her chin she swept her longer, shoulder-length highlighted curls out of her eyes and padded barefoot over to the fridge to refresh her sweet tea. She'd been to Violet's Vintage Clothing up on Main Street a few days ago and bought flowing bohemian skirts, peasant blouses, and several pairs of jeans. Oh how she loved jeans rather than the khaki slacks that Steve preferred her to wear. Tomorrow she planned to shop at Designs by Diamante, a local jewelry shop that Maggie said had gorgeous chunky bracelets and beaded necklaces. It had taken some time, but she was finally rediscovering her personal style. And it felt so damned good.

But then Trish looked down at the amber liquid in her glass, absently thinking she needed more ice. Lost in thought, she frowned, tried to focus on her glorious newfound freedom, but her mind took her to a place she didn't want to go, opening a door she wanted to slam shut forever.

Why had she been so stupid? Wasted *twenty years* of the prime of her life with a man who didn't give a shit? From countless hours of pondering the question, Trish knew the answer remained complicated. Her marriage had been like a tire with a small leak, deflating slowly, showing signs but ignored until it was totally flat. Hope and determination trumped the sad truth until Trish was finally smacked in the face with a sharp shot of reality: her husband was a lying, cheating, mean jackass.

When hot moisture filled her throat, Trish doused it with a gulp of cold tea, refusing to shed another tear related to that poor excuse of a man. She placed the glass down and inhaled a deep, shaky breath. The divorce had taken the better part of a year since Steve fought her every step of the way, acting as if everything belonged to him because he was the big-ass breadwinner who never allowed her to pursue a career.

Or have a child.

Trish put her hand on her stomach and felt a hollow ache of longing. She'd wanted children, but Steve always asked to put it off and then suddenly it was too late. When she'd learned that Heather the hussy was pregnant, depression hit Trish like a sledgehammer, and for the first time in her life she'd felt the destructive stirrings of rage. She remembered going over to the house to get the last of her possessions and maybe break a few things in the process. Heather had been standing in the front yard watering the lush flower bed Trish had nurtured and grown over the years. She'd felt like grabbing the hose and dousing Heather with water until she cried uncle, but when Heather turned around, revealing the big baby bump, something shifted in Trish's brain. There was a child involved. An innocent child. Whether Heather trapped Steve or the pregnancy had been an accident, the result was the same. The child deserved the best that life had to offer, and in that moment Trish decided to stop fighting and sign the divorce papers. She'd gotten royally screwed, but she didn't care.

All she wanted to be was . . . *done.*

Gripping the edge of the counter, she said, "Don't you dare give that despicable excuse of a human being the power to continue to hurt you. Those days are over." She pushed back from the counter and mentally picked herself up and brushed herself off. Trish knew it was going to be a process, but little by little, step by step, she was reclaiming the free-spirited, creative woman who had become a mere shell of her former self.

So Trish settled for a lump sum and their two-family rental home, took Maggie's advice, and relocated to Cricket Creek, Kentucky, where life moved a little bit slower. As long as she lived conservatively and made a little money, she'd be fine.

Although her life hadn't gone in the direction she'd expected, the exhilarating rush of freedom from an overbearing jerk was well worth the occasional bouts of loneliness. A table for one really sucked sometimes, but it was a helluva lot better than sharing it with someone who simply didn't care. Plus, she had Maggie, who was a shining example of how you didn't have to become boring at midlife but could actually get better. Her friend was not only busy with her real estate projects but also married to a famous rock star. Sweet Maggie and a rock and roll legend! Life was just crazy. "Why can't something really cool like that happen to me?" she wondered aloud, then shrugged. Hey, who knows, maybe it would? It certainly could.

When she heard Digger's deep bark, she rushed over to the window feeling like a giddy schoolgirl, but hey, she needed to take what she could get. She should really do the adult thing and introduce herself, but as Anthony jogged closer she could see the trickle of sweat sliding down his tanned chest. Oh boy, he had a nice covering of dark hair leading to an enticing line pointing south.

Trish heard a groan and realized the sound had come from her throat. How long had it been since she'd experienced a long, hot kiss? Would she feel the strong arms of a man wrapped around her ever again? "I need to get my groove back," she said firmly.

Anthony paused at the edge of the patio leading to his rear door, and with his back to Trish he doubled over with his hands on his knees, giving her a very nice view of his very fine butt. She angled her head, admiring the view. She'd bet the farm that sexy Anthony would be a tiger in the sack. After a moment he picked up a tennis ball and tossed it in the air for a very happy Digger.

"This is silly," Trish mumbled. She was not only his neighbor but his landlord and she really should just open the door, march out there, and introduce herself. She couldn't locate his lease, so all she knew was the name he signed on the rent checks. Steve had initially rented it through Maggie's real estate company, so perhaps Maggie could give her a copy of the lease. She made a mental note to ask her friend. She certainly wasn't about to interact with her ex-husband and ask him for them.

Trish took a deep breath and squared her shoulders. She fluffed her hair and actually had her hand on the doorknob when her phone rang. Telling herself the call could be important, she hurried over to answer. Damn, meeting her hot neighbor would have to wait.

Looking at the caller ID, Trish smiled. "Hi, Maggie. What's up?"

"I've got a job for you!"

Trish gripped the phone tighter. Maggie had been pushing her to follow her dreams, but could she really have found her a writing job? "Really? What?"

"Well, our local newspaper, the *Cricket Creek Courier*, had fallen on hard times and was about to fold, but Clyde and Clovis Camden, twin brothers who live in Whisper's Edge, bought it! A few of the Whisper's Edge residents are going to help staff the paper, but they're in need of a reporter for the Life and Travel section, so I suggested you."

"Oh, that's wonderful, Maggie. Thanks so much."

"I'll e-mail you where to send your résumé, but I'm

pretty certain you'll get the job. If you want it. I know it won't pay much, but it should be fun and perhaps lead to some other freelance work."

"Oh, I'll get right on it. I'm thrilled!" After ending the call she did a little jig. Sure, the *Cricket Creek Courier* was a small press in a small town, but Trish didn't care. She wanted the job. With determination, she maneuvered her way past boxes that still needed unpacking to her small office where she had set up her computer and printer. This could be the fresh start, the new beginning she desperately needed to turn her life around and find some much deserved joy.

"Who needs a man, right?" she mumbled, but her traitorous thoughts immediately conjured up a vision of her superhot, shirtless neighbor. Trish fanned her face and then grinned. "Apparently, I do." She'd forgotten to ask Maggie for his lease papers, but she wasn't going to call back and bother her busy friend. Knowing that getting involved with her sexy neighbor wouldn't be the smartest move, she tried to conjure up a visual of . . . somebody, *anybody* other than him. Brad Pitt? George Clooney? Oh, how about bad boy Colin Farrell? *Come on, guys, help a girl out.*

Damn, it didn't work.

4

Rise and Shine!

DIGGER DROPPED THE TENNIS BALL AT TONY'S FEET AND sat back on his haunches. "Do you ever get tired?" Tony asked. Digger answered by giving the yellow ball a nudge with his nose. Tony chuckled at his panting dog, whose tongue lolled out the side of his mouth. Exhausted, Digger still begged for more. When Tony turned and headed toward the back patio, Digger barked a protest.

"Come on, Dig, I'll get you a *treat*," Tony promised, knowing Digger would follow at his heels. They could both use a big drink of cold water. Tony glanced up at the kitchen window of his neighbor. He thought he'd seen the curtains flutter earlier, indicating she'd been looking out. Her red Cadillac SRX Crossover sat in the apron in front of the detached garage, so he knew she must be home and it was about time he introduced himself to his neighbor who was also his landlord. Reaching up, he swiped at some sweat with his forearm. First, he needed a shower.

When Tony opened the back door, Digger bounded past him and then danced in a circle in front of the glass jar holding doggie treats shaped like bacon. Tony tossed Digger one and then added an extra, feeling terrible that he'd been neglecting his trusty companion who had been by his side ever since he found him half-starved and digging in the Dumpster in the alley behind Marino Pizza. Gloria had protested keeping the sorry-looking dog, but all it took was one look into Digger's soulful eyes and Tony'd been a goner. When he'd first considered the apartment, the lease had said no pets. Tony was going to look elsewhere, but Maggie McMillan apparently knew his landlady and he was relieved when she agreed to allow him to keep his dog.

Tony filled Digger's big water dish and then pulled a sports drink from the fridge, downing the blue liquid so fast that his head hurt. When Digger looked up at him with adoring eyes, Tony reached down and scratched behind his ears. Digger had remained a calming factor in Tony's chaotic year from hell. And thank God for Reese, who had been a voice of reason when anger at Gloria threatened to consume Tony.

"Dude, she fucked you over, but don't let her ruin your life," Reese had said.

"Easier said than done," Tony mumbled, and then shoved his fingers through his damp hair. He'd waited until his midthirties until getting married, wanting to be sure before taking the plunge. Too many of his friends had gone through tough divorces and he didn't want to join those ranks. In the beginning, his marriage had been everything he'd dreamed of and then some. Gloria was passionate and loving until the recession hit. When she could no longer spend money freely and when Tony had to devote most of his time trying to save Marino Pizza, she became sullen. Bitchy.

Unfaithful.

Ten years of marriage with only half of them being happy cost Tony a business that had been in his family for nearly fifty years. He'd been too blinded by his adoration and so sure of their love that he hadn't even considered a prenup. What a dumb-ass he'd been.

"Ah, don't go there," Tony growled, drawing Digger's attention. He did that little dog eyebrow questioningly thing, making Tony laugh. He really needed to thank his landlady, but first he needed a shower. Digger followed Tony up the stairs to the master bedroom. Being furnished was one of the other draws of the two-family house. Until Tony had signed a year lease, the two-bedroom unit could be rented on a weekly or monthly basis as a vacation getaway because of the close proximity to the river. Fishing and boating were supposed to be pretty good at this wide section of the Ohio River—not that Tony would get the chance to find out anytime soon.

The hot water sluicing down his tired body felt heavenly. Tony had started running when Reese suggested exercise would help clear his head and strengthen his body. Reese was right. Tony suddenly found himself in the best shape he'd been in since he could remember. With a groan of pleasure Tony lathered up and took a leisurely shower instead of the quick in-and-out he usually performed each morning. Twisting the showerhead to massage mode, he turned and braced his hands against the smooth tile, allowing the thick shots of water to pelt his neck and back. He would have stayed in the spacious stall longer, but a cold beer was calling his name followed by flopping on the couch to watch a baseball game or an action flick. Oh, and greeting his landlord.

After toweling dry he had to chuckle when he found Digger sleeping in the big bed. He didn't have the heart to wake him with a scolding for getting up on the mattress, something Tony only allowed when invited. Damn, the bed looked inviting. Maybe he'd stretch out for a quick nap. Yeah, he'd just take a fifteen-minute quickie, getting just enough rest to enjoy the lazy evening he had planned.

* * *

The sound of an engine rumbling followed by the hiss of brakes interrupted Tony's slumber. He rolled to his side, opened his eyes, and blinked at the digital clock on the nightstand. "Seven o'clock? In the morning?" He sat up and shoved his fingers through his hair, waking Digger.

"How the hell did that happen?" When he heard the sound of a thump followed by a female yelp, he hurried over to the window. "Holy shit . . . ," Tony said. Digger joined Tony, putting his paws up on the windowsill. They watched neighbor Trish drag a big trash can with one hand while she attempted to hurry down the gravel path leading to the front road where a garbage truck stopped. She waved her free hand as if asking them to wait. They did and Tony couldn't blame them.

Trish wore a red silky robe that hit midthigh, and if Tony wasn't mistaken there wasn't much underneath. The plastic wheels on the trash can didn't take well to the gravel and bumped along, swinging wildly sideways a couple of times when hitting a larger rock. She must have hit something sharp, because she yelped again, paused slightly, and then soldiered on until she reached the end of the driveway. The city worker made quick work of dumping her trash into the truck, but when Trish turned away and started back up the gravel drive at a slower pace, Tony didn't like when the truck failed to move on down the road. He knew why. They were doing what he was doing . . . enjoying the view.

Just when Tony considered yelling something out the window, the truck rumbled on down the road. Trish decided to move from the gravel to the grass and pulled the empty can behind her. Tony decided that he should be a gentleman and stop watching her in the sexy red robe, but just when he was going to turn away from the window, the lid from the can blew off. She gave her leg an angry smack and chased it. He chuckled but then swallowed hard when she bent over, revealing a quick glimpse of red panties.

But he suddenly remembered he was naked and standing in full view at the window. "Damn it!" He quickly stepped back and his mood shifted from amusement to agitation with Trish's reminder that it had been a long-ass time since he'd felt his blood stir at the sight of a woman. Tony turned away sternly, reminding himself that he needed to concentrate on his restaurant not only for his sake but for Reese's and Tessa's sake as well. Any kind of romantic entanglement would just get in the way of his goal, and he seriously doubted that his gorgeous neighbor would want a one-night stand.

Digger gave him that I-have-to-go-out whine, breaking into his thoughts. "Okay, Dig, give me a few minutes to gather my wits about me and get dressed."

A short while later he located a pair of gym shorts and then led the way down the stairs. "Don't go too far," he warned, but as luck would have it just as Tony let Digger out, a rabbit hopped across the yard. Totally ignoring his need to pee, Digger chased the bunny making a beeline for the woods. "Digger!" Muttering a curse, Tony pushed the screen door open and ran outside, stubbing his toe in the process. He hopped for a moment and then started running across the back lawn. He rounded the garage but suddenly tripped over a knee-high garden hose that seemed to come out of nowhere. Taking a swan dive, he face-planted into the grass, rolled, and then scrambled to his feet, only to be doused with freezing cold water.

"What the hell are you doing?" Tony shouted. He looked up into wide blue eyes.

"W-watering my roses."

"I'm not a rose," Tony growled, and swiped at the water running down his face.

"Well, you certainly have thorns."

He wasn't amused. "Can you blame me?"

"I can try."

Tony flashed her a grumpy look and then scrambled to his feet.

"Look, I'm really sorry. I . . . I didn't see you coming. I just turned the water on and was pulling the hose around to my rose garden that I recently planted." Trish swiveled to demonstrate and shot him with another cold spray. "Sorry! I water before the heat of the sunshine," she added with an apologetic wince. "It was getting late, so I was in a bit of a rush or I would have seen you, I guess." She shrugged. "You did come out of nowhere."

"I came out of the house."

"Well, again, sorry. I was sort of in a zone, trying to decide what flowers to plant next. Oh, by the way, I'm Trish Daniels." She stuck out her hand. She gave him a friendly smile. The red robe had been replaced with jeans and a loose T-shirt, but her feet were bare with pink-painted toenails and he somehow found that little detail sexy. It was a good thing he'd just been hosed down with cold water.

"Tony Marino," he responded briskly, and gripped her hand briefly. "I've got to go get my dog before I go to work." He jammed his thumb over his head and felt a flash of guilt when her smile faded. He knew he was being a complete ass and so added, "Uh, nice to meet you."

"Sorry about your scraped knee and shoulder. If you need Band-Aids, I can run in and get you some."

Tony glanced down at his knee. "I'll be fine."

"Suit yourself." At his brisk tone she nodded and turned away. There was something about the set of her shoulders that almost made him walk over and apologize. It wasn't her fault that she'd awakened a longing that he wanted to keep at bay. But instead, Tony pivoted away and started walking toward the woods. And then he felt it . . . a blast of cold water hit him in the ass.

"Sorry, my bad," she called to him, but then giggled. Her feminine laughter washed over him and for a moment he felt himself smile. He missed that kind of laughter and he paused, almost turned around. But instead, he walked toward the woods and whistled for Digger, telling himself to keep his distance. If she thought he was a jerk she'd keep her distance too. He'd already felt a strong pull of attraction. It was better that way.

He felt his damp ass and chuckled. It wasn't going to be easy.

5

Bringing Sexy Back

GABBY TAPPED HER TOES TO HER PLAYLIST AND THEN gave the wrist corsage a critical once-over. "Needs more baby's breath." She reached for a sprig and then separated the pink rosebuds. "Much better." She nodded but then rolled her shoulders to get the kinks out. Listening to lively pop music helped keep her moving through the large order of corsages and boutonnieres for the seniors' prom at Whisper's Edge. The theme was early 1950s, re-creating the era when most of the residents were in high school. Proceeds from the prom would go to local charities, so Gabby had given them a good price in exchange for some much-needed publicity. Gabby sang along with the refrain as she danced her way to the cooler to store the corsage.

"Nice moves, Gabby."

Gabby froze and then looked over at Reese standing in the doorway. "Thanks." She hoped her light response hid her embarrassment. "I try."

"Don't stop on my account."

"I'm not," Gabby responded nonchalantly but felt

heat creep into her cheeks and silently cursed her fair skin. She hoped he didn't notice.

"I could join you." When Reese walked toward her Gabby wondered how he could make merely walking somehow look sexy. "I have some moves of my own," he added. "How's this?" he asked, and did a silly little dance spin.

"Simply amazing." Gabby tried not to grin but failed. She really needed to stop cranking up the music so she could hear the bell ding over the front door. She shrugged as if Reese's appearance didn't create a flutter in her stomach. Although she often had to wear sweaters, she was suddenly grateful that she had to keep the store pretty cold for the health of the flowers, because she could certainly use a cooldown just from looking at him. She barely refrained from fanning her face. Was it possible that Reese had gotten even hotter in just a couple of days?

Apparently, it was. . . .

Maybe her stomach fluttered because Reese looked so darned masculine in the midst of all the flowers, Gabby reasoned, but then she had to go and compare her reaction to that of seeing Drew.

"So, what are you working on?" Reese walked closer and nodded toward the long table littered with snips of colorful ribbons, discarded leaves, and stem wire.

"Seniors' prom," Gabby replied. When her music shuffled to Bruno Mars crooning a sexy song, she hurried over and clicked Pandora off.

"Ah . . . senior prom?" Reese leaned a jean-clad hip against the front counter. "It still stings that you turned me down."

"Going to the prom?" Gabby sputtered. "Are you serious?"

"I asked."

"I didn't have a date. You were simply poking fun. Joking."

"What? I wouldn't make fun of you, Gabby." Reese frowned. "Why would you think *that*?"

Gabby raised her hands skyward. "Because you were supercool and I was a nerd." She hadn't fit in with the rougher crowd or the middle-class students either. Instead, she sat at the lunch table full of misfits who became her friends. Gabby didn't care about clothes she couldn't afford or meaningless trends. Well, most of the time, anyway.

Reese arched a dark eyebrow. "More like I was super badass and you didn't want anything to do with me." His tone remained teasing, but something flashed in Reese's eyes that gave Gabby pause, making her wonder if there might be more than what he was saying.

"Oh well, thank God that high school is over, right? Would we really want to do that again?"

Reese shrugged slightly. "I might have done a thing or two differently."

Gabby wasn't sure what Reese meant by his comment, but he didn't seem to want to elaborate. "Well, by *seniors*, I was referring to the senior citizens at Whisper's Edge. It's a dance where they raise money for charity. A lot of the town attends." She grinned. "I was actually invited."

"Sounds like a blast." Reese rolled his eyes.

"Hey, don't be fooled. I recently provided flowers for a birthday bash. Trust me, the Whisper's Edge residents know how to throw a party. All I can say is beware of the punch."

Reese chuckled. "So, are you going?"

"I don't have a date," Gabby answered without thinking.

Reese arched an eyebrow. "Does that mean I have a second chance to take you to the prom?"

Surely he wouldn't tease her about prom for a second time. Caution warred with attraction and when he gave her a crooked grin, attraction won hands down. "It's this Saturday night. Don't you have to work?"

"I'm pretty sure that Mom and Uncle Tony will be able to cover for me." He paused and then said, "In fact, I know they will. Until the grand opening of the actual restaurant, we'll be pretty slow, but we planned it that way. We wanted to get all of the kinks out with a soft opening. And, you know, hopefully get a little buzz going with how good the pizza is. Restaurants rely on word of mouth and can also go under pretty quickly with bad press."

"Well, if all of the pizza is as good as the one I had, you don't have a thing to worry about."

"Thanks, I hope you're right."

"So . . . so, what brings you here?"

"I wanted to know if you liked the cannoli," he said.

"I . . . I did," she replied, but it wasn't the cannoli that suddenly popped into her mind. She looked at that amazing mouth of his and swallowed hard. "I bet it would be really delicious."

"Would be?" He frowned slightly.

"Oh yes, I'm sure," Gabby said, and then suddenly snapped out of it. "I mean, yes, it was," she amended, and started fussing with the flowers strewn across the table.

"The best you've ever had?"

Gabby nodded slowly and her heart thudded. "I have to say . . . yes." She looked up and met his gaze.

"Good. I was hoping you'd say that." He walked closer until he stood right in front of her.

Gabby wanted to back up, but her feet would not budge. She tried to look away, but her eyes refused to as much as blink. She could feel the warmth of his body so close to hers and she remembered how intoxicating it felt to be wrapped in his strong arms. When he reached forward her heart hammered in her chest. He leaned even closer and caressed her hair with his fingers. If he kissed her she was afraid she'd be powerless to resist, but she stood there motionless. Waiting . . . hoping.

"Here."

Gabby blinked at Reese. "What?"

"This was tangled in your hair." He took a small step back and handed her a sprig of baby's breath.

Gabby's emotions bounced around like a pinball. Was he toying with her? Flirting? "Reese, why are you really here?"

"Flowers."

"Flowers?"

"Isn't this a flower shop?"

"Um . . . yeah." Trying to be flippant, Gabby responded by giving him a shove. But the moment her palms met his rock-hard chest, she wanted to fist her hands in the cotton of his shirt and yank him forward . . . and kiss him as if there were no tomorrow. Instead, she took a big step backward and came up against the craft table. For a moment she thought he was going to step forward. She imagined him putting a palm on either side of the table, trapping her, leaning in for a hot kiss. For another long, heated moment she wanted him to.

Reese licked his bottom lip and his chest rose and fell more than simply standing there warranted. Gabby wished she could read his mind. She studied his face, noticing a small scar on his chin, a tiny mole on his cheek, and flecks of gold in his eyes. "Well?" The deep timbre of his voice felt like a caress, causing her breath to catch.

"Well . . . what?" Gabby had the urge to reach over, tug his shirt from his jeans, and feel her hands on his skin. A hot shiver ran down her spine at the thought. When had merely standing in the presence of a man affected her in this way?

The answer was easy: *never*.

"I need two dozen flowers."

Gabby heart plummeted. "Well, now what did you do wrong?"

"Wrong?" He frowned for a second and then grinned. "Not for a woman. We want to dress up the tables in the restaurant with fresh flowers. Tessa bought small vases and wants to fill them with whatever flower you suggest.

I'm guessing it should be something that will last. And include shades of red, I think she said."

"Oh. . . ." Gabby cleared her throat and tried to switch her brain back to business. "Well, um, carnations or mums can last for several days or more if you snip the stems at an angle and keep the water fresh and the vases clean. Plus, they come in a variety of shapes and colors."

Reese nodded. He still stood close. Too close. And then not close enough. "Mom suggested that you could leave a business card by each vase."

"That's sweet of her."

He smiled softly. "Well, we'd like you to reciprocate by having our flyers on your counter."

"Easy enough. Like I said, I already know the pizza is fantastic." She swallowed hard. "And the cannoli."

"Good." Reese hesitated and then said, "I'll throw in an endless supply of cannoli in exchange for talking us up. And I'll soon have other decadent desserts for you to sample."

"You're going to make all of them?"

"With my own two hands. Pretty amazing for a badass like me, huh?"

Gabby tilted her head to the side. "You're not just a delivery guy, are you?"

"Part owner. Sous-chef. And my real claim to fame: maker of amazing desserts."

"Anything else?"

"I graduated from the Brooklyn Culinary Institute, but my specialty is desserts."

Gabby sighed. "Why on earth did you lead me to believe otherwise?"

Something flashed in his eyes. "I didn't. You assumed."

Had she? Gabby supposed she'd never given him the chance to tell her any of that before. "I'm sorry."

"It's fine." He shoved his hands in his front pockets and glanced around before bringing his gaze back to her. "You were preoccupied with dou . . . uh . . . Mr. Mayor.

By the way, how was your big date eating something so much better than pizza?"

Gabby shot him a grin. "In my opinion there's nothing better than pizza."

"Good answer, but you failed to address the question."

Was Reese jealous? The thought shot another thrill down her spine. "After getting the prom order I've been too busy for a date." Actually, she'd turned Drew down, giving that same excuse. She still wasn't sure if it was true, though.

"Well, I'm sure he won't give up." Reese looked at her closely as if gauging her reaction to his comment. "But at least he isn't the one taking you to the senior prom."

Gabby laughed. "Well, if you're serious, the prom is a fifties theme, so dress like James Dean or something."

"Yeah, I used to have that whole rebel-without-a-cause thing down pretty well, I guess," he said lightly, but his gaze flicked away again.

"Hey," she said, trying to draw his attention away from the pain of his past. She knew where much of his angst had stemmed from. And she remembered the sweet kid he'd once been. "Reese, I understand how it feels to lose someone you love."

His gaze returned to hers. "Your mom didn't have a choice. My dad did."

"But I imagine that the emotion feels somewhat the same."

"There's more anger involved."

"There were times when I was really angry at my mother for dying," she quietly admitted, although she hadn't told anyone until now. "I threw a few things against the wall. It's not surprising you reacted with rebellion."

"Yeah, well, it really wasn't fair to do that to my mother." Reese sighed and then scrubbed a hand down his face. "She had enough to deal with. I should have been there for her instead of acting out."

"You were a kid." When Gabby witnessed the pain shining in his dark eyes, she had the urge to pull him into her arms and offer comfort. Instead, she stepped forward and put her hand on his forearm. "Don't be so hard on yourself." She intended the gesture to be comforting and platonic. It wasn't. The warmth of his skin, beneath the taut muscle, sent a hot zing through her that she couldn't deny. Her breath caught and her heart thumped harder. She raised her gaze to meet his.

Did Reese feel it too?

When he studied her for a long moment, the awareness between them felt like a tangible thing. She had the urge to run her hands over the contours of his chest and then tilt her head up in silent invitation. Gabby's reaction to standing close to Reese felt so strong that she couldn't move even if she wanted to. Goodness, if a touch, a kiss could make her feel this way, what must it be like to . . .

Make love?

But then Gabby felt a flash of fear tingle down her spine. Feelings this intense carried the power to hurt with them, but when she would have stepped back Reese reached out and ran a gentle fingertip down her cheek. The gesture was so surprisingly tender that she longed to lean her face into his palm and lose herself in the sweet moment. Oh, there had been so many nights when she'd longed for someone to hold her, to comfort her, and to dry her tears. Feeling as if he was seeing too much, Gabby glanced away only to have Reese tuck a fingertip beneath her chin and guide her gaze back to him.

"Okay, I won't."

"What?"

Reese smiled. "Be so hard on myself."

The brightness of his smile chased away the darkness of the past. "Good."

"I've never seen you with short hair," Reese said, softly changing the subject. "I remember your hair being halfway down your back most of the time worn in a long braid or ponytail that I always wanted to tug."

"Sometimes you did." She gave him a slight grin.

Reese remained silent for a moment and then said, "Yeah, but later what I really wanted to do was run my fingers through your hair to see if it felt as soft as it looked." He shook his head. "I just said that out loud, didn't I?"

Gabby chuckled. "Unless I was reading your mind."

His eyes widened. "Oh God, I hope not!" But then he smiled as he reached over and picked up a lock of hair. "Just as I thought," he observed in a husky tone that had Gabby all but melting. "Why did you cut it?"

"Locks of Love." She tried to smile, but all her lips managed was a wobble.

"I've heard of it."

"Yeah, it's an organization that provides hairpieces for kids who are suffering from hair loss because of illness and can't afford a wig. I donated a twelve-inch ponytail in honor of my mother, who had lost her hair to chemo." She paused. "And then I shaved the rest off."

"I bet your mother was so touched by the gesture."

"At the Locks of Love donation, yes. But when I shaved my head she was so upset. My mother rarely uttered a foul word, but she cussed a blue streak! Said I shouldn't have done that and then we both hugged and cried like crazy."

"I bet you were beautiful even with a bald head."

"I have pictures of us." Her smile trembled again and swiped at a tear and then sniffed. "Ah . . . well, *anyway*, when my hair grew back in I decided that short layers were so much easier and so I've kept it this way."

"It suits you. Shows off your pretty face and gives you a sassy side. I like it."

Gabby tilted her head. "Are you flirting with me?"

"Trying my best but I'm not sure I'm all that good at it. Is it working?"

"I think so."

Reese smiled. "I'd send you flowers, but . . ."

Gabby giggled. "There's always cannoli."

"Ah, so I had you at the cannoli? I've got several decadent desserts up my sleeve." He wiggled his fingers.

"You're not wearing sleeves," Gabby joked, but when she looked at his tanned, muscled arms and the hint of the tattoos peeking out of the short sleeves that were stretched by his biceps, she suddenly wondered what he would look like shirtless. The thought brought warmth into her cheeks and she was glad that he couldn't read her mind either. A hint of what she was feeling must have shown on her face, because his playfulness faded and was replaced with something sultry and . . . hot.

Gabby had dated here and there while in college, but with the death of her mother and starting her business, she'd put any thoughts of romance on hold. Drew was the first guy Gabby had set her sights on and wanted to date. Still, she couldn't recall ever experiencing this kind of longing or desire so potent.

"If you keep looking at me like that, I might get the idea you're going to throw yourself at me again."

Gabby fisted her hands on her hips and leaned forward. "I did *not* throw myself at you! Would you stop saying that?"

"No," Reese said, and then grinned.

Gabby found herself smiling back. She remembered that after his father left, Reese rarely smiled. He'd obviously done some healing over the years. She understood. After tragedy strikes, you have to pick up the pieces and keep going.

Reese arched an eyebrow. "Well, let me go on record and say that I wouldn't mind if you did."

Whoa. Reese really was flirting with her. "I'll make a note of it."

"Good. Feel free. You know, don't hold back. My arms will be wide open." When he demonstrated Gabby considered taking him up on his offer. Although his tone remained teasing, Reese dropped his arms to his sides and stepped closer, making her pulse kick into overdrive. He might have matured, but he still had that wicked bad-boy edge that felt like a walk on the wild side. And she would do well to remember that. "And hey, if you'd like to stop by the restaurant sometime this week and check out the color scheme so you can plan the flowers, I'll reward you with lunch."

"I just might take you up on your offer."

"Good. The offer includes dessert."

"You're making your offer hard to resist."

"That's the plan." He didn't step closer, but Gabby felt as if he did.

"Oh, but hey, listen, if Saturday night is a problem with work, let me know. I'll understand."

"It won't be," Reese answered firmly. His eyes dropped to her mouth and for a second Gabby thought he might kiss her this time. But just when her eyes started to flutter shut, the bell over the front door dinged.

"Hello!"

"Miss Patty!" Gabby stepped away from Reese as if getting her hand caught in the cookie jar. She greeted her friend who lived in the Whisper's Edge retirement community. "What brings you in?"

"I was over at the bakery ordering a big cake for the dance and thought I'd pop in and see your pretty little face." Miss Patty gave Reese a once-over. "Well, hello there, handsome."

"Miss Patty, this is Reese Marino. He and his uncle own River Row Pizza and Pasta."

"Well, bless your heart for bringing some delicious pizza to Cricket Creek."

"You've had a slice?" Reese asked.

"Sure did at our last craft class. I have to tell you that the crust was to die for. Hand-tossed, I'm guessing?"

"You betcha. I can do some serious flipping-in-the-air action. The sauce is our own too."

"It's so good."

"Thank you." Gabby couldn't help noticing Reese's obvious pride in the restaurant.

Miss Patty gave him a sassy smile. "You didn't deliver it, though, sugar. I would have remembered. Although the man who did was mighty fine too. I'm predicting you'll be getting a lot of business from Whisper's Edge." She gave him a wink and then turned her attention to Gabby. "I think I might have a date for you for the dance!"

"Too late," Reese responded in a playful yet decidedly make-no-mistake tone that had Gabby hiding a grin. "Gabby's going with me."

"Well, now." Miss Patty arched an eyebrow and then tucked a lock of silver hair behind her ear. "Do tell."

"Reese offered to take me to the prom." A giddy little surge of joy at the announcement took her by surprise.

"Yeah, she's making up for turning me down the first time."

"Are you crazy, child?" Miss Patty gave a low whistle and then winked again at Reese. "Just make sure to save this ol' gal a dance. And make it a slow one."

Gabby wagged a finger at her friend. "Did you forget that you're taken, Miss Patty? Clovis might not take too kindly if you dance with another man."

"Humph." Miss Patty held up her left hand. "Do you see a ring on it?"

Laughter bubbled up in Gabby's throat, but then her eyes widened as a diamond caught her eye. "Yes!" She took Miss Patty's hand. "Oh my goodness, did Clovis ask you to marry him?"

"There's no fool like an old fool," she answered, but her eyes glistened with tears. "But he sure as shootin' did."

Gabby grabbed Miss Patty and gave her a huge hug before looking at the ring again. "Congratulations! The ring is lovely."

"Got it from Nicolina. Clovis told me he wanted a one of a kind just like me."

"Funny coming from him since he's a twin."

"I know; I warned those two not to pull any shenanigans with me. They love fooling people, but I can tell the difference. Clovis said he wanted to ask me to marry him at the dance in front of the whole world. Well, our little world, anyway. He also said he was going to put an announcement on the front page of the *Cricket Creek Courier* now that he and Clyde own it. Silly man."

"Oh, how sweet!"

Miss Patty rolled her eyes. "Ha, because he likes to be the center of attention! But he just couldn't wait to ask."

Gabby put her palms to her cheeks. "That's so romantic!"

"Oh . . . he's got game, that one. So does his doggone twin brother." Miss Patty waved a dismissive hand through the air, but a soft glow of happiness seemed to radiate from her.

"Congratulations," Reese said.

"Thank you, young man. But that doesn't mean I don't get my dance. I'm just sayin'."

Reese inclined his head. "I'd be honored."

"Why, thank you." Miss Patty turned back to Gabby. "The other reason I stopped in was to offer to help make the corsages. Etta Mae and Joy could help out too. Even though Etta Mae can be a pain," she added behind her hand. "Our fingers aren't as nimble as they used to be, but we're still pretty crafty, thanks to Savannah's craft days. Given instruction we could lend a hand, especially since you're charging so little."

"I would like that," Gabby admitted, and felt a wave of relief. She needed help at the shop, but she didn't have the funds to hire anybody just yet, not even a delivery person. At times she felt overwhelmed.

"And, well, I do have a bit of a favor to ask," Miss Patty continued.

"Shoot," Gabby urged.

"Joy is a little bit down in the dumps lately. Her cat passed away."

"Oh, that's so sad."

"Poor thing was walking around Whisper's Edge sideways. The cat, I mean, not Joy. But anyway, she really is good with crafts. She's had to step in for Savannah once in a while. If you could use a little part-time help, Joy would do a bang-up job. I know she's too prideful to ask, but if we come in and help out would you consider offering her a small job? It's not even about the money—she's set with retirement—but I think just being needed would do her a world of good."

"Miss Patty, I really can't afford to pay much until business picks up."

"She wouldn't need much. Just some pocket change. You know, for lunch and a martini at Sully's now and then. Shew, we had a couple the other day and we were walking sideways too. Clint, that handsome son of Sully's, had to drive us home and all but carried Joy into her house." Miss Patty shook her head. "Poor Joy got the wrong impression and tried to kiss him! Can you imagine her thinking she was going to get lucky with that young hunk of man-cake?"

Reese's eyes widened as if picturing this happening.

"Thank goodness she doesn't remember," Miss Patty added. "Being that she's already down in the dumps and all. But will you consider giving her a little work now and then?"

"Sure, Miss Patty, I'll consider it. In truth I could use the extra help."

Miss Patty smiled. "You are such a sweetheart. We'll come by later, if that's okay?"

"I'll provide some pizza," Reese offered. "And a sampling of my desserts."

"I won't even touch that line." Miss Patty winked at Gabby. "But listen, I really want to have some of your pizza at the dance. I'm thinking about ten or so, but we insist upon paying. The food is part of the budget."

"Just give me a call."

"Count on it." Miss Patty gave them a wave and then headed out the door.

"Well, she sure is a character," Reese commented. "I'm thinking this party is going to be fun."

"Like I said, beware of the punch."

"Does she always try to set you up on dates?"

"Once in a while. Now that Savannah is engaged, they seem to have set their matchmaking sights on me."

"Savannah?"

"The social director at Whisper's Edge. I'll be doing the flowers for her wedding. Miss Patty is one of the bridesmaids."

Reese chuckled, but he didn't seem to like the matchmaking idea. "Hey, by the way, I want to let you know that I can make some deliveries for you."

"You're already busy. I can't ask you to do that."

"You didn't." Reese gave her shoulder a squeeze. "I offered."

Gabby nodded and felt a warm rush of emotion. She and her mother had spent so many years sticking together as a team. Having witnessed her mom getting hurt by seemingly well-meaning men had Gabby treading cautiously. This business meant the world to her—she'd invested everything in it, and she couldn't trust it to just anyone.

Reese must have sensed her sudden withdrawal. "It's just an offer, Gabby. Keep it in mind and don't hesitate to ask for help. I know firsthand how difficult it is for an established business to stay afloat. Starting a new one is even harder. Don't be afraid to ask for a hand."

"I'm not afraid."

"Yes, I think you are. But I know that where we come from, trust has to be earned." His dark eyes captured hers. "I plan on earning it from you." He walked closer, leaned down, and kissed her on the cheek. "Let me know what your lady friends want on their pizza, okay?"

Gabby nodded and watched Reese walk out the door.

Closing her eyes, she swallowed the moisture gathering in her throat. She knew that if she didn't want to spend her days—and nights—alone, she had to let down her guard and open her heart.

She only hoped she could dig deep for the courage.

6

Long As I Got My Suit and Tie

"MOM, DO YOU REALLY HAVE TO ROLL THE CIGARETTE pack up into my sleeve?" Reese looked down at his mother's head and sighed. "This is bordering on overkill."

"Just hold still, I'm almost finished." She glanced up at him and then went back to her task.

"I don't want Gabby to think I smoke."

"The pack is obviously candy, Reese." She angled her head over to a white bag perched on a table. "I have a pack of my own over there. Who knew they still made them? I had a field day in that new candy store up on Main Street. I bought Mary Janes and Bit-O-Honey. They even had Neapolitan coconut squares."

"Those are horrible. So are those wax bottles filled with that nasty syrup." Reese shuddered. "Why did you buy those?"

"Ol' times' sake, I guess. You'd better be careful or I won't share the Bull's Eyes."

Reese chuckled. "Now, those I like. And I want the vanilla French Chew and those ice-cream cones with the marshmallows on top."

"Tony already claimed those. He's such a big kid. I even have one of those candy necklaces." She paused and gave Reese a meaningful look that he instantly understood. "I'll never forget when you spent half of your candy cash buying one of those for Gabby."

"What can I say? I'm a nice guy," Reese responded lightly, but he remembered too. When his father had still been around working as a mechanic at Fred's in town, life had been pretty good at least as far as Reese knew it back then. Gabby, on the other hand, rarely went to the candy store and even as a ten-year-old, Reese realized it was because her mom couldn't afford it. Gabby was so grateful for the small gift that she hugged him. Reese shook his head and smiled. He could still see the happy smile on her sweet face when he handed her the small white bag containing the necklace. . . .

"For me?" Gabby asked. When Reese nodded she put down the watering can that looked too heavy for her to manage but she did somehow.

"Just, you know, a little something." Reese lifted one shoulder and watched her open the bag.

Her eyes lit up. "Oh, my favorite! Did you know that?"

"No . . . I just kinda guessed," he scoffed, but he was so glad that he was right.

"Well, you're a good guesser! Thank you, thank you! I don't want to touch the necklace, because my hands are dirty." She pointed to the tomato plants she'd been watering. "As soon as the tomatoes are ready to pick, I'll give you some. Shouldn't be too much longer."

Reese smiled even though he wasn't all that fond of tomatoes. "Thanks. That's really cool." He was trying to think of something else to say when his mother called him for dinner. "Well, I'd better get going."

Gabby nodded and then stepped forward and gave him a brief hug. "Thank you for the treat. It was super-nice of you."

"Ah, it was nothing," Reese protested, but he really liked seeing her eyes light up. But just so she didn't think he was wimpy or anything like that when she turned around, he gave her long braid a quick tug before hurrying home for dinner.

"Whatcha thinkin'?" his mother asked, drawing Reese's thoughts back to the present.

"Just that it's pretty great that the old-fashioned candy store reopened after being closed down for so long." His response wasn't entirely honest, but Reese wasn't ready to explore his feelings about Gabby with his mother just yet.

"Yeah, it closed when Cricket Creek was struggling. It's still called the Sweet Spot, but did you know it was little Ronnie Carlton who reopened the candy shop? She worked at the toy store on Main Street for a few years and since it's right next door I guess it was a smart move. I think you went to school with her?"

"I did," Reese replied. "Ronnie was on student council and all that stuff. Kinda geeky but cute. I think she and Gabby were friends." In fact, Reese knew that they were friends. Gabby might have avoided him, but Reese had always tried to look out for her. Even after their friendship faded, a bond remained that couldn't be broken. "I'm sure that store brings back memories for lots of folks around here."

"It does," she responded, but her smile appeared a little bit forced. "Funny how something as simple as a piece of candy can take you back, ya know?"

To before Dad left us hung in the air between them, making Reese fidget once more. This time his mother remained silent as if lost in her own thoughts. His parents had seemed to love each other so much. Why his father emptied the bank account and left remained a mystery. The only reason they knew there wasn't foul play involved was that an occasional envelope with cash would arrive but never with a return address.

"There, I think that about does it." When Reese saw his mother's fingers tremble slightly, he silently cursed his father. Wanting to bring her good mood back, he said, "Are you really coming over to take pictures of Gabby and me?"

She brightened. "Of course! You might not be in a tuxedo, but I finally get to take prom pictures." She backed away and gave him a once-over. "You need to slick your hair back."

Reese put his palms up in protest. "Nope, I'm drawing the line."

"Come on. Just a little bit of gel?" When Reese answered with a sigh, she smiled. "Do you have any upstairs in your apartment?"

"Mom, I don't put that goop in my hair."

"You used to."

"I used to do a lot of things."

"I'll have to make a superquick trip to my house. Man the phones for Tony. I'll be right back."

A moment later Tony pushed his way through the double doors from the kitchen, but he stopped in his tracks when he spotted Reese. He put the tray of salt and pepper shakers down and folded his arms across his chest, giving Reese an accusing glare. "Are those cigarettes?"

"Yeah, you got a problem with that?" Reese couldn't help asking him. "Want one?"

"Well, hell yeah, I've got a problem with it! And no, I don't want one."

"Suit yourself." Uncle Tony never did intimidate him with the glare even though Reese let him believe it. In truth, Reese had complied with his uncle's rules out of respect rather than fear. It had been tough watching his uncle's marriage crumble. It remained another example of someone not keeping her promise to a person she supposedly loved. Gold-digging Gloria he could understand but not his father's desertion. Reese pushed that thought from his mind. Thinking about his father still put him on edge, and he wanted to enjoy his date with Gabby.

"Reese, are you shittin' me, man?"

"Don't get your panties in a wad. If I did smoke I wouldn't put the pack in my sleeve. It's just candy. I'd show you but it took fifteen minutes for Mom to get them to stay rolled up like this. Apparently, this was considered cool back in the fifties."

Relief softened Tony's expression and he grinned. "Oh, so who are you? Lenny or Squiggy?"

"I was going for James Dean. Who the hell are Lenny and Squiggy?"

"Never mind. I'm old."

"No, you're not. Well, not *that* old, anyway."

Tony pulled a face. "I sure as hell feel like it." He rolled his shoulders. "Sorry I got so wound up. I'm kind of stressed. I'll be so damned glad when the grand opening is over."

"You want me to stay tonight? Gabby will understand." Reese didn't want to give up his date with Gabby, but his family meant the world to him. And he owed Uncle Tony big-time for being there for him when he was going down the wrong path very quickly.

"No! Hell no. I've got everything in the kitchen under control. Tessa and I can hold down the fort. You need to have some fun, Reese. Oh, and I put an ad in the paper for a delivery guy."

"I don't mind doin' it."

"No way. We need your expertise more in the kitchen and doin' other business-related things. I did hire a few more servers today too. We'll train them this week."

"I know the drill." Reese nodded, hating the fatigue etched on his uncle's face. "Uncle Tony, you need to take some time off too."

"I will once things are up and running smoothly."

"I'll hold you to that. Digger's gonna forget what you look like."

"Tell me about it. I did take him for a run the other day," he said, and then chuckled.

"What's so funny?"

"Nothin', I just finally met my neighbor. Well, actually she's my landlord."

"And?"

He answered with a bemused expression followed by a shrug.

That was a strange reaction. "Wait. Is she hot?"

"I dunno."

"Come on, Uncle Tony."

"Yeah . . . yeah, she's hot. I guess. Whatever."

"You should, you know, hang out with her or somethin'," Reese said casually but watched his uncle's reaction closely. Since the divorce two years ago, his uncle had yet to venture out on even one date. It was about damned time.

"Like I got time for that," Uncle Tony scoffed, but there was something in his eyes that said he wished he did. Reese inhaled a deep breath and was about to encourage the idea, but his uncle's expression suddenly darkened and so Reese left it alone, for now, anyway.

"But hey, look, all the prep work is done for tonight. I just got the order for ten pizzas for the dance. I'll have Tessa deliver them. I think she wants to take some pictures."

Yep, both Uncle Tony and his mother needed to have more of a social life. "I'll put some flyers and coupons next to them. Apparently, our reputation is already good at Whisper's Edge."

"Whoa, yeah!" Tony lifted his palms in the air. "I delivered a couple of pizzas last week. Got my ass pinched! What was up with that?"

Reese thought of Miss Patty and laughed. "I think I might know the guilty party."

A few minutes later his mother raced back through the door. "Got some!"

Reese looked at the purple jar. "Is that gonna make me smell like a girl?"

"Hush, I'm only going to use a little bit."

"Meaning yes." He sighed while she played around with his hair. "Uncle Tony, are you gonna help me out here?"

"Tessa, just don't make him look like Squiggy."

She chuckled. "I won't! Look, I'm going to slick it back so it looks like you have shorter hair."

Reese didn't even bother to protest this time, deciding to let her have her fun. After finishing up she stood back and admired her work. "How do I look?"

"Perfect! Now, when I show up with the pizza I fully expect to see you and Gabby out there cutting a rug."

"Mom, I have no idea what that means."

"It's an old-fashioned term for dancing. Granddad used to say it when he'd jitterbug with Grandma, right, Tony?"

"Somehow I don't think I'll be doing anything called jitterbugging."

"I can do it. Want a quick lesson?"

"I would but I'm pressed for time!" Reese replied, but grinned.

"Well, at least do the twist," she said, and demonstrated.

"Just have fun," Uncle Tony advised. " 'Cause next week we'll be like chickens with our heads cut off."

Reese gave his mother a hug and headed out the door, surprised that he felt a little bit nervous as he walked over toward Flower Power. Since Whisper's Edge wasn't too far away, Reese had suggested walking, especially after Gabby said the punch would be spiked. He wanted his days of getting in trouble in Cricket Creek to remain behind him.

When Reese caught his reflection in a picture window of a vacant shop, he paused and shook his head. He sure looked like a vintage teenage troublemaker. "So much for changing Gabby's opinion of me," he grumbled. Then he turned the corner and Top Hat, the tuxedo rental shop next to the bridal boutique, caught his eye. This section of the shops had earned the name "Wedding Row" for a reason. He gazed at the mannequins displayed in the window and then on a whim he opened the door and went inside.

"May I help you?" the friendly clerk asked, but then she took off her reading glasses and gave Reese a curious look.

"I'm going to a fifties dance."

"Ah, that explains a lot. Wait. You're going to the Whisper's Edge prom? Aren't you a little bit young?"

"I'm going there with Gabby, the owner of the floral shop down the street. She was invited because she's providing the flowers." Reese extended his hand. "I'm Reese Marino. My uncle and I just opened River Row Pizza and Pasta."

"I'm Marcy Duncan, shop owner. Oh, Gabby is such a sweetheart! I send all of my prom and wedding parties over to her for the flowers. And thanks for bringing pizza to Restaurant Row! I've been meaning to try it."

"Nice to meet you, Marcy. We're still only doing a soft opening with takeout and delivery, but the actual sit-down restaurant will open next weekend. We'll have a daily selection of an authentic Italian dish and a few staple items on the menu."

Marcy tapped her temple. "Smart decision."

"Yeah, hopefully it will all go smoothly." Reese pointed to his chest. "Gabby wanted me to do the whole James Dean thing, but I'm having second thoughts. I'm a little pressed for time, but you wouldn't happen to have a tux that has a bit of a retro look, would you?"

"Oh, we usually measure and have to order sizes in," Marcy explained. "The suits we have here are mostly for picking things out." She nibbled on the inside of her lip for a second and then snapped her fingers. "Wait. Are you about six feet tall, about a thirty-two-inch waist?"

"Close. Six one, but you've got the waist size right. You're good."

"My shop is fairly new, but I've been doing this for a while. Look, I just got in a *Mad Men*–inspired line. Partly because of the popularity of the show, skinny ties and fitted suits are in vogue," Marcy explained with a smile. "The lapels are narrow and the suits are tailored. Perfect for your body type. You're going to rock this style." She whipped out a measuring tape and did a quick once-over. "I think I've got you covered."

"Bring it on," Reese said with a grin.

"I'll gather what you need and hang it in the dressing room. We'll have you looking debonair in no time."

Reese chuckled. "Well, that will be a first."

Marcy grinned. "But not the last. You know who you remind me of?"

Reese shook his head.

"A young Antonio Sabato Jr. Don't worry. You're going to pull this off. Sweet Gabby is going to be swept off her feet."

"You think so?" Reese suddenly realized that was exactly what he wanted to do.

"I know so."

7

Sweet Memories

GABBY LOOKED DOWN AT THE COLORFUL ARRAY OF dresses strewn across her bed and groaned. Nothing was right for the retro dance. "I really should have gone shopping," she lamented with a sigh, but there just wasn't enough time in the day to get all of her work done and shop as well. If Miss Patty and her crew hadn't jumped in to help out, she'd still be downstairs making corsages. Hiring Joy was going to really be a godsend.

Gabby had originally planned on wearing one of her sundresses that looked a bit retro, but suddenly nothing seemed right. She glanced at the digital clock on her nightstand and felt a little surge of alarm. Reese would be arriving soon. She'd just have to pick one out and go with it, but just as she reached for the buttercup yellow eyelet dress, she heard a knock at the back entrance to her apartment. Crap. He was early. She cinched the belt on her robe tighter and hurried through her kitchen to let him in. She'd have to offer him a beer while she got ready.

Gabby opened the door and shook her head in surprise. "Addison!" She stepped aside to let her friend and fellow Wedding Row shop owner in. "Hey, girl, it's good to see you. What brings you here?"

Addison held up a dress sheathed in plastic. "Maggie told me you were going to the dance at Whisper's Edge. I know you probably already have a dress picked out and this is so last minute, but I just got a shipment of bridesmaids' dresses at the shop. These look like the famous Marilyn Monroe halter-top dress. I thought this white one would be perfect, so I hurried over." She pulled the plastic off and held the dress up. "What do you think? It even has the pleated skirt. But hey, if you're not interested my feelings won't be hurt."

"No, it's so pretty! Addison, you won't believe it but I was just lamenting my lack of choices of what to wear. I've just been swamped lately."

Addison smiled. "I figured that. And since you have a date with Reese Marino . . ."

"How did you know I was going with Reese?"

"Are you kidding? New travels faster in Cricket Creek than it did when I lived in L.A. Just like I know that Drew Gibbons has set his sights on you too."

Gabby chuckled. "The Miranda Lambert song is right about everybody dying famous in a small town."

Addison chuckled. "Well, I don't mean to butt my nose into your business, but I've learned that's kind of par for the course here. But mostly in a good way. Everybody just cares. Let me see, I guessed you to be about a size six?"

Gabby nodded. "Yes, but I'm so doggone short. Do you think it will be too long?"

Addison angled her head to the side. "The beauty of this style is that it can be a little bit long on you and still look good. It's not a petite but we can adjust the halter top. As long as it fits in the waist, we're good to go. Like I said, it's totally your call." She wiggled it back and forth. "But do me a favor and at least try it on."

"Okay." Gabby nodded and then took the dress from Addison. "If Reese arrives will you keep him entertained?"

"No problem."

"Thank you, Addison!" After feeling like a bit of an outcast in high school, she found it was nice to have friends in Cricket Creek. She'd just been so shy and insecure back then. Gabby hurried to her bedroom, shed her robe, and put the dress on. When she gazed at her reflection in the full-length mirror, she put her hand on her throat. Was it too sexy? "Addison, will you come in here and tell me what you think?"

"Sure!" A moment later she appeared in the doorway. "Oh, Gabby! A little bit long, but other than that it's perfect on you."

"Does it show too much skin?"

"Not in my opinion." Addison shook her head. "Unless of course you stand over a wind tunnel," she added with a grin. "Oh, but seriously, put a few curls in your short blond hair and you will actually do a pretty good impression of a young Marilyn Monroe. Rock some red lipstick and you will be the belle of the ball."

Gabby turned back to the mirror and held the full skirt out and then pivoted to see her back. She bit her bottom lip between her teeth.

"It's no different than the sundresses I've seen you wear." Addison pointed to the bed. "I see some dresses in there that show just as much skin. There's just something about this iconic style that is sexy. But in a classy way. Put on those strappy heels over there and you will complete the look."

"Okay, I'll wear it!" She twirled around, causing Addison to laugh, and then walked over and gave Addison a hug. "You've become such a good friend. What do I owe you for the dress?"

Addison waved a hand. "Nothing! Just talk up From This Moment for me and we're even. I'm carrying more than just wedding attire, and this dress showcases that for me."

"Thanks so much!"

"Now I'm going to get out of your hair so you can get

ready. Have fun, Gabby! I want a full report over coffee soon. Or maybe a glass of wine? I love my husband, but I could use a girls' night out."

"You bet." After Addison let herself out, Gabby hurried into her bathroom to do her makeup and hair. Fifteen minutes later she had soft curls in her layered hair and her bangs lifted off her forehead in a retro style. She added more drama to her eyes with a smoky shadow and black liner. Rummaging through her makeup drawer, she couldn't find deep red lipstick but spotted a dusky rose in a free promotion she'd gotten with a purchase. Gabby blotted her lips and shook her head at her reflection. Although she wouldn't normally have chosen such a dramatic shade, it was perfect for tonight.

After spraying on a light floral scent, she went back into her bedroom and slipped on white sandals that added a few inches to her height. She put a few essentials in a little beaded clutch purse and decided that she was ready.

"Phew!" She took a deep breath and glanced at the clock again. Reese was a little bit late, but she tried not to worry. He most likely worked up until right before he had to leave.

Gabby glanced shyly into the mirror and was surprised at the glamorous woman staring back at her. She put a hand on her chest and felt the rapid beat of her heart. When had she been this excited about the evening ahead? "Probably never," she murmured, and then suddenly wondered what Reese would think. Was this look a little bit too much? Would he think she was be coming on too strong?

A moment later the doorbell chimed. Swallowing hard, Gabby smoothed her skirt and then fluffed her hair.

She was about to find out.

With each step that she took toward the door, Gabby tried to calm her heartbeat and was mildly successful until she swung open the door. "Oh my . . . ," she breathed, and then felt a stab of panic when Reese turned around. "Wh-where are you going?"

"I must have the wrong address. I don't have a date with Marilyn Monroe."

Laughing, Gabby put a hand on his shoulder, tugging him back around. "Don't go, Joe DiMaggio." She hoped he thought the breathless sound of her voice was an imitation of Marilyn, but in fact she was just . . .

Breathless.

When Reese entered her kitchen she leaned against the sink and said, "And I thought I had a date with James Dean."

"Are you disappointed?"

Her heart thudded when she looked at him. "Not in the least." Reese seemed to fill the room with his presence. It wasn't that he was tall, dark, and supersexy. What drew her to him was the humor, the intelligence shining in his eyes. And he cared about her. He always had.

"I would have brought you flowers, but . . ." He shrugged those wide shoulders of his, sending yet another thrill through Gabby.

"I held back a wrist corsage, but I didn't know I'd need a boutonniere."

Reese pointed toward the door. "My jeans and T-shirt are over at Top Hat. I could go back and morph into James Dean."

"Oh no, I like this look."

Reese stepped closer. Gabby caught a whiff of his aftershave and had to suppress a sigh of pure feminine delight. "You do?"

Gabby nodded slowly while she tried to make her vocal cords work. "A lot."

"I could say the same thing," Reese said, and then ran a fingertip over her bare shoulder.

"Then say it."

The slow grin he gave her was wicked and full of promise. "I like this look."

A hot tingle slid down Gabby's spine. She wanted to

touch him but worried that if she put her hands on him she'd end up grabbing his narrow lapels and yanking him forward for a long, hot kiss.

"I do have something for you, though."

Gabby tilted her head in question and watched him pull a little cellophane bag from his pocket. She smiled when she saw what it contained. "Oh my goodness!" It was just a candy necklace but represented so much more. Emotion filled her throat as she accepted the gift. Tearing it open, she dumped the necklace into her palm and then looked up at Reese. "Thank you," she gushed, and then wrapped her arms around him and squeezed.

Reese returned the hug and when he pulled back he reached over and wiped away a teardrop with the pad of his thumb. "It wasn't my intention to make you cry." He appeared so worried that Gabby reached up and put her palms on his cheeks.

"I'm touched by the gesture and the memory. The one blessing in growing up poor is the realization about the little things in life."

"And what would that realization be?" Reese wanted to know.

Gabby dropped her hands but continue to look up at him. "That they aren't little at all."

When his gaze dropped to her mouth, Gabby felt a giddy sense of anticipation. He was going to kiss her. And she wanted him to, but a sudden knock at her door had them both jumping at the sudden break in the spell. Reese looked over at the window and grinned. "It's my mother. She wants to get her prom pictures."

With a little whoop of delight Gabby hurried over to the door. Swinging it open, she exclaimed, "Tessa! Come in!"

"Oh, would you just look at you two?" Tessa put fingertips to her lips and shook her head. "Reese, where did you get that tux?"

"Top Hat," he said with a chuckle. "I decided that my

rebel-without-a-cause days were over." He turned in a circle. "How do I look?"

"So handsome! And, Gabby! My goodness, you look like a sweeter version of Marilyn Monroe. Simply gorgeous! May I take some pictures?"

"Could we even begin to stop you?" Reese asked with a chuckle.

Tessa laughed. "Not on your life."

The next thirty minutes were spent snapping pictures everywhere, even in the flower shop. Just when they thought they were finished, Tessa spotted another location that was perfect. Finally, Reese put his hands up in surrender. "Mom, we do have to get going."

"Okay, but I'll get some more when I deliver the pizza." She gave them each a big hug. "Have fun tonight!"

Reese leaned down and kissed his mother on the cheek. "I intend to."

"Your mother is such a lovely person," Gabby said. "She must be so thrilled that you've moved back to Cricket Creek."

"Can you tell?" Reese asked with a smile, but then sobered. "She's gone through a lot. So has Uncle Tony. I intend to do everything in my power to make the restaurant a success."

"It will be."

"I hope you're right. I just wish it were six months down the road and we were up and running smoothly with all of the kinks out."

"Don't wish your life away," she said in a teasing tone.

Reese looked at her. "Good point. From here on in I vow to savor the moment." He extended his arm. "Are you ready?"

"Absolutely."

8

That's Life

TRISH ABSENTLY PLAYED WITH THE STRING OF PEARLS around her neck and tapped her toes to Bill Haley and the Comets singing "Rock Around the Clock." She sat tucked in the corner while discreetly taking notes on her first official assignment for the *Cricket Creek Courier*. Covering the Whisper's Edge prom was proving to be much more entertaining than she first anticipated, but then after meeting Clyde and Clovis Camden why should she be surprised? If she still lived in Cricket Creek when she was in her twilight years, she vowed, she would take up residence in Whisper's Edge. These people knew how to have fun.

Trish took a sip of her drink and smacked her lips. Of course the spiked punch certainly helped loosen things up. The drink reminded her of the hooch served at parties back in her college days. Since she'd driven, she put the drink aside to nurse and turned her attention back to the crowd. A moment later a cute girl in a peach chiffon dress and a bouffant hairdo stepped up to the microphone.

"How y'all doin'?" she asked, and had to wait for the

shouts and whistles to die down. "As just about all of you know, I'm Savannah Perry and I'll be your hostess tonight. Just a few things. We have the table of prizes to bid on." She pointed in that direction. "Check it out, because there's some really nice stuff!" She started ticking things off. "Dinner at Wine and Diner, Cougars baseball tickets, a gorgeous necklace from Designs by Diamante, donuts for a year from Grammar's Bakery, flower arrangements from Flower Power, the list goes on and on. Everything has been generously donated, so one hundred percent of the proceeds will go to the charities listed on the poster in the far left corner of the hall. If you want to get in on the jitterbug dance contest, it costs five bucks with half of the money going to the winner. See Kate about that. Kate, wave your hand. Thank you. Song requests are accepted and a nice tip for our Dan, our DJ, who has also donated his services, will help ensure that your favorite song gets played. I think that's about it for now. Y'all have a good time!"

Trish watched from her corner smiling and then laughing at some of the antics of the seniors. Some were already practicing their jitterbug, a few of them doing quite well. It was, however, the entrance of a young couple that captured Trish's attention. The girl, although dressed like Marilyn Monroe, actually reminded Trish more of the girl-next-door innocence of Sandra Dee. The guy with her, tall and handsome in a devilish kind of way, gazed at the girl with such adoring eyes that it made Trish's breath catch and a lump form in her throat. There was something familiar about him and then she realized that he resembled her neighbor Tony . . . another handsome devil that she couldn't get out of her thoughts, not that she was really trying. Fantasizing about him was harmless, right?

Trish watched the young couple sway to a sultry Sinatra song. She sighed. Had Steve ever looked at her that way? Somehow she didn't think so. And if he ever did, what had she done that made him stop?

"Oh . . . quit it," Trish chided herself. As she watched the silver-haired seniors laughing and having a good time, Trish was hit with the realization that she still had a lot of life to live. Seeing the energy and hearing the laughter told Trish that her life, though not what she had expected it to be, was far from over and she needed to take steps to get back in the game. Trish just wasn't quite sure how to go about it. With another sigh she bent her head and went back to taking notes.

"Nobody puts Baby in the corner."

Trish looked up to see Clyde Camden shaking his head at her. "I'm trying to be discreet while reporting."

"Oh, bull hockey." Clyde held out his hand. "Let's dance."

"Oh . . . no . . . I—" Trish attempted to protest, but Clyde shook his dyed-black head and wiggled his fingers.

"Let's go, Trish. Make my night and dance with me." He gave her a charming smile that flashed white against his George Hamilton tan.

"You don't seem to be hurting for dance partners." Clyde and Clovis were the resident hotties, and now that Clovis was taken, Clyde reigned king. She fully expected him to puff out his chest at the compliment, but his smile faded. "Oh . . . except for the one you want."

Clyde looked at her in surprise.

"I've been watching, remember. What's the name of the pretty lady you've had your eye on all night?"

"Joy."

"Pretty name too. Why is she keeping you at arm's length?"

"She thinks I'm just a player," he answered glumly.

Trish arched an eyebrow. "Is it true? I have heard rumors, Clyde."

"Yes, but the right woman could tame me."

Trish had to hide her smile since Clyde sounded so sincere. "So, why are you asking me to dance rather than Joy?"

"I'm trying to make her jealous."

Trish frowned. "I'm not sure that's the right tactic."

Clyde grinned. "Just roll with it, okay?" He wiggled his fingers again. When Trish stood up he grinned. "And make it look good, okay?"

Trish smiled. "I can, in fact, dance." And she loved it. Before her marriage fell apart she and Steve had gone swing dancing on a regular basis. Trish somehow doubted that Heather Hooter could perform a spirited Lindy Hop.

"Perfect! Jitterbug?"

"You betcha."

A moment later Clyde and Trish had commanded the dance floor so thoroughly that a circle formed and the crowd stood back to cheer them on while they jitterbugged to "Chantilly Lace." Breathless, Trish would have sat down, but when "Tequila" came on she just had to join in, doing the hand jive and shouting, "Tequila!" By the time she finished doing the bop to the song "At the Hop," Trish had worked up a sweat. "Shew, Clyde, I have to take a break. This might be your chance to go over and take Joy some refreshment." Trish leaned close to his ear. "And I do have to say that she was watching you. I think your little ploy might have worked. You should go over and see before somebody else beats you to the punch, if you'll pardon the pun."

Clyde took out a handkerchief and blotted his forehead. He straightened his tie and rolled his shoulders. Trish thought it charming that he appeared so nervous. "Wish me luck."

Trish grinned. "Good luck, Clyde. And thanks for dancing with me."

"Anytime. Girl, you sure can cut a rug."

Trish smiled as she walked over to the refreshment table. While she'd been dancing, pizza had been delivered. She noticed it was from River Row Pizza and Pasta, scheduled for a grand opening this weekend and her first restaurant review assignment. After grabbing a bottle of water, she returned to her corner to watch the upcoming jitterbug dance. Clyde had asked her to enter, but Trish wanted to sit back and observe. Reporting was fun and after the dance she planned on going home and starting to write about the event while it was fresh in her mind. With the newspaper only being weekly, there wasn't any deadline pressure, giving Trish the opportunity to also query some magazines. For the first time ever she could take her writing seriously and it felt pretty damned good.

When Trish arrived home she noticed that no lights were on at Anthony's side of the house. She'd barely spoken to her neighbor, but whatever he did, he must be a workaholic. She instantly felt sorry for his dog and decided that she would just take it upon herself to let him out. She knew she should ask permission but kept forgetting to get the lease from Maggie so she still didn't have his phone number. Surely he wouldn't mind her letting his penned-up dog out for relief and some exercise.

Trish hummed along to "Rock Around the Clock" while she changed into yoga pants and a tank top. A glance at her phone told her it was after eleven. When she'd left the party it was still going strong and she had to chuckle at the energy over in Whisper's Edge. They'd tired her out! After all of the exercise and excitement, she decided that she'd enjoy a glass of wine to unwind while she let Digger romp around for a little bit. She knew that the Irish setter needed the exercise, but she was also sure he would stay close to the house. Since it was dark, there was little chance of anything coming by that he'd want to chase. After that she planned on looking over her notes and perhaps starting her story.

Armed with a glass of wine, she glanced down at the key chain and felt a little bit guilty opening his door. Perhaps she'd wait for a little longer for Anthony to return. But when fifteen minutes passed and the wine kicked in, Trish decided to do the dog a much needed favor. She wouldn't go into his apartment, just let the dog out for a few minutes and then go about her business.

"Hey, Digger! Come on out, boy."

"Woof!" Digger didn't need any other encouragement and bounded out the back door. After giving Trish an excited dance in a circle, he headed out to the grass. She watched, hoping he wouldn't venture too far. Trish wondered where Anthony worked that he would keep such long and often late hours. "Not the kind of job to have when you own a pet," she grumbled. Trish had always wanted a dog, but Steve had been adamantly against it. She'd never argued, but now she suddenly wondered if she should look into getting a puppy.

"Come on, Digger," Trish shouted, and let out a breath of relief when the dog eagerly ran her way. And then she saw why. He had a yellow tennis ball in his mouth. "Oh, so there's the one that you couldn't find the other day. Yes, I watch you and your cutie-pie master play. Where is he, anyway?"

Digger dropped the ball at Trish's feet and then looked at her expectantly.

Trish sighed. "Okay, one toss. But then you have to go inside. Lucky you have a full moon so you can see enough to do this," she said, and then gave the ball a soft toss not too far away. Digger brought it right back and waited. Trish ended up playing with him for about fifteen minutes, but when she yawned she shook her head. "Time to go in, Dig. Surely Anthony will come home soon."

To her relief Digger obediently entered the house as if knowing he'd better if he wanted to get the chance to play outside again. Humming to herself as she locked the door, Trish felt in much better spirits. She needed to force herself to get out there, take more chances, and be more social. The residents of Whisper's Edge certainly were an inspiration.

Too tired to go over her notes, Trish got ready for bed. Just as she slipped between the sheets, she heard the rumble of an engine. Looking at the clock and seeing it was well after midnight, she shook her head. "Dig, I'm glad I let you out."

As she heard the car door shut and the alarm beep, she had the urge to go over to the window and peer out, but she didn't want to risk Anthony seeing her peeking at him, so she stayed put. But when she closed her eyes she had a vision of him shirtless and looking mighty fine.

9

Catch Me If You Can

When they crossed the road and headed back up to Wedding Row, Gabby felt a stab of disappointment. The night that she never wanted to end was almost over. They'd walked in silence for about the last five minutes, making Gabby wonder what was on Reese's mind. Had tonight been as special for him as well? They'd talked about childhood memories, snowball fights, playing tag, and chasing fireflies on warm summer evenings. Reese still had that lopsided grin, the sideways tilt to his head when he laughed. And when they'd slow-danced, being in his arms had felt almost . . . magical.

Gabby glanced over at Reese, thinking for the millionth time how handsome he looked dressed in the suit. The skinny tie had long ago been removed and placed in his pocket and his jacket was now slung over his shoulder, but that somehow added to his sexy appeal. They strolled down the sidewalk along the riverside, pausing halfway to sit on a park bench and look out at moonbeams dancing across the water.

Gabby wanted him to reach over and take her hand, but he didn't. She knew he was moving cautiously, catching up and letting her get to know him. She told herself that she was glad and yet all she could think about was if he was going to kiss her good night.

"It's a gorgeous summer evening," Gabby commented.

He nodded but continued to gaze out over the water as if deep in thought.

"Tired?" Gabby ventured, wondering if something was wrong.

"A little. It's been a long week and next week is going to be pretty crazy."

"Are you worried about opening the restaurant?"

Reese glanced at her and then looked down at the pavement. "Yeah, Uncle Tony needs this to go well. And so does my mom. They're both such good people and haven't been dealt an easy hand."

Gabby put her hand over his and squeezed. "I'm sure it will be successful. Your uncle has been in the business for a long time. He knows what he's doing."

"That's true." Reese shrugged. "But it was different in Brooklyn. I mean, yeah, we took a hit during the recession. The rising cost of operating Marino Pizza made times tough, and competing with chains was becoming more and more difficult. But Uncle Tony wouldn't even consider buying into a franchise when he made the decision to come to Cricket Creek. He wants complete control and I don't blame him."

"Oh, I know. Flower shops have to compete with grocery store purchases that are a lot more convenient. But people in Cricket Creek support each other, Reese. You'll be fine six months down the road."

Reese raised her hand to his mouth and kissed it. "Thank you."

"For what?"

"For being you." He gazed at her for a moment and then said, "We should probably get going."

Gabby nodded and then stood up. Something was still on his mind, she could tell. All too soon Flower Power came into view. Gabby's heart started beating harder. Should she invite him in? It was late, but she remained closed on Sundays so she could sleep in. But letting him into her apartment at night meant moving forward in this relationship. Right? Before Reese walked back into her life, Gabby had thought that Drew Gibbons would be her perfect match. Gabby suddenly heard her mother's warning to find Mr. Strong and Steady echo in her mind. Not knowing what to do as they rounded the side of the building, she glanced over at Reese once more, trying to read his mind.

At the bottom of the steps she said, "I had a lovely time tonight, Reese. Thank you for going with me."

"You're welcome," he replied in a soft tone, and then sighed. "Ah, Gabby, damn . . ."

"What?" Gabby felt her heart skip a beat.

"Don't send me away."

"I . . ." She looked up at his handsome face bathed in the moonlight and swallowed hard. She didn't want him to go and yet . . .

"Okay . . . all right." He inhaled a deep breath but took a step closer. "No, it's not all right."

"Reese, what's wrong?"

"Ah . . . Gabby." He looked up at the night sky and shook his head before gazing at her again. "All I could think about was holding your hand on the walk home. And now . . . now all I want to do is kiss you and yet I can feel you pulling away."

"I'm not pulling away. I . . . I wasn't sure what you were thinking."

"Can't you feel it, Gabby? This thing between us?"

She swallowed. Of course she felt it. Longing. Desire so potent that it consumed her thoughts . . . scared her. And Reese was so dangerously sexy. She could lose herself in his arms. Fall deeply in love with him. Dare she risk it?

"I'll go. I'm glad you had a good time."

Gabby nodded, but when he reached over and caressed her cheek, it was her undoing. Gathering courage, she gave him a slow smile.

"Gabby, what are you doing?"

"I think I'm about to throw myself at you."

Grinning, Reese put his suit coat over the nearby railing, took a step back, and opened his arms wide. "I'll catch you."

With a little laugh Gabby launched herself at him. As promised Reese caught her easily. And then he kissed her. Playful at first, spinning around while she clung to his shoulders, but then suddenly she threaded her fingers through his hair and kissed him with the pent-up passion she'd been feeling since the first touch, the first kiss. He was temptation. Danger. And she wanted him with an all-consuming hunger.

Gabby tossed away the caution that she'd been holding over her head like an umbrella for such a long time. And she simply let go and gave in to the moment.

Let it rain. . . .

His lips felt so warm so soft . . . so seductive. She opened her mouth for more, dipping her tongue in to taste, to tease, to tempt. He kissed her on and on beneath the canopy of stars, the light of the moon. Crickets chirped, frogs croaked, and a cat meowed, oblivious to Gabby's life-changing moment. This wasn't a kiss stolen in high school or the nearly being kissed in her shop. This kiss was deliberate. Delicious. Wanted. Needed.

Still kissing her, Reese carried her up the steps to the landing leading to her back door.

"My . . . keys," she said, breathless and between kisses. "In . . . my . . . purse." She slid down his body to a standing position but had to cling to him for support. Fumbling with the clasp, she managed to get her purse open, but with a low, sexy chuckle Reese took the keys from her trembling fingers and opened the door.

As soon as they were inside he swept her off her feet, making her giggle until he smothered her laughter with another sweet, hot kiss. He let her slide slowly down his body and then kissed her bare shoulder, holding her close. Gabby tilted her head to the side, giving him better access to her neck, and he took full advantage. His hands spanned her waist and then moved upward to caress her bare back, causing a hot tingle to slide down her spine.

Gabby wanted to reach up and untie the halter, allowing her breasts to tumble free, but she knew that having his hot mouth on her bare breasts would be her undoing. As much as she longed to take him into her bedroom and make wild passionate love to Reese, she knew it was too much too soon.

"God, I want you, Gabby."

"Reese—"

He put a fingertip on her lips. "No, you don't have to say it. I know it's too soon. As much as I want you right now, I want this to feel right. I want you to be ready to take that step."

"Thank you." She splayed her hands on his chest and smiled up at him. "Because, Reese, if you keep kissing me like that I won't be able to resist much longer."

Reese groaned up at the ceiling. "I don't know if I should think of that as good timing or really bad timing."

Gabby giggled low in her throat. "You'd better go before those fancy buttons on that shirt go flying."

His eyebrows shot up. "So you want to rip my shirt off?"

Gabby felt heat creep into her cheeks. "The thought went through my mind."

Reese closed his eyes and sucked in a breath. "You're killing me, girl."

Gabby leaned her forehead against his chest. She knew that one tug on his hand and she'd have him in her bed, sexy as hell and gloriously naked.

Reese gently tilted her chin upward. "Hey, if the time was right we'd already be making love. As hard as this is to do, I'm walking out the door. Because another minute of you looking at me like that and I won't be able to go. My resistance is only so strong and I'll have to kiss you again."

Gabby nodded because if she spoke it would be to tell him to stay.

"But I want to see you again. This week is going to be a crazy one, but let's find time to get together, okay?"

"I'd like that," Gabby replied, and then walked him to the door. He leaned in and kissed her briefly but sweetly and then headed out into the night.

Gabby immediately felt a sense of loss after he left. What would it be like to be his girlfriend? To make love to him and wake up wrapped in his arms? She looked over and spotted the candy necklace on the table and smiled. "Amazing," she whispered.

While she got ready for bed Gabby relived each kiss, smiled at some of the jokes he'd told and stories of his mother and uncle fighting over spices in the kitchen. Gabby remembered how troubled he'd been as a teenager and marveled at the man he'd grown into. And yet there was still an edge of sadness lurking in his eyes. As horrible as it was for Gabby's mother to die, it must be so very hard not to have closure with his father. Gabby shook her head, wondering how a man could up and desert his wife and child. She remembered Mike Parker as being a nice guy who seemed to love his family. They weren't rich, but he provided a steady income and had a reputation as being a good mechanic. But Gabby was no stranger to seeing men leave her mother. Her father did even before she was born. Men left. It was a fact of life.

Well, Gabby had promised her mother that she'd find Mr. Strong and Steady and she intended to keep her promise.

Oh, but it had felt so good letting go of her worries, her inhibitions, if only for a little while. Her thoughts drifted to Drew, and Gabby knew that kissing him wouldn't come close to the chemistry she felt with Reese. Kissing Drew might be pleasant. Safe. And yet when she tried to envision kissing Drew, she didn't feel the slightest longing to do so. Kissing Reese felt explosive. Dangerous. And so she reminded herself to tread carefully.

Chemistry wasn't everything. She also reminded herself that she hadn't dated all that much, so she was pretty clueless when it came to being in a long relationship. Gabby also knew that some of her restless longing stemmed from helping Addison plan flowers for weddings. Seeing happy couples so much in love had Gabby wishing that someone special would look at her with adoring eyes.

"Just slow down," she said sternly before turning off the light.

But like it or not, her thoughts of Reese and being in his strong arms stayed with Gabby and sleep eluded her for a long time. Out of frustration she grabbed a pillow and hugged it close, but it was a poor substitute for a warm, sexy male body. Going slow might be smart, but it sure wasn't nearly as much fun.

10

Water Under the Bridge

"DAMN IT, UNCLE TONY, I CAN'T GET THIS ICING TO THE right consistency," Reese complained.

"Somebody woke up on the wrong side of the bed."

No, the problem was waking up in an empty bed. Reese shot his uncle a glare. Thoughts and dreams of Gabby Goodwin had caused him a few restless nights.

"Forget about the Italian cream cake and go see Gabby," his uncle said in a gentler tone.

"Are you kiddin' me? We open in less than two hours."

"Yeah, so go see her now. You've been a grump-ass all week long."

"Like you haven't been?" Reese challenged.

"Would you two quit bickering?" Tessa said. "I'm going to box both your ears if you don't."

Tony put the pan of lasagna in the oven and then wiped his hands on his apron. "You look like you need to tell us something. Everything okay out in the dining room?"

Tessa nodded. "The flowers Gabby brought over are lovely. Everything is stocked, set up, and ready. Cara, the cute little hostess, arrived early and both servers are already here."

"Then what's the problem?"

"Tony, it's only ten and we already have people coming by. I hope we're not slammed."

"Oh, I don't think we will be. With no advertisement?" He waved a dismissive hand through the air. "No way. I mean, I hope we're steady, but I don't see how we could be slammed."

"Word can carry pretty fast in Cricket Creek," Tessa warned. "Do you think we should call in some extra help?"

"Who?" Reese asked, and his mother shrugged.

"I don't know. Maybe some of the people who applied for the server's job?"

"Without proper training and at this late notice?" Tony asked.

"I guess I'm just nervous," Tessa admitted. "I'm sure it will be fine."

An hour later they had a line out the door.

Reese wiped the sweat from his brow and then spread sauce on pizza dough with lightning speed. They hadn't stopped and people kept coming in. His mother ran here and there trying to do everything at once. Uncle Tony looked as if he was ready to have a meltdown. This was precisely the scenario they didn't want to have happen.

A moment later Reese looked up to see Gabby walking through the kitchen door.

"I don't mean to barge into the kitchen, but my goodness, you have a huge crowd out there." She jammed her thumb over her shoulder. "Is there anything I can do to help?"

Reese glanced over at his uncle and then shook his head. "Gabby, you can't close the flower shop."

"Please, at least let me help through the lunch rush. Joy is at Flower Power right now, so I can spare a few hours."

"I can't ask you to do that," Reese said.

"You're not asking, I'm offering," she said with a meaningful look. "Just like you've delivered some flower arrangements for me and put my flowers on your tables with a business card. All I want in return is for you to save me a piece of the Italian cream cake," she added with a smile, and then rubbed her hands together. "Now, how about giving me an apron so I can start busing tables?"

Tessa tossed her an apron. "You're an angel."

"I'm happy to help," Gabby said, and then hurried out into the dining room.

"She's a keeper, that one," Tessa called over to Reese.

Reese smiled. "Tell me something I don't know." He wanted to go out and give her a hug, but the orders kept coming. When the dining room proved to be too full, they were suddenly bombarded with takeout orders and delivery. Reese made a mental note to talk to his uncle about setting up additional outdoor patio seating. While patrons seemed to be taking the long wait and other mishaps in stride, Reese worried that this could hurt their business. First impressions meant everything. By the frown on Uncle Tony's face, Reese could tell he feared the same thing.

Gabby rushed in to help do dishes next to Ryan, a high school kid who looked as if he was going to have a panic attack when the pots and pans piled up like a mountain of stainless steel that might come to life like a Transformer. At one point the dishwasher clogged and when Tony went over to fix it, Reese had to rescue a too-crisp pizza. When he turned his back, Jamie, the new server, had already picked it up. Reese crossed his fingers, hoping that the customer liked it that way.

No one could have predicted this big of a crowd. Just when Reese thought it couldn't get any worse, Gabby came rushing through the double doors, put down some dirty dishes, and headed over to Reese. He didn't like the look on her face. Uncle Tony noticed it too and raised his eyebrows. "What's wrong?" Reese asked.

"I overheard that the woman sitting in the far corner is a food critic for the local paper."

Reese swallowed hard. "And?"

"I think her pizza was overdone and she ordered salad, but apparently you're out. Do you think you should send her some dessert or something?"

"Yeah, do that," Tony agreed.

"Maybe you should go out there and sweet-talk her," Reese suggested. "Take the dessert out yourself."

"I can't, Reese. I'm making more lasagna for tonight. And I'm a big ball of sweat. I'd likely offend her."

"I'll take the dessert out," Gabby offered. "Where's the Italian cream cake?"

"I was saving the last piece for you," Reese protested. "Take her something else."

"No, you can make more. Where is it?"

Reese gave Gabby the generous slice of cake and couldn't resist giving her a quick kiss. She blushed and he thought it was so damned cute. He watched her hurry out into the dining room, wondering what cool thing he could do for her to show how much he appreciated how she jumped in to help.

A minute later Gabby came back in with the cake still in her hand. Reese felt his stomach drop to his shoes. "Did she refuse the dessert?"

Gabby shook her head. "No, she'd already left. I'm so sorry, Reese." She put a hand on his arm. "Hey, I heard lots of people out there saying some great things about the food. I'm sure it's fine. She'll give you a good review. She seemed really nice."

Reese nodded. "Well, it's water under the bridge now," he said with more conviction than he felt. "Listen, we should have a little bit of a lull before dinner. Do you need to leave?"

"No, I already called Joy and told her to lock up. I can stay and pitch in."

"At least stop and eat," Tony said to her.

"Now, that I'll do," Gabby promised. "But first I'm going to run to the market and pick up whatever y'all need for salads. Make me a list while I go clear some tables."

Tessa watched her push through the double doors. "She's still as sweet and caring as ever. I remember when she was just a little girl she would bring us tomatoes from her garden, so proud of her produce!" She tilted her head. "She'll make a good mama someday."

Reese rolled his eyes. "Mom . . ."

"I'm just sayin'." Tessa turned and pushed through the doors and then reentered with a frown.

"What?" Tony and Reese asked at the same time.

"Nothing," Tessa answered, but Reese hurried over and looked out the door.

Reese spotted Drew sitting at a table chatting up Gabby. He wore a suit and tie and didn't have a hair out of place. Reese, on the other hand, had pizza sauce splattered on the front of his shirt and smelled like garlic. When Drew put his hand on Gabby's arm, it was all Reese could do not to storm out there and toss the jackass out the door. Until now Reese didn't know he had a jealous bone in his body, but he sure as hell was seeing green. He turned away before he did something stupid.

"She's just being polite," Tessa said.

Reese shrugged and went back to putting pepperoni on the large pizza. He tried not to let it get to him, but the thought went through his mind that though Gabby might find him desirable, was somebody like Drew what she really wanted for the long haul?

As if reading his mind, his mother poked him in the chest. "Hey, that guy's got nothin' on you. Remember that, okay?"

Reese gave his mother a quick peck on the cheek. "I will." He watched his mother walk through the door and then glanced over at his uncle. Both of them were such hard workers with such big hearts and both had been stomped on by the one each trusted the most. How did that even happen?

Reese sprinkled shredded provolone over the sauce, trying to keep his focus on the task at hand. He remained all too aware that life can come at you in unexpected ways and when you don't even begin to see it coming. But when anger had consumed him, sucking him under like quicksand, Uncle Tony had stepped up, providing the stability and discipline he so desperately needed at the time, allowing his mother to pick up the pieces of her life, heal, and go on. Once the restaurant was up and running smoothly, Reese was determined to push his mother into filing for divorce and getting the closure she so richly deserved.

When Gabby walked back through the doorway, Reese gave her a smile. He might be wearing sauce instead of a suit and he wasn't the mayor of Cricket Creek, but he wasn't about to stop pursuing Gabby Goodwin. She'd held a special place in his heart for a very long time, and now that he was back in Cricket Creek where he belonged, he was determined to show her that there was much more to him than met the eye.

When the seemingly never-ending rush finally subsided, Reese insisted that Gabby go home and rest. As much as he longed to see her later, Reese knew that the cleanup and prep work for tomorrow would keep him there well into the night. He retrieved the cake and insisted on sending some lasagna with her as well.

"Hey, thanks so much for helping," Uncle Tony said to her, and Tessa rushed over and gave her a hug.

"My pleasure," Gabby insisted. "I've learned that small businesses need to stick together. And hey, I'm impressed at how much work goes into running a restaurant. Like I told Reese earlier, I heard lots of great comments on the food. I can't wait to try the lasagna." She held up her foam box. "I'm thinking midnight snack."

Reese leaned over and gave her a kiss on the cheek. "I'll call you."

She nodded. "I'd tell you not to work too hard, but that would be silly."

"Reese, walk her out the door," Uncle Tony urged. "You need a breather."

Reese gave him a grateful grin and then opened the

kitchen door for Gabby. Once they were outside he took a deep breath of evening air. "Wow, now, that was quite a day."

Gabby placed a hand on his arm. "It's nearly over. Things will calm down now. A new restaurant in a small town is a big deal."

"I just hope that the reporter is kind to us. I think she got one of the few mess-ups of the day in spite of the huge crowd. Talk about bad luck."

"Like I said, she seemed nice enough."

"Do you know her name?"

Gabby shook her head. "Can't say that I do. She must be new in town."

"Ah well . . ." He inhaled another breath and then smiled at her. "I've thought about you nonstop all week, you know."

"I know now." She smiled. "And your text messages were a little bit of a clue."

Reese scrubbed a hand down his face. "I wish I could leave."

"I wish you could too. But I understand."

Reese ran a fingertip down her cheek. "Would you do me another big favor so I can make it through the night?"

"What would that be?"

"This. . . ." Reese took her hand and led her around the side of the building bathed in the semidarkness away from curious eyes. After gently prying the to-go box from her fingers, he put it on the ground and then pulled her into his arms. "I've waited all day, no, all week for, this." He bent his head and captured her mouth with the kiss that he'd been thinking about since she walked into the kitchen. To his delight Gabby wrapped her arms around his neck and kissed him back. She felt warm, pliant, *willing*, making it so hard to pull back and let her go home. "Well, that was stupid."

She tilted her head to the side. "The kiss?"

"Oh no. Gabby, the kiss was amazing. But no way will

it last me all night long." He rubbed his thumb over her moist bottom lip. "It only makes me want more." With a sigh he pushed away from the wall and said, "But I have to get back in there. We'll start getting some late night pizza orders."

"When will I get to see you?" Gabby wanted to know.

The question pleased him so much. "I'll find time. I promise."

"I'll hold you to it."

When she turned to go Reese put a hand on her shoulder. He wanted to ask if he could come by her place later, but he didn't want it to sound like a booty call, so he refrained, reminding himself to go slowly, but it was killing him. "Come over tomorrow for lunch?"

Gabby nodded. "Okay." She bent down to pick up the box and then eased up on tiptoe to give him a light but slightly lingering kiss on the lips.

Reese groaned and looked up at the sky. "This sucks so bad."

Gabby laughed and gave him a flirty wave as she walked away. Reese stood there watching her until she turned the corner. He knew he had a goofy smile on his face, but he just couldn't help it. If this was what it felt like to fall in love . . . well, it felt pretty damned good. Reese shook his head. With any luck it would only get better.

11

Busted

TRISH LOOKED UP AT THE MOONLIGHT AND SIGHED. SHE felt a little bit guilty after sending the lukewarm review of River Row Pizza and Pasta off to her editor. But even though the *Cricket Creek Courier* was a small publication, Clyde and Clovis made it abundantly clear that they wanted polished, professional articles written with an honest point of view. Trish even cut the new restaurant some slack since it was apparent that they were overwhelmed and understaffed, but that being said, she couldn't overlook the scorched bottom of her pizza with a crust so crisp that it crunched when she chewed. A crying shame because the thick sauce had delighted her taste buds and the stretchy, high-quality provolone melted in her mouth. To be fair she mentioned those positive things as well along with the homey, friendly atmosphere that felt old-world Italian. The fresh flowers were a nice touch and the piped-in music wasn't too overbearing.

Still, halfway through the day and they were already out of something as basic as salad. Patrons waited while tables remained cluttered with dirty dishes. In fact, she'd wanted to try one of the homemade desserts but felt as if she needed to vacate her table, allowing someone waiting to have a seat.

Trish tipped her wineglass up and took a sip of her Merlot and then patted Digger on the head. "Still, Dig, I feel kind of rotten." Maybe she wasn't going to like being a critic after all.

Trish also felt a bit guilty that she'd been letting Digger out several times a day with an extended playtime in the evening. At first it wasn't an issue because a teenager had stopped over to let the dog out but hadn't shown up for the past few days. She knew she needed to get ahold of Anthony and ask permission, but the man was never home. She'd tried to get his phone number from Maggie, but her friend was out of town for the week, probably off on some fancy rock star vacation, and so she still didn't know anything more about her mysteriously absent tenant—except that he left early and came home late, leaving his dog alone for way too many hours. The thought crossed her mind that he might have a girlfriend, and she frowned.

Reaching down, she scratched Digger behind the ears. She and the dog, both lonely, had bonded over the past week and when she did see Anthony she was going to ask formal permission to keep letting Digger out when he would otherwise be penned up for long periods of time.

After draining the last of her wine, she gave the dog one last scratch. "Time to head inside, Digger. It's getting late." Trish yawned and then stood up. Digger knew the drill and trotted toward his back door entrance, but this time he hesitated and gave her a sad look with his big brown eyes, making her halfway tempted to bring him inside with her. But she knew that'd be going too far. Maybe she really would have to look into getting a rescue dog of her own. Then Digger would have someone to play with. "I know, I know, this loneliness stuff is for the birds." Trish let him in and then locked the door.

After entering her side of the house, she locked up and then headed upstairs. Once she was finished getting ready for bed, she grabbed the self-help book she'd been reading and tried to get interested in the chapter on how to declutter the negative thoughts from her mind. She tried, really tried, but after rereading the same page twice she decided that she just wasn't in the mood to declutter her brain. "Maybe tomorrow," she said with a sigh, and put the book on top of a stack of several other self-help manuals. Perhaps she needed to read something more exciting like murder mysteries . . . oh, or maybe erotica.

And then she heard it. A noise.

Barely breathing, she sat very still and listened. Straining, she closed her eyes as if doing that would somehow make her hearing better. She should have listened to her mother's warnings about loud music as a teenager, because her hearing wasn't as sharp as it used to be. Aha, there it was again. A scratching and tapping noise seemed to be coming from the backyard. Switching off the light, she crept over to the window and peeked out but couldn't see anything. Trish made a mental note to have one of those gotcha lights installed.

Was someone trying to break in? Trish grabbed her cell phone and decided to creep down the stairs and see what was going on. But what if someone was already in the house? Her heart hammered in her chest and she wished she had a baseball bat handy. Instead, she picked up the empty wine bottle, thinking that might do the trick if push came to shove.

And then she heard a crash that had her nearly jumping out of her skin. She hurried across the kitchen floor and peeked beyond the vertical blinds, squinting, and then finally spotted the culprit.

"A raccoon!" And he'd just knocked over her garbage can. Relieved but grumbling, she fumbled with the latch and tugged, knowing she needed to shoo him away or there would be garbage all over the pavement in front of the garage. Trish made another mental note to get a garbage can with a sturdier lid that locked down. She tugged hard on the sliding glass door, grunting while wondering why it wouldn't budge. "Oh . . . right," she whispered, remembering the sawed-off broomstick inserted to keep out intruders, probably overkill in Cricket Creek but big-city habits die hard.

Finally, she opened the back door and stepped outside a few feet to the edge of the patio. She noticed the pretzels that she'd accidentally left outside that had been the late-night snack for the raccoon before moving on to bigger and better things. She shouted, "Go away! Go on, get out of here." She brandished the wine bottle even though she wouldn't dare go any closer. When the raccoon boldly looked over at her, Trish started waving her arms and jumping up and down, wielding the wine bottle like a sword. "Go! Get!" She stomped her bare foot and winced. "I'm warning you," she said, hopping on one foot.

"Is there a problem?" asked a deep male voice that had Trish yelping. She stopped in midjump, mid-crazy-wine-bottle wave, and landed like a ninja ready to pounce and turned toward . . . "Anthony?" Digger came out with him and barked at the raccoon before trotting over as if to protect her.

"You seem surprised. I live here, remember?" Shirtless, he wore weathered gym shorts. His dark hair was wet as if he had just gotten out of the shower. When he gave her an amused grin, Trish realized she was still in the crouched ninja pose. He frowned at the wine bottle.

"I . . . it was . . . I heard a crash." She pointed toward the garage with the neck of the bottle. "A raccoon knocked over my trash can."

"Oh. Interesting, uh, weapon." When his gaze lingered on her for a second, Trish remembered she was in a pink tank top and shorts . . . and no underwear. "Unless you were going to lure him away with a glass of wine?"

"It's empty," she said. "I . . . I should go pick the trash up."

"You go back inside. I'll get it."

"No, it's my trash," Trish protested.

"Hey, it's dark and there might be other critters out there."

"I've got this," Trish boasted, wanting to show that she was no longer dependent upon a man. But she swallowed, thinking of the beady eyes staring back at her waiting to pounce. No, she could do this. . . .

"I insist," Anthony said, and started to cross in front of her patio at the same time Trish hurried forward before her courage disappeared. She ran smack into him and on instinct, or maybe it was divine intervention granting her secret wish, the solid impact of his chest sent her stumbling backward. The bottle flew from her fingers, luckily landing on the edge of the grass, and she grabbed his shoulders for support. At the same time his hands shot out and steadied her around her waist.

"Oh my!" Trish said, suddenly becoming acutely aware of his warm skin. He smelled of masculine soap and minty toothpaste. She would let go . . . as soon as her equilibrium returned, and she hoped it wasn't anytime soon. For now she held on for safety reasons. "S-sorry."

"For what?"

"Running into you."

"Can't say that I'm sorry," Anthony admitted, keeping his hands put. He flashed Trish a sexy grin and for a heart-thudding moment she watched a droplet of water slide from his wet hair to his cheek, landing on the corner of his mouth. When he licked the droplet off, Trish almost moaned. For a moment she wished she could pinch herself to see if this was really happening or she was dreaming.

She watched his Adam's apple bob in his throat, and for another heart-pounding moment, she thought he might . . . well, maybe . . . kiss her?

"Sorry. I probably shouldn't have voiced that out loud, but it's been a long day." He suddenly dropped his hands and took a step backward as if wanting to create some distance between them. Digger started running around as if thinking this was time for fun and games. The happy dog brought the tennis ball over, but instead of putting it at Anthony's feet, he nudged Trish's hand. With a giggle Trish tossed it.

"He seems to like you. Funny because he was a rescue and it sometimes takes him a while to warm up to somebody."

Trish shrugged, wondering if she should confess that she and Digger had a thing going on, but she didn't. "Look, seriously, you don't have to pick up the trash. I need to put getting a better garbage can on my to-do list." *I'd like to put you on that list too* went through her mind, and she felt heat in her cheeks. "I would wait until morning, but I don't want to attract any more critters."

"I'll do it." Light from his kitchen cast a soft glow, and when he took another step backward, Trish got a really nice view of his chest. Anthony stood close enough for her to touch him, and Trish sure wanted to and fisted her hands at her sides in an effort not to do just that. Damn . . . it had been so long, and having her hands on his warm skin had been such a tease to her senses.

Anthony had one of those nicely ripped, but not too bulky, athletic bodies along with an enticing dusting of dark chest hair that had her heart hammering. He didn't immediately head over to clean up, just stood there as if he wanted to say more, but Digger ran over and started getting into the trash.

"I'd . . . I'd better get over there before he eats something he shouldn't. I feel bad enough that he's been cooped up so much lately. Katie, the dog walker I hired, left for volleyball camp and I haven't found a replacement." Tony sighed. "I let him out early in the morning and then sometimes not until late at night, but he's been so good about not making a mess. Hopefully, I can make it up to him after things settle down for me."

"I wondered what happened." Trish nodded. When was a good time to confess you'd been secretly carrying on an affair with someone's dog? She thought she would go join him and help while learning more about what was keeping him so busy, but a sudden cool breeze reminded her that she was scantily dressed and bending over might not be such a good idea, so Trish decided she'd better go back in the house. "Thanks so much, Anthony," she said quickly. "I'll get a new can tomorrow."

Once she was back inside, Trish put her hand on her chest, feeling the rapid beat of her heart. Biting her bottom lip, she smiled and savored the little feminine thrill sliding down her spine. She already knew Anthony Marino was one sexy man, and there was something deeper about him that sucked her in, making her want to know more about him. He had a killer smile and the coming-to-her-rescue thing was a total turn-on. As much as Trish wanted to become independent, she couldn't help liking the notion that he would come to her aid if need be.

But then she sighed when she remembered that she'd forgotten to ask him where he worked or if it was okay for her to let Digger out to play during the day. "Tomorrow," she said, and then went back upstairs, hoping that sleep wouldn't elude her. With any luck she'd have a steamy dream about her oh so dream-worthy neighbor.

Sunday passed by without any sign of Anthony, and feeling sorry for Digger, Trish let him out to romp around in the backyard while she worked on an article about Heels for Meals, a local charity benefiting families in need. Next on her list of restaurants to critique was Wine and Diner, but since she'd already eaten there she knew the review would be a positive one. She thought once again about the Italian restaurant. She'd have to head there again to see if they'd settled down and improved. The review would be in the paper tomorrow and she was excited for her words to be in print but still felt a little bit of nagging guilt that the review wasn't all that positive.

In addition to writing a lot of local articles, lately Trish had also been considering writing a novel but had yet to put the plot forming in her head on paper. When she'd once mentioned the idea of writing fiction to Steve, he'd scoffed at the notion, telling her she'd be wasting her time. Well, one thing that Trish had learned about her life since her divorce was that she'd wasted a lot of precious time *not* doing things she'd always dreamed of doing.

Those days were done. Knowing that made her want to dance a little jig.

Trish had decided it was about time to head inside when her cell phone rang. Looking at the screen, she smiled. "Hi, Maggie!"

"Hey," Maggie said, "I'm finally back in town after a week in Nashville with Rick. He's looking for new talent to sign at his recording studio."

"Sounds like fun."

"It was but I'm so behind with my work. So, what is it you were calling about?"

Trish watched Digger chase after a bird. "I haven't been able to locate the lease for Anthony Marino. Steve might still have it, but I thought you would be able to e-mail me a copy?"

"I'm sure I can do that. I believe it was a two-year lease."

"Oh, good. Hey, listen, do you know what he does for a living? He's rarely here."

"You don't know? He and his nephew own River Row Pizza and Pasta."

Trish's eyes widened. "Oh my God."

"What's wrong?"

"Maggie, I had no idea. I just did a review of his restaurant for the paper."

"You sound like you're in a panic."

"My pizza was burnt, and, well, let's just say I didn't slam them or anything but the write-up was, well, lukewarm at best."

"Oh no. . . ."

"It comes out tomorrow morning. I don't suppose I could go out and buy up all of the papers in the city, could I?" She tried to joke, but her stomach was doing flip-flops.

"Was it that bad?"

Trish winced. "It certainly wasn't glowing. Oh, I feel terrible!"

"Hey, you were being honest. That's your job as a reporter."

"I doubt if he'll see it that way." Trish closed her eyes and inhaled a deep breath. "Maggie, what should I do?"

"Maybe he'll take it better than you think. Or maybe he doesn't read the local paper."

"Maybe . . . ," Trish said in a small voice. "I guess I'll find out soon enough. What else do you know about him?"

"Not much, I'm afraid. His sister, Tessa, lived with her son, Reese, in the trailer park that Tristan and I recently bought. We're going to build starter homes on the site. I sold Tessa a little bungalow up in town."

"Oh, well, thanks, Maggie. I hope he's not too angry. I'll let you know how he takes it. You might need to find me another tenant asap!" she added with a wince. After ending the conversation, Trish called for Digger. She gave the dog a sorrowful pat on the head and he seemed to sense something was wrong. He put his head in her lap and looked up as if trying to let her know things would be okay.

"Thanks, Dig. But I don't think your master is going to take this very well." She sighed and felt a lump form in her throat. "You'd better get inside," she said, and some of her newfound joy dampened. "Sometimes I just have some really rotten luck."

12

Running on Empty

"UNCLE TONY, CALM DOWN BEFORE YOU BLOW A GASKET."

Tony slapped the newspaper against his leg. "Calm down? Did you read this review?"

Reese nodded. "It's not that bad."

"Ha! Highly anticipated but lacking in service? Overbaked pizza? Out of the basics? Unprepared? How could this be worse?"

"You're taking that out of context. She says some good stuff too."

Tony snorted. "What, that the flowers were a nice touch? Not to mention that she's my neighbor! My landlord. If I wasn't under lease I'd pack up my shit and move out rather than pay Trish Daniels another damned dime!"

Tessa pushed through the double doors. "Pipe down. The customers can hear you."

Tony inhaled a deep breath. "I'm tryin'."

"Look, I have an idea. Why don't you take her a fresh pizza? A big tossed salad with your amazing dressing and a slice of the turtle cheesecake Reese made last night?"

"Are you kiddin' me? You want me to bring her a dozen roses from Gabby's too? A bottle of Chianti?" To add insult to injury Tony had been thinking about his sexy little neighbor along those lines. Ha! That's what he got for trusting a woman.

Tessa shook her head. "Look, this really sucks and I'd love to give her a piece of my mind, but, Tony, you need to stop seeing red and think about how to handle this professionally. Maybe after eating an amazing meal from here, she'll write another review? I mean come on, she did say that we were obviously not prepared for such a big crowd. And she was right."

"You tried to tell me, Tessa. I was too bullheaded to listen." He sighed. "This is the only local paper and it is delivered all over Cricket Creek. People read it. This hurts."

"I think Mom's right. Take her a pizza. We're not too busy. You need to go home and cool off. Go for a run with Digger. If we get in a pinch later we'll call, okay?"

Tony looked over at Tessa and she nodded. "Do it. You have the meatballs ready for tonight's special. Mondays are always slow for delivery too. We can handle pizza orders and we're fully staffed in the dining room. I interviewed two more servers today and someone else for kitchen prep work. You're worn out, Tony. Go home."

Tony sighed, suddenly feeling so damned tired. At this point in his life, he should be almost coasting on cruise control instead of starting over. Sometimes it just really got to him. At times he felt like breaking down. Like now.

"Tony?" Tessa asked softly. "Are you okay?"

"Define okay?" he asked with a low chuckle.

Tessa walked over and gave him a hard hug. "Hey, we're Marinos. Made of strong stuff. One little crappy review isn't going to bring us down!"

"I'm making the pizza now," Reese said. "Since we don't know what she likes, I'll just do basic pepperoni. Mom, the cheesecake is in the fridge."

"I'm on it," Tessa said.

Thirty minutes later Tony left the restaurant armed with the food. He only hoped he could keep his cool and not give Trish a piece of his mind. He turned on some music and tried to calm down and it almost worked until he parked his SUV and spotted Trish out in the backyard tossing a ball to Digger.

"What?" How in the hell did his dog get out? And then it suddenly all made sense why Digger liked Trish so much. She'd been letting him out without his permission! Not only had she tried to wreck his business, but she'd invaded his personal space. Tony narrowed his eyes and tried not to notice how cute she looked in worn jean shorts and a faded Cincinnati Reds T-shirt. She'd been critical of his restaurant. She was *not* cute. Her ponytail swinging back and forth with curly tendrils escaping wasn't sexy, nor were her bare feet or tanned legs.

After opening the car door, Tony picked up the pizza box and grabbed the big plastic bag laden with food. He turned and witnessed Trish bending over to pick up the ball Digger had dropped at her feet and then tossing it in the air, laughing when Digger deftly caught it in his mouth.

"Good boy!" Tail wagging, the happy dog immediately brought the ball back for another toss. They were both so engrossed in the activity that they didn't even notice him standing in the driveway until he slammed his door to draw their attention. Digger happily bounded over to greet him.

Trish stood there with wide eyes, looking as if she wanted the ground to swallow her up.

Good, Tony thought as he took long, angry strides in her direction. To her credit she didn't back up even though she swallowed hard and then licked her bottom lip. "I . . . can explain."

Tony tilted his head to the side. "Explain why my dog is outside or explain why you felt the need to trash my restaurant to the public?"

"I didn't trash your restaurant!" Her chin came up. "I wrote about my personal experience at your establishment. I write the truth! What other reason would there be for reviews?"

"It was evident that we didn't expect such a large crowd. You could have come back later in the week."

"That's not how it works! Look, I'm sorry but it's not my fault that my pizza was scorched and the service was slow or that you were out of salad."

Okay, this wasn't going the way he'd planned. After inhaling a deep breath, Tony said, "I brought you a real example of our pizza. I've been in this business for a long time. My family had an amazing pizza parlor in Brooklyn until I was forced to close. I know how to make a killer pizza." He thrust the box forward and handed her the bag. "There's salad with our homemade Italian dressing and turtle cheesecake that my nephew baked this morning. Everything we do is made by hand, including our sauce. Our crust is hand-tossed. You won't get a better pizza anywhere. Period."

Trish took the box and looked at him with stormy eyes. "Tony, had I known it was your restaurant—"

"I don't need you to sugarcoat anything. Just eat the damned pizza. It speaks for itself." He motioned to Digger. "Come on home."

Digger looked at Trish and seemed to do a confused doggie frown, as if sensing something was terribly wrong. He sat by Trish's side.

"Are you for real, Digger?"

"You have been gone so much ... we kind of ... bonded."

In his anger about the restaurant, Tony had forgotten to be pissed about Digger. "That didn't give you the right to open my door and let my dog out. Did you go inside my place too? Snoop around?"

"Of course not! Look, I couldn't find the lease papers and I didn't have your phone number. He was whining one day and my heart went out to him."

"You realize what you did could be in violation of my lease." He just came up with that one on the spur of the moment.

"You . . . you want to move out?" Her eyes widened and she rubbed her lips together. "Seriously?"

No, not really, and he actually hated the stricken expression on her pretty face. He knew his reaction was knee-jerk and a product of his pent-up anger at so many things that was making him react this way. "Maybe." He motioned for Digger. "Let's go." When Digger sat there on his haunches as if in protest, Tony shook his head and started walking toward his side of the house.

"Tony?"

He kept walking, taking large steps, knowing it would be hard for Trish to keep up.

"Look, I can understand your anger with me."

Tony stopped, but the emotion in her voice wouldn't allow him to face her. He wanted to hold on to his anger, not forgive her.

"I really am sorry."

He didn't want her apology. Her kindness. He didn't want to feel that pull of attraction, the need for a woman in his arms . . . or in his bed.

"But I would like your permission to let Digger out to play."

"No."

"You're being unfair. He's a good dog and needs to get out and exercise. Why deny me . . . I mean him that?"

Tony tried to ignore the twinge he felt at her small admission. "We've hired more staff," he answered tightly. "I'll try to get home more often."

"And if you can't? Do I have your okay?"

"I'll think about it," Tony said, unwilling to give in so easily. That's what he'd done with Gloria. Looked the other way; extended forgiveness when he should have walked out. And where had that gotten him? She'd stripped him of his business and his pride, turning him into an unhappy shell of his former robust lifestyle. The first time he'd felt anywhere near his old self was when he flirted with Trish. And that could be dangerous. After his divorce he vowed never to give a woman the power to bring him to his knees ever again.

No, he'd stay as far away as he could from Trish Daniels, which was going to be difficult since she lived next door. Digger stared at him with those big brown eyes and Tony sighed. "Don't look at me like that. I'll come home more often. I promise."

But as he took Digger on a long run through the woods, he couldn't stop thinking about Trish. It pissed him off! She was making him feel things he didn't want to feel. God, he remembered the touch of her skin, the scent of her hair, the sound of her laughter. Although Trish would probably never believe it, he'd been a romantic guy, bringing flowers for no reason. He loved holding hands, kissing . . .

And sex. Amazingly hot sex. When he made love to a woman he did it slowly, thoroughly, exploring every inch of skin, getting as much pleasure out of giving as receiving. He'd given his all and then some to Gloria, but it wasn't enough. Her betrayal cut him to the quick, stripping him of his pride, his confidence. But even worse was the fear of trying again. Tony saw the same fear in the eyes of his sweet sister. How could people be so cruel . . . so callous, heartless?

Anger exploded in his head like fireworks and he pushed harder until his breath came in ragged gasps and his lungs burned. His calves protested, but he ran through the pain, even welcomed it.

Tony refused to slow down until he neared the clearing that led back to the house. He veered off the worn path to cross the narrow part of the creek, using rocks for stepping stones. When Digger stopped to lap up some water from the creek, he pushed on. Not knowing if the water was safe for Digger to drink, Tony turned to call to him, tripping when he failed to see a tree root in his path. Twisting his ankle, he went down with a grunt followed by a curse.

Pushing up to his feet, Tony gingerly put weight on his foot, only to curse a blue streak. Digger looked at him with worried eyes. "It's okay, Dig. I don't think it's broken, only sprained." But when he tried to walk it hurt like hell.

"Well, isn't this just great?" Tony hobbled around hoping he could find a sturdy stick that he could use as a damned cane but came up empty. With another curse he sat down on a fallen tree and looked at his ankle that had already begun to swell. He knew from experience that he needed to get ice on it pronto or he was going to have a helluva time working. "Damn it all to hell and back."

Digger looked at him and then, as if hit with sudden inspiration, took off toward the house, pulling a Lassie. If Tony hadn't been in so much pain he might have laughed. Just as he thought, about fifteen minutes later Trish came into sight. She spotted him sitting on the fallen tree.

"Oh my gosh, what happened?"

"I tripped. Sprained my ankle," he answered sullenly.

"Can you walk?"

"Does it look like it?"

She fisted her hands on her hips. "You don't have to be an ass."

Yes, he did, or he would give in to the feeling of being glad to see her and the concern in her eyes. "I'll be able to hobble home in a few minutes. You can go back to writing something mean."

"Okay," she said, and to his horror she turned on her heel. Digger barked as if trying to tell her this wasn't the drill. She was supposed to help!

"Wait . . . um . . . I guess I could use some . . . uh . . ."

"Help?" She whipped around to face him. "Is it so hard to ask, Tony?"

"Apparently." He inhaled a deep breath and used the edge of his T-shirt to wipe the sweat from his brow.

"Well, then, don't ask. I'm offering." She knelt down and gently examined his ankle. "You need to ice it, pronto."

"I know," he answered tartly, but when she looked at him with sympathy in her blue eyes he softened.

"I realize it's going to be hard for you to swallow, but you're going to have to lean on me, you big beast." She glowered at him and as long as he kept her pissed at him he felt safe.

"You mean sexy beast, right?"

"No."

He eased up to his feet. "But you were thinking it."

"I was not! But I do have to tell you that I ate your pizza."

"And?"

"You were right. It was killer. The salad dressing was perfection. I tasted the cheesecake and it was divine. I'll finish it later in small, guilty bites."

"So now you're eating crow."

Trish gave him a deadpan stare. "Just when I think I could like you . . ." She sighed. "Now put your arm over my shoulder."

"I'm sorry I'm really sweaty."

"I don't think you are sorry at all. I think it will give you great pleasure to drip your sweat all over me," she grumbled, but then suddenly fell silent, making him wonder if her comment conjured up the same visual as it did for him.

Tony swallowed hard. "You're right about that." He knew he needed to stay pissed at her and to keep his guard up, but she was making it so damned difficult. "So, what are you going to do about the fact that you gave River Row Pizza and Pasta a bad review?" he asked, trying to remind himself that his sexy little landlord was the enemy.

"You'll see," she replied.

"That's it? All you're gonna say?"

"Yep."

When she failed to elaborate Tony fell silent, partly because he was starting to warm up to her all over again and partly because his ankle hurt like hell. He was never so glad to see the house come into view.

Once he hobbled inside, Trish helped him over to the sofa. She gently propped his foot on pillows and then examined it once more. "It looks pretty bad. Are you sure you don't want to go to the emergency room?"

"I'm sure." Tony nodded, wincing when she slowly unlaced his running shoe.

"Sorry, but I'm going to have to tug it off."

"I'm tougher than I look," he tried to joke, but couldn't suppress a hiss of pain when she removed his shoe.

"I'm sorry, Tony!"

"Sure you are," he joked, but when she pressed her lips together in sympathy he managed a small smile. The thought ran through his head that Gloria had never been this compassionate or caring, but he shoved it aside. He'd been fooled by a woman once. He wasn't going to allow that to happen again.

"I'll go get a bag of ice," she said, and then hurried into the kitchen. Digger trotted after her like a shadow, and in truth Tony was glad that she'd taken it upon herself to let him out. She filled his water bowl before getting the bag of ice. While he wasn't about to get involved with her, Tony knew he should give her permission to hang out with Digger.

After placing the bag over his ankle she also handed him a bottle of water and asked, "Need anything else before I go?"

"No, I'll just find something on television and try not to think about how I'm going to work with this damned injury."

"Where's your cell phone?"

"On my dresser in my bedroom."

"If you don't mind, I'll go get it."

Tony nodded, but the thought of her in his bedroom had his brain sliding into dangerous territory. When she handed the phone to him their fingers brushed and Tony was shocked at his reaction to a slight touch. He scowled to hide his feelings. "Okay, you're off duty now," he said in the grumpiest voice he could muster.

Something akin to hurt slid into her eyes and he felt like an ass. She swallowed, blinked.

"Sorry. I'm just pissed that this happened at the worst of times. I didn't mean to take it out on you."

"Don't worry. I'm used to it," she responded in a false breezy tone.

Somehow Tony didn't think she was talking about him and then he recalled Maggie saying that she was divorced from Steve and wondered if she was referring to her ex. The thought of anyone talking to her in a nasty tone suddenly bothered him and he shook his head. "Seriously, I'm sorry, Trish."

His quiet, sincere tone surprised him as much as it did her and she shrugged slightly. "It's okay," she murmured, but there was suddenly a haunted quality in her expressive eyes and it hit him that she was most likely as damaged from her divorce as he was from his. "I'll give you my number in case you need anything," she offered, and waited until he nodded before rattling it off.

"Hey, seriously, I'm really sorry," he repeated, and she gave him a nod.

"Yeah, me too," she said. "Believe me."

Tony wasn't sure what she meant, but he could feel her withdrawal. Something in him wanted to bring her easy smile back, but warning bells rang in his head and so he remained silent, though when she turned to leave he stopped her. "Hey."

She turned around slowly.

"You have my permission to hang out with Digger."

She rewarded him with a small but bright smile. "Thank you," she said softly, and then walked away.

After she was gone Tony felt strangely alone but pushed the feeling aside with an angry edge. Being alone was way better than hurt and betrayal.

But when he closed his eyes and tried to doze he thought how amazing it felt to have Trish in his arms if only by accident. What would it be like to have her in his life?

In his bed?

"Not gonna happen," he grumbled. He reminded himself that he needed to stay focused on his restaurant. He had way too much on the line, and the two people he cared about the most were depending on him. Getting involved with Trish would be a distraction that he didn't need or want.

13

Raise Your Glass

"WHY SUCH A LONG FACE, CHILD?"

Gabby tied the raffia onto the Mason jar and then looked over to where Joy was sweeping up leaves that were scattered on the floor. "I didn't realize I appeared so sad," Gabby admitted.

Joy walked over to the craft table and sat down. "Are you wishing you hadn't turned down that handsome young Drew again? I'll watch over the shop if you really want to go to the Cougars baseball game. It's such a nice night for it. If you turn him down once more he might stop asking, you know."

"I know." Drew had been in the shop three times in the past week, but she just couldn't bring herself to say yes to a date.

"Gabby, Drew Gibbons is the most eligible bachelor in Cricket Creek and he's obviously set his sights on you. Aren't you interested?"

"I thought so . . . but I don't know." Gabby shrugged. "I should finish this arrangement and get it over to Addison."

"I can take it to her."

"That's okay."

Joy put her hand over Gabby's. "Sweetie, you need to get out and have some fun. It's Friday night, for goodness' sake. I don't understand. Listen, if you want to talk to me about something . . . *anything*, I promise I won't breathe a word to anybody." She made a show of crossing her heart.

Gabby smiled. "Thank you, Joy." Her mother had been her only real confidante, and it wasn't easy sharing her innermost thoughts with anyone else, although she'd recently become closer to Addison now that wedding season was in full swing. She didn't find it easy to open up with her personal problems, but the earnest look in Joy's eyes had Gabby wanting to confide in her.

"Talk to me, child."

"Oh, I don't know. I think perhaps doing the flowers for several weddings has me wondering if I'll ever find someone and get married."

"Oh, Gabby, you're a lovely, vivacious young woman. If the right man hasn't come along, he will."

Gabby hesitated and then asked, "How do you know if he's the right one?"

Joy tilted her silver head to the side. "I'm guessing this has something to do with Reese Marino?"

"How did you know?"

"I'm seventy-five years old and I've done some living. The way your eyes light up when he stops by tells the story. He gives you butterflies, doesn't he?"

Gabby nodded.

"And Drew doesn't."

Gabby sighed and then nodded. "No, not really. I mean, he's nice and everything, but . . ." She shrugged.

"So you want to be attracted to the young mayor rather than the resident hellion."

"He says he's put those days behind him."

"Ah, but reputations die hard in a small town, don't they? And maybe you're not so sure?"

Gabby nodded again.

"And it doesn't help that young Reese still looks the part. He's a hottie, that one."

"The kind my mama fell for and it never worked out," Gabby admitted. "It wasn't always easy growing up in Riverbend Trailer Park. We used to be called river rats by some. When Drew finally took notice of me, well . . . it made me feel validated. Accepted rather than looked down upon."

Joy's chin came up. "Anybody who ever looked down upon you because of where you're from isn't worth your time of day."

"I know you're right." Gabby tapped the side of her head. "Up here. But sometimes I still feel a little bit on the outside looking in. Forgive me, I don't mean to sound shallow."

Joy shook her head. "Honesty is never shallow, Gabby. We all have our stories, our fears. I know I sure do. Fear is a necessary form of protection from doing something foolish, but don't allow fear to rule your life. That's all I'm saying."

"I hope you'll share some of your life with me while we work together. I'll soak up your wisdom like a sponge."

Joy tossed her head back and laughed. "You mean learn from my mistakes?"

"Oh, I'm sure you made mostly good choices."

Joy gave her a soft smile and her eyes appeared misty. "Yes, mostly."

Gabby was hit with sudden inspiration. "Joy, did you walk to work?"

"Surely did. What's that got to do with the price of tea in China?"

Gabby arched an eyebrow. "Well, I'm thinking about running upstairs and getting a bottle of wine. Are you interested?"

"Is the pope Catholic?"

"I'll take that as a yes." Gabby laughed, already feeling better.

A moment later Addison entered the flower shop. "What's up, girls?"

"We were just talking about you," Gabby said. "I have the tabletop arrangement ready for you to show your client."

Addison sighed. "That's why I came over. She's changed her mind about the colors . . . again. I brought swatches."

"No big deal," Gabby said with a shrug. "If it were my wedding, I'd want everything to be perfect too. Hey, Joy and I were about to open a bottle of wine. Would you like to join us?"

"I'd love it," Addison answered brightly. "Reid went to the baseball game with Braden and his dad, so I have the night free. Hanging out with the girls sounds like fun. Hey, do you mind if I go grab Maggie? She's about to close up and I know that Rick is at the studio in a recording session."

"The more the merrier!" Gabby announced, and Joy nodded her agreement.

"Sweet. I'll stop by my apartment and get a couple more bottles of wine. I have some hummus and pita chips if you want me to bring a snack?"

"Sure, hey, why don't we move this to my back deck?" Gabby offered. "I think I can round up some munchies too. I'll lock up down here, so come around the back entrance, okay?"

"Gotcha," Addison said, and grinned. "This is nice! See you in a few minutes."

"Let's lock up," Gabby said to Joy. "A glass of wine is calling my name."

Joy cupped her hand to her ear. "I hear it too!" she said with a tinkle of laughter.

"Then let's go." Gabby brought the Mason jar filled with wildflowers up to her apartment. She felt a nice little bubble of excitement at the prospect of entertaining friends.

"Your apartment is lovely," Joy commented. "Kind of an eclectic mix of style and furniture."

Gabby laughed. "It's called thrift store chic," she admitted. "My mother and I learned to repaint and repurpose before it was the in thing to do. There aren't many things in here used for their original intention."

Joy grinned. "Ah, like the wooden ladder over there used as a bookcase? And the wicker trunk for a coffee table?"

"Yes, and it doubles as storage space." Gabby pointed to a stack of antique hatboxes stacked in the corner. "Those are filled with random things that I just can't part with."

"Secret junk drawers?"

"Exactly!" Gabby pointed at Joy and laughed. "I just love exploring the dusty corners of cluttered antiques shops, and there are a few in Cricket Creek that I frequent. It might sound weird but I find more pleasure in something worn and used than shiny and new."

Joy shook her head. "Not weird at all. There's a certain comfort in antiques, I suppose. Maybe it's the history, I don't know, but I understand completely. Have you been to the Purple Frog Café up on Main Street yet?"

Gabby shook her head. "Where is it? With a name like the Purple Frog, it has to be fun."

"Oh, you'd adore it." Joy nodded. "My good friend Barbara Smith opened it just last week. It's a coffee shop, but it's also a wonderful mix of antiques, trinkets, and handmade knickknacks."

"I'm sure I'd love it." Gabby waved her hand in a circle. "After all, nothing in here matches, not even my silverware or dishes."

"I like it. Full of vibrant color and personality, just like you!"

"Thank you, Joy! I always did like a bold mix of colors. I suppose it comes from working with flowers. Is Chardonnay okay? I have a bottle of red too."

"Oh, Chardonnay sounds refreshing for a warm summer night. Thank you for the invitation, Gabby."

Gabby smiled as she poured the wine and then

handed Joy a glass. "I have a nice deck out back. Someday I hope to have a house with a big yard so I can plant a garden, but for now this is perfect for me." She dumped some pretzels in a bowl, then sliced up some cubes of cheddar cheese.

"May I do anything?" Joy asked.

"Just grab those napkins and get the door and we're set!"

"Oh, this is so pretty!" Joy pointed to the white bistro table and matching chairs. "I just knew there would be flowers everywhere. Oh, and tomato plants! You certainly have a green thumb."

Gabby laughed with delight. "It started with seeds in a milk carton when I was a kid and grew from there. I still like to garden from seeds."

Joy nodded. "There's a certain satisfaction in seeing a plant sprout from a seed, isn't there?"

A few minutes later Addison arrived. She had Maggie with her, along with a woman Gabby didn't recognize. "I'd like you to meet Trish Daniels," Addison said. "She and Maggie were friends when they lived in Cincinnati and she recently moved to Cricket Creek."

"Welcome, Trish. I'm Gabby and this is my friend Joy."

"Nice to meet you and thanks for having me," Trish said with a wide smile.

"Oh, you work for the newspaper, don't you?" Joy asked.

Trish nodded and it suddenly hit Gabby that this was the woman who had written the rather stinging review of River Row Pizza and Pasta. Gabby knew she was doing her job, but it was a little hard not to hold it against her. Still, she seemed like such a genuine person that she wanted to give her the benefit of the doubt.

"I live in Whisper's Edge near the Camden twins," Joy explained. "So I've heard about you."

Trish nodded. "Those two are quite a pair. I danced with Clyde at the prom the other night."

"I saw you," Joy said hesitantly.

"You know he was trying to make you jealous, right?" Trish asked.

Joy waved a dismissive hand through the air. "Right. . . ."

Trish raised her eyebrows. "I'm serious. He told me so. Seems like there's never a dull moment with the residents."

"You got that right." Joy laughed her agreement. She seemed to really perk up with the news that Clyde was trying to make her jealous. "We might be a retirement community, but there's nothing boring about Whisper's Edge—that's for sure."

"So, are you going to give Clyde the chance he wants?" Trish persisted, and they all waited for Joy to answer.

"He's such a player, that one. I think I'm going to make him work for it," Joy answered. "Make sure he's, as the kids, say . . . *legit*."

"He sure seemed to be," Trish said. "And the man can dance."

Joy laughed. "Oh, he can do everything to hear him tell it."

"I'll get more glasses and bring a corkscrew," Gabby said. She also turned on some music and brought out an ice bucket. Pretty soon wine was flowing and they were all laughing and chatting away.

"So, does anybody have any *other* juicy gossip?" Joy wanted to know. "I sure didn't think I'd be the center of attention."

Addison shook her head. "Not that I know of, anyway. I'm just glad there's nothing out there about me this summer." She grinned at Maggie. "I'm sure you feel the same way. You know the story, right, Trish?"

Trish took a sip of wine and nodded. "You mean the gossip that you were having an affair with rock star Rick Ruleman while engaged to his son?"

"Yeah . . . that one," Addison said with a roll of her eyes.

"You should have seen my face when I saw the famous kiss picture in *People* magazine," Maggie said. "And now I'm married to the man."

Trish leaned back in her chair. "Did you ever think in a million years that you'd be married to a famous rock star?"

"No!" Maggie laughed, and then gave her friend a nudge with her elbow. "You just wait. The right guy will come along when you least expect it."

Addison nodded in agreement. "After two very public broken engagements, I opened a bridal shop that led me to butting heads with Reid and now I'm married to him. Go figure. Life can be crazy."

"So, any advice for us single ladies?" Joy wanted to know.

Gabby was also listening closely, figuring she could use all the advice she could get from this eclectic group of ladies.

Addison nodded. "I know this sounds totally cliché but you've got to follow your heart." She tapped her chest. "I mean, seriously."

"What if your heart's been shattered, stomped on. Put in a blender?" Trish asked.

Gabby's eyes widened. She didn't know Trish yet, but she seemed like such a sweet person. Who could want to hurt her so badly?

"Pick up the pieces," Addison suggested. "I had to and I know it's not easy by any means."

"How do you get past the fear?" Trish asked. "I really want to get my groove back."

Maggie raised her hand. "I've got this one. I had to get over the fear of falling for a rock legend who dated women half my age."

"How did you do it?" Gabby wanted to know.

Maggie raised her eyebrows. "You have to let love take the wheel. Steer you in the right direction."

Trish shook her head. "But, Maggie, I'm terrified. I

feel as if I'll steer right off another cliff. Crashing and burning isn't fun."

Maggie put her hand on Trish's arm. "You were married to a jerk. Don't give him the power to keep you from finding happiness." She wiggled her eyebrows. "Your neighbor Tony Marino sure is a hottie. Has he forgiven you for the review yet?"

Gabby watched for Trish's reaction.

Trish sighed. "I don't think so, but he should *soon*. I've written a follow-up review that's glowing. I explain that I was in the restaurant at a bad time and that the food is really quite wonderful. It was actually an interesting article to write because it involves giving the restaurant a second chance. I didn't apologize because I didn't want to discredit myself as a food critic, so I wrote it from the angle of giving a well-deserved second chance."

"That was a good way to go about it." Gabby felt instant relief. She was starting to like Trish and didn't want to hold her review against her even though she realized she was only doing her job.

"So you think he will?" Maggie persisted.

"Forgive me?" Trish shrugged. "The man might be gorgeous but he's got a hard head. I guess I'll see. I have a couple more things up my sleeve that may sway him too. But he refuses to stay off his sprained ankle."

"So, have you been playing nurse?" Joy asked.

Trish rolled her eyes. "I've tried but he's been so grumpy."

"You could get a naughty little nurse's outfit and sashay over there." Joy stood up, put a hand on her hip, and demonstrated, bringing all to laughter. "I just bet that would cheer him up."

"He's a tough nut to crack," Trish admitted. "But hey, I don't blame him. After divorce the romantic rug gets pulled out from beneath you so to speak. I sure am struggling."

"Oh . . . wait. So this is the uncle that Reese lived with in Brooklyn?" Joy looked over to Gabby for confirmation.

Gabby nodded. "Reese and I grew up together until he left for New York."

Trish's eyes widened. "Oh my gosh. I thought you looked familiar. You were at the restaurant helping out, weren't you?"

"Yes, I walked over to get lunch and entered chaos. I knew I had to try to pitch in," Gabby replied.

"Thanks for being so understanding about the review and not tossing me over the side of the deck."

Gabby poured more wine in her glass and offered the bottle to Trish. "I grew up being judged and so I try to keep an open mind. Like you explained, you were just writing an honest piece."

Trish sighed. "I love to write but I'm not so sure I'm cut out to be a critic. I was horrified when I realized Anthony and Reese owned River Row Pizza and Pasta."

Maggie shook her head. "I know it had to be horrible, but I would like to have been a fly on the wall when Tony found out."

"Oh, I defended my position to him, but in truth I wanted the ground to swallow me up. Plus, he found out I'd been unlocking his door and letting his dog out on a daily basis. He was steaming," Trish said, but grinned.

"You fancy him, don't you?" Joy asked.

Trish stabbed a cube of cheese with a toothpick. "That arrogant, mule-headed Italian?" she scoffed.

"A very sexy Italian," Maggie pointed out. "And so is his nephew." She arched an eyebrow at Gabby, who tried to hide her blush by taking a sip of her wine.

"So that's a yes," Addison said to Trish, and they all laughed. "What about you, Gabby? I know you had fun at the dance with the younger arrogant, mule-headed, sexy Italian. Any news there? Now that I'm married I have to live vicariously through you single ladies."

"Ha!" Joy slapped her knee. "We all feel so sorry for you being married to Reid Greenfield," she said in a singsong voice.

"Thank you. I'll admit it's tough," Addison answered with a laugh. "But speaking of mule-headed, I had to take *that* whole situation into my own two hands or we wouldn't be married. The days are done when women have to wait for the man to make the move." She gave Gabby a pointed look. "So, Gabby? Have you been seeing Reese since the dance?"

"He's always working," Gabby answered with a shrug. "Especially since Tony sprained his ankle." She left out getting the flirty text messages that made her smile throughout the day and dream of Reese at night.

"So, in other words, not nearly enough," Addison pointed out.

Gabby bit her bottom lip but nodded her admission. He always seemed to be on her mind.

"Well, now," Joy said. "Addison has the right idea. Sounds like these men need a nudge in the right direction. Sometimes you do have to take the situation into your own hands, if you know what I mean."

Maggie nodded and raised her glass. "I'll drink to that. Cheers!"

They tapped their glasses together and laughed.

"I suddenly feel like pizza. Anyone want to join me at River Row Pizza and Pasta?" Joy asked with a grin.

"Sounds like a good plan," Maggie said with a firm nod. "Let's go, girls!"

"I'm in!" Gabby joined in the laughter, feeling more carefree than she'd felt in a long time.

14

Cloudy with a Chance of Meatballs

"UNCLE TONY, YOU SHOULD GET OFF THAT FOOT AND ICE it down," Reese suggested when he noticed the grimace of pain on his uncle's face.

"I've got to mix the veal into the ground beef."

"I'll take over," Reese insisted.

"You've got desserts to bake."

"You know what? I'm thinking about heading up to Grammar's Bakery in the morning. Cheat a little bit so I can do the prep work for you. They'll still be homemade desserts."

"No way."

Reese raised his hands in the air. "You need to stop being so damned stubborn. At this rate you'll be hobbling around for the rest of your life. Sit your ass down and I'll grab you a beer. I'm capable of making meatballs."

"You are a meatball," Tony answered with a dark scowl. "You know I can take you even with the bum ankle."

"In your dreams."

"You wanna go?" Tony asked, but the fight was gone from his voice as he hobbled over to a metal folding chair and sat down.

Reese brought a bag of ice over and handed him a Bourbon Barrel Ale.

"This is some good stuff."

"I'm always looking out for ya." Reese had stocked up on his uncle's new favorite beer. He scooted another chair over so Tony could prop his foot up. "Chill for a few minutes, okay? I told you we should have had Ryan stay and help out."

"We need to cut back on costs until we're in the black. Besides, the kid worked his ass off and it's Friday night. We're likely to get some delivery orders soon or I'd get the hell out of here myself."

"At least the dinner rush is over," Reese said.

A moment later Tessa hurried through the door. "You'll never guess who stopped in for a late dinner."

Reese and Tony looked at her, waiting.

"This is where you guess," she said, clearly excited.

"Mom, just tell us. I'm not in the mood for guessing."

"You're no fun. It's Gabby, Trish, Addison, Joy, and Maggie! They ordered a large pepperoni with mushrooms and bell peppers and an order of cheese sticks."

"I'll get on it." Reese tried not to appear as though the news made his heart pound. He hated that he'd been so busy all week and hoped that douche bag Drew wasn't making a move on Gabby, but he was fairly certain that he was.

Tessa chuckled. "You know that both of you can stand there looking all big and bad but you're both so transparent."

"I'm sitting," Tony corrected, and glared down at his ankle.

"You like Trish, Tony. Just admit it."

"Are you kiddin' me?" Tony growled. "Are you forgetting Trish trashed our food? She might be out there to do 'nother story for all we know."

"You're so full of it, Tony, and you know it. She's out there laughing and cutting it up with her friends. I think they've been drinking a little bit," she added in a stage whisper. "Joy, the older one, just got up and started dancing to Sinatra. She's a card."

Reese watched the sudden wistful look pass over his mom's face. When was the last time she had a girls' night out? "Mom, why don't you take a bottle of wine out there, on the house, sit down, and have a drink with them?"

Tessa put a hand on her chest. "We're too busy. I need to start the prep for tomorrow."

"Have Cara roll the silverware and fill saltshakers. She's not busy right now."

Tessa looked at Reese for a second. She swallowed hard but then nodded. "You know what? I think I will!"

Reese felt emotion fill his throat. His mother was such a good person. She deserved to have some fun once in a while. "Go! I'll bring the pizza out when it's done."

When she walked out into the dining room with the wine, Reese heard the ladies cheer.

"You're a good kid, Reese."

Reese shrugged. "I love her so much, ya know?"

"I do know."

Reese watched the play of emotion on his uncle's face. "I know you love her too."

"We all got handed a raw deal in some ways, but we're luckier than most. We have each other's back. That's what families do."

"Always," Reese said, and then cleared his throat. "By the way, I'm not a kid, you big oaf."

Tony laughed and then tipped his beer bottle up to his lips. "Get your ass to work."

Grumbling under his breath, Reese started making the pizza, but when he heard the sound of his mother's laughter drift back into the kitchen he smiled. He'd never be happy about Uncle Tony having to shut down Marino Pizza, but he sure was glad to be back in Cricket Creek near his mother.

"Make sure the pizza is perfect for Miss Critic out there," Tony grumbled.

Reese shot him a look. "Was Mom right? Do you have a thing for her?"

"Hell no! Trish Daniels is a thorn in my side and gonna stay that way. She squirted my ass with water from a hose last week."

"I like her already."

"You would. She's even stolen the affection of my dog!" he grumbled.

"Ah . . . so you do have a thing for her."

Tony set the beer bottle down with a thump. "Now, how do you figure that?"

"Because you're protesting way too damned much."

Tony's answer was a grunt. "Right. Like I want another woman to screw me up even more than I already am. Not gonna happen. I'm done, Reese. You can stick a fork in me."

"Maybe you shouldn't have that piss-poor attitude." Reese hesitated because he and his uncle hadn't really discussed this before. "I mean, it's been two years now."

"Two years of struggling to get back on my feet, financially . . . emotionally. You were there, Reese. Man, I don't know if I could ever put myself out there again."

Reese slid the pizza in the oven and turned around. "Well, I carried that damned chip on my shoulder for a long time. You'd be surprised how much better you feel when you let the anger go. It's like a big-ass weight lifted, ya know?"

"I know you're right. I just can't shake the anger."

Reese angled his head toward the crutches. "Why don't you hobble out there and say hi?"

Tony glanced toward the double doors. "No, let Tessa have center stage."

Reese nodded his agreement, but something flicked in his uncle's eyes and he knew it was an excuse. Gloria had done a serious number on him. But it wasn't right for Uncle Tony to live the rest of his life looking back. Somehow they all three needed to break free of the past in order to move forward.

"Hey, Reese, don't look at me like that. I need to get this restaurant up and making money. The last thing I need is to get tangled up with a woman." He tipped his bottle up and took a long pull of his beer.

"Really? Because I think it's exactly what you *do* need."

Tony grimaced and then rearranged the ice pack on his ankle. "Like I said but you don't seem to hear me: not gonna happen."

Reese put the cheese sticks on a serving plate and poured some of their homemade marinara into a small bowl. "Keep an eye on the pizza while I take this out there, okay?"

Uncle Tony gave him a grumpy nod. "Whatever."

Reese pushed through the doors with the food. His gaze immediately fell on Gabby. She tossed her head back and laughed at something that Joy said, but when she looked his way her laughter stopped and she swallowed hard. Was she nervous? Excited to see him? He sure as hell wished he knew. "Here you go, ladies. Your pizza will be out in just a few minutes."

"Do you need me in the kitchen?" his mother wanted to know.

"No, Mom, Uncle Tony and I have it under control. You just sit and relax."

"Is he staying off that ankle?" Trish asked.

"Of course not, unless you count right this minute," Reese replied. To his surprise Trish pushed back from the table.

"Pardon me while I go give him a piece of my mind," Trish said firmly.

"Good luck with that one," Reese said with a surprised shake of his head. He suspected that the wine they'd been consuming had given her a bit of liquid courage. Good thing. She was going to need it.

A moment later Reese heard raised voices. "I'd better get back there and run interference," he said with a shake of his head. "I'll bring your pizza if I come out of there alive. If I'm not out in five minutes, come looking for me."

The ladies all laughed and just as he imagined when he entered the kitchen, Uncle Tony and Trish were nose to nose arguing.

"No, I didn't take the anti-inflammatory because it upsets my stomach."

"You have to eat in order for that not to happen," Trish argued.

"I don't feel like eating with my damned ankle throbbing."

"That's why you need to stay off it, Anthony!"

"You're my landlord, not my mother. Don't call me that."

"Then I'll call you what you really are."

"And what would that be?"

"A jackass."

Reese stood there wondering what to do. Neither one of them realized he'd entered the kitchen.

"Is that right?" Tony crossed his arms over his chest and glared at her. He picked up his beer and then frowned when he realized the bottle was empty. "Why don't you do something useful and get me a beer?"

Trish fisted her hands on her hips. "When hell freezes over."

"You're just full of charm, aren't you?"

"And you're full of—"

Reese cleared his throat, deciding it was time to put an end to this heated exchange. "Um, I came back here to get the pizza," he explained, and headed over to the oven.

"Hope it's perfect so Trish doesn't turn her nose up and write something mean."

Reese watched her eyes flash. "You know what? I'm out of here. Pardon me for caring." She turned on her heel and stormed out.

"Um, that went well," Reese said, and shook his head

at his uncle. "Don't you think you were a little bit harsh? She did come back here to see how you were doing."

"I don't need her mothering me."

"I don't really think that's what she has in mind," Reese said. "You know you might be screwing up what could be a good thing?"

"Haven't we had this conversation already?"

Reese slid pizza onto a metal tray and then turned to face his uncle. "Cut her some slack, Uncle Tony. She seems pretty sweet."

"You call that piece of work sweet?"

"Yeah, and you were a complete dick. Get your sorry ass out of here and take her some dessert."

"I don't want to get involved with the woman. Any woman. But especially *her*." He angled his head toward the door.

"Then you're dumber than you look."

Reese picked up the pizza and walked out into the dining room. He noticed that Trish had left and felt sorry for her. "So Trish went home?"

When Gabby nodded Reese shook his head.

"Why don't you sit down and have a slice of pizza?" Without waiting for an answer, his mother stood up and vacated the spot next to Gabby. "The dining room is closed and we don't have any deliveries. I'll go back and help clean up the kitchen with Mr. Grump," she added with a nod toward the kitchen.

While Reese wanted to argue, the temptation to sit next to Gabby was too strong and so he agreed. "Let me know if you need me back there," he called over his shoulder.

A few minutes later his mother sent him a text message saying all was under control and that he should offer to walk Gabby home. He smiled, liking the idea.

"This pizza is so good," Joy said. "I can't wait to try some other items on your menu too."

"I agree wholeheartedly," Addison added.

"Thanks." Reese felt a measure of pride and smiled.

"Of course pretty soon my butt is going to be the size of a Buick," Joy added, making them all laugh. "Especially with those delectable desserts."

A moment later Clyde Camden walked into the restaurant. Reese remembered him from the dance. At least he thought it was Clyde. It could have been his twin.

"Oh, I'm sorry but the dining room is closed," Cara told him. "Would you like to order carryout?"

Clyde glanced over at Joy. "No, thank you. I've found what I'm looking for."

Reese saw Gabby give Joy a discreet little nudge and had to hide his grin. Clyde was one smooth operator. When he looked at the pink color in Joy's cheeks, he thought he should start taking notes.

"You were looking for me?" Joy put a hand on her chest.

"I knew you were working late and didn't want you to walk home in the dark. I passed Trish and she let me know you were here."

"There are streetlights along the way, Clyde. And it's not far to Whisper's Edge. Not much crime happens in Cricket Creek."

"I think that's a lovely gesture," Gabby piped up, and this time Joy nudged her back. "Don't you think so, Addison?" Gabby persisted.

"Absolutely," Addison agreed. "I'm about ready to leave too. She motioned to Cara. "Could we have the check, sweetie?"

"This is on the house," Reese offered.

"No way," Addison argued when Cara handed her the tab. "And this one is on me. I had such a great time tonight," she said as she slid her credit card into the plastic slot. "Let's do this more often."

"I agree," Gabby said, and Reese was glad to see that she was fitting into the community. There was a new confidence about her that he found appealing . . . and very sexy.

"Me too," Joy added, but then frowned. "Will y'all check on Trish? She seemed a little bit upset."

"Uncle Tony is going to bring her a peace offering," Reese promised. "He's just in a crummy mood with his sprained ankle." And other things. . . .

"Those two just seem to be dancing around their mutual attraction," Joy said.

"Like someone else I might happen to know?" Clyde arched an eyebrow and gave Joy a knowing look.

"I don't know who you might be referring to," Joy shot back, but Clyde only grinned while he politely offered his hand.

Cara brought Addison her card back and then turned to Reese. "Is it okay if I go, Mr. Marino? I think I have all of my prep work finished."

"Cara, you can call me Reese," he said with a grin. "Yes, you can go. Nice job tonight, by the way."

"Thank you." She gave him a shy smile before taking off.

"Someone has a crush," Gabby observed.

Reese waved that off, but he had to admit that it felt nice to be seen as the boss in front of Gabby. He'd come a long way from his troubled teenage years. He sure hoped she could see that and believe that he would only continue to grow as a person.

"I'll see you guys later," Addison said. "Gabby, I'll stop by tomorrow and we can chat about the new colors for the flowers."

"Sounds good."

"Nice to see you, Reese. I agree with Joy. I'm going to need extra days at the gym now that you're open. But it will be worth it and I'm not a fan of working out, so you should really be flattered."

"Thanks, Addison," Reese said with a chuckle. After she left he turned to Gabby. "So, may I walk you home?"

"Taking notes from Clyde?"

"Absolutely."

Gabby dipped her head rather shyly but then smiled. "Yes, I'd like that."

Reese couldn't remember when something as simple

as walking down the street made him so happy. But having Gabby's small hand tucked in his felt so calming and had the power to put his mind at ease. The soft evening breeze brushed her hair against her cheeks and she laughed in a carefree way that had Reese hoping she was feeling some of the same sense of relaxation. "You have a very beautiful, genuine smile, Gabby. You always did."

"Thank you. There's nothing pretentious about me—that's for sure." She shrugged. "What you see is what you get."

"I like what I see."

Gabby tugged on his hand. "You're such a flirt."

"I'm simply stating the truth. I don't even think I know how to . . . flirt."

"I guess you never had to. Girls just fell at your feet."

He was quiet for a minute when they stopped at the corner that led to her shop. "But not you."

She shook her head.

"You do know that back in high school those girls were attracted to the darkness. The bad-boy reputation. None of them had any real interest in me as a long-term boyfriend. And they really didn't want to be my prom date."

Gabby stopped in her tracks and looked up at him. "So you really did want to take me to the prom?"

"I did. I thought you were the one girl who would accept me as I am . . . or at least was. I wasn't nearly as badass as everybody thought I was and, I don't know, I guess I thought you might have seen right through me. In fact, I was just pretty much lost without any real direction—unless you counted downward," he added with a short chuckle. "I sure didn't have any goals. But Uncle Tony got me past a lot of that . . . him and my grandparents."

"What did it take?"

"Love, Gabby. They loved me without judgment and without hesitation. Not that Mom didn't, but she needed her own time to heal." He grinned down at her. "She sure did enjoy tonight. It's been so great hearing her laughter. She was so full of energy and fun when I was a kid." Reese shook his head. "I just wish she would file for divorce and totally break free of my . . . of Mike Parker."

"Maybe she still has some hope."

"Gabby, how could she ever forgive what he's done?"

"Love is a pretty powerful thing. Who knows?"

Reese shrugged and they started walking again. "Let's not talk about anything negative. I'm enjoying just being with you too much to have anything bring me down."

"Believe me, I understand."

When they reached Flower Power he wanted her to ask him up. "It's late. . . . Are you too tired to hang out for a little while?"

"No, not at all. Having Joy to help me out has made such a big difference. She's such a sweet lady," Gabby said as they walked around the side of the building to the back entrance to her apartment. "I hope this thing with Clyde works out." She stopped at the bottom of the steps to dig her key out of her purse.

"He seems pretty sincere," Reese commented. "Why would she hold back?"

"From what I understand Clyde has a reputation of being quite the ladies' man. I guess she's afraid of getting her heart broken." Something flashed in her eyes and she turned to walk up the stairs.

Once they were inside, her mood shifted and the walls went up. Reese felt her slipping through his fingers. She stood with her back to him and he could feel her hesitation, sense her indecision. "Are you nervous?" he asked softly.

"No." Gabby whirled around. "Why would you think that?"

"I can feel you pulling back. Are you upset with me because I've been so busy?"

"Of course not. I understand completely."

Reese wanted to step closer, draw her into his arms, but he didn't. "Then why are you still fighting this so hard? I was hoping you'd come over to the restaurant this past week. Damn, Gabby, I looked at the door so many times hoping you'd walk in."

Gabby closed her eyes and swallowed. "I'm sorry. I wanted to. . . ."

"Then why didn't you?" Reese tilted his head to the side and waited for her to answer.

"Because I'm afraid of making the wrong choices."

"Me being one of them? Because I'm not the town mayor? Do you wish it was him here instead of me?"

"No. I don't think of him throughout the day, Reese. I think of you. Only you."

"So do you want me to stay?"

By all accounts Reese should have been angry at her almost reluctant admission, but she was being completely honest, and honesty was the stepping stone to trust. Once she trusted him, believed in him, then the rest would come easy. "I understand fear, Gabby. When you grow up poor, fear is always breathing down your back. I can't even begin to imagine what it must have been like to lose the one person in your life who was your rock. My father left, but I still had my mom, my uncle, and loving grandparents."

"Grandparents?" Gabby's lips twisted. "When my mom's parents found out she was pregnant with me, they kicked her out. I've never even met them. She didn't even want to tell them that she was sick. If it hadn't been for the help from people here, I don't know what we would have done." She closed her eyes and inhaled deeply. "And sometimes it's hard to help Addison plan weddings. I see all of these big, happy families and my heart aches."

Once again Reese fought the urge to draw her into his embrace. "Listen. I'm going to tell you something and I want you to remember it always." He paused until she nodded. "I care about you, Gabby. I always have. I will be here for you no matter what." He clenched his jaw and then said, "Even if you don't choose to be with me.

All it will ever take is a phone call and I'll run to you. Fix a flat tire. Take you to the dentist . . . bail you out of jail," he added with a chuckle. "Anything. Do you get that?"

She nodded and then pressed her lips together as if to keep them from trembling.

"And if anyone ever hurts you, there will be hell to pay. I'm just sayin'."

She nodded again, slowly.

"And if you want me to leave, I'll go . . . but not far."

"Well, you only live right around the corner," Gabby reminded him, and he laughed.

"True." He took a step closer but didn't touch her. Difficult since he could smell her perfume, feel the heat of her body. He felt her soften, open up slightly. "But you didn't answer my question. Do you want me to stay?"

15

Stuck in This Moment

GABBY LOOKED INTO HIS EYES AND KNEW HE WAS BEING completely sincere, and it warmed her heart. The cold knot of fear started to melt and she smiled. "How can I say no to a man who is willing to bail me out of jail?"

Reese tossed his head back and laughed. "You can't!"

"Have you always been this amazing?"

"Yes, I've just somehow managed to keep it a secret."

"Well, your secret is safe with me. I mean, I don't want all of the women in Cricket Creek to know."

"There's only one woman in this town I want." He looked at her with those soulful eyes of his, but he didn't touch her. Gabby knew that he was waiting for her to make the first move.

And so she did.

Gabby put her palms on his chest, loving the solid muscle beneath her hands. She could feel the rhythmic thud of his heart, the heat of his skin through the soft cotton. He remained very still, waiting, allowing her to take the lead. He'd made it clear how he felt about her, how much he cared without expecting anything in return. His admission gave her a heady sense of freedom to let her fear go and to simply live in and embrace the moment.

When Gabby slid her hands up Reese's chest to hook around his neck, he closed his eyes and his breath hitched just slightly but enough for Gabby to know how much this meant to him. This vulnerable side of Reese shot straight to her heart. Instead of kissing him as she intended, she unlaced her fingers and took him by the hand.

Reese opened his eyes and tilted his head in silent question.

"Come with me," Gabby said.

Reese swallowed, nodded, and followed her through her living room, down the hallway, and into her bedroom. Once inside, she turned and before she could reach out to him he pulled her into his arms. His lips captured hers in a tender, sweet exploring kiss that ended with him trailing his tongue over her bottom lip.

With a little groan Gabby fisted her hands in his shirt and tugged upward, needed to feel his skin. Ah . . . warm, silky smooth. She needed more, so much more. As if reading her mind, he pulled his shirt over his head and tossed it and then stood there letting her run her hands over the contours of his chest. "You're gorgeous," she breathed. And he was. Lean with defined muscle, with tattoos that added an edge of danger, of excitement. He was sexy as sin, but what drew Gabby to him was how he looked at her. How he cared. Beneath the tough guy image remained the little boy who had used his money to buy her a candy necklace.

Reese stood very still and let her touch and explore. Needing to taste, she leaned forward and kissed his chest. When she licked a pebbled nipple he sucked in a breath. His reaction made her feel sexy, powerful, and then with a throaty laugh she pushed him back onto the bed. He looked so masculine against the light blue comforter and piles of colorful pillows. "Would you mind very much if I undressed you the rest of the way?"

"No" was his immediate reply. "I wouldn't mind at all." He came up to his elbows. "In fact, do whatever you want to. I'm all yours."

"I was hoping you'd say that." Gabby reached over and turned on the small bedside lamp, giving the room a soft glow. She removed his shoes and socks, but instead of reaching for his belt buckle she trailed her fingers over his chest. He sucked in a breath and his ab muscles tightened. Gabby wasn't a virgin, but her brief sexual encounters were limited to her college days. She thought her inexperience would make her nervous, but with Reese she felt relaxed, safe . . . and when she saw the heat in his dark eyes and the obvious bulge beneath the zipper of his jeans, she felt a sultry sense of power that made her feel like a sexy siren. She let one finger dip beneath his leather belt, sliding back and forth before she reached for the buckle.

"God, Gabby, what are you doing?"

"Whatever I want, remember?" She leaned over and kissed him and then trailed her tongue down his chest, kissing and licking.

"I didn't think torture was part of the plan," he protested gruffly.

With slightly trembling fingers she slid the zipper down and then ran her fingertip over the hard ridge beneath the black cotton of his boxer briefs. With a moan he tilted his hips upward so she could tug the denim downward. A moment later his boxers and jeans landed on the hardwood floor and he was completely, gloriously naked.

Gabby drank in the sight. The soft glow of the lamp gave his tanned skin a golden cast. When Reese came up to his elbows again, muscle rippled. She wanted to touch him, taste him, and feel his skin against her naked body. She wanted to straddle him and sink her body down onto his thick, erect penis. She never knew that this kind of longing could be so powerful, so intense.

"Take your clothes off for me," he pleaded.

Gabby nodded slightly, but the need to touch him was so strong that she reached over and ran her fingertip over his mouth and then trailed south over his abs and to the hard, hot ridge of his penis. She touched him lightly, but he tensed and sucked in a breath.

"God . . . Gabby."

She'd never thought much about oral sex, but she suddenly wanted him in her mouth, against her tongue. When she leaned forward, though, he shook his head. "If you do that . . . God, I'll lose it and I want to be buried deep inside you. Gabby, I want you naked. I want your skin sliding against mine so damned badly."

Gabby reached down and pulled her blouse over her head and then, while watching him, she unclasped her bra. He sucked in another breath, and while Gabby was wild with wanting him, she forced her fingers to go slowly, seductively. After tossing her jeans to the side, she stood there in nothing but a lacy thong. She toyed with the sides until he rose to a sitting position and with a low groan reached over and ripped the lace as if it were made of paper. "I'll buy you a dozen more," he promised, and putting his hands on her ass, he pulled her forward, pressing his mouth intimately against her.

"Reese!" When a flash of sharp pleasure hit her, she gasped. The abrasive tingle of his dark stubble rubbed against her thighs, making a hot shiver slide down her spine . . . and his mouth, oh, his mouth! "God . . ." When his tongue flicked over her she felt her knees buckle. Cupping her ass, he held her steady. "No . . . ," she gasped again. "You said . . . ," she continued in a throaty protest, but then threaded her fingers in his hair and moaned.

"I *have* to do this. . . ." His soft lips covered her while his hot tongue teased with light flicks. . . . And then she exploded with a rush of pleasure that had her clinging to him, dazed.

Wrapping his arms around her, he lowered her to the bed. She felt his weight leave the mattress and would have protested, but her voice had decided to take a holiday. All that came out of her mouth were low breathy sounds. She vaguely realized he was putting on a condom and she wondered how, when she was so satisfied that she could want more. Her limbs felt heavy and her heart pounded a slow thud. But when his skin brushed against hers, she sighed and was surprised when her body responded with another deep longing to have him make love to her.

Reese kissed her, slowly, deeply, and with such passion that she wrapped herself around him, loving the sensation of skin against skin. He dipped his head and captured a nipple in his mouth, licking, sucking, and when he nipped lightly she groaned and arched her back.

"Your breasts are beautiful."

"Too small."

"No . . . perfection. Just like everything else about you. Are you ready for me, Gabby?"

"Yes, oh yes. . . ." When she nodded he eased her thighs wider and then rocked against her, entering her slowly. She knew he was holding back to please her and she felt such tenderness for him that she pulled his head down and kissed him. He moved in a slow, steady rhythm until Gabby urged him faster. She wrapped her legs around his waist, and her pulse pounded while the pleasure started to build, intensify, reaching higher. When she felt him stiffen and his muscles bunch and quiver, she let go, crying out while wave after wave of sweet bliss washed over her.

Reese kissed her, holding her close, and then rolled to the side, taking her with him. Gabby rested her cheek against his chest, feeling the wild beat of his heart.

"Gabby, my God, making love to you was even better than I imagined, and I thought that would be impossible," he said gruffly.

"So you've thought about it?"

"Maybe a little." His laughter rumbled beneath her cheek. "Okay, a lot. But mostly just about you, period."

Gabby raised her head and smiled. Threading her fingers into his hair, she pulled him in for another long, heated, bone-melting kiss and then sank back onto the pillows. He came up on his elbow and traced a fingertip down her cheek and over her bottom lip. She licked his finger, making him smile.

"I want to stay with you tonight, Gabby. Hold you in my arms all night long. See your face first thing in the morning."

"Wow, do you know what's amazing?"

"You?"

Gabby giggled. "That someone as tough and sexy as you are has such a tender, romantic side." She traced her finger over his armband tattoo. "Who knew?"

"I sure didn't. You bring it out in me, Gabby. So . . . I take that as a yes?"

"On one condition."

"Name it," he said so seriously that she giggled again.

"That you wake me up in the middle of the night and do this all over again. . . ."

His answer was to pull her against him and kiss her gently, tenderly but with an underlying heat that made her melt into the pillows.

They snuggled for a few minutes, but when Gabby started to doze she said, "I'm fading fast."

"Me too. Being with you like this is so relaxing."

"I've got a new toothbrush in the medicine cabinet. I need a bottle of water. Want one?"

"Please," he said.

"Anything else?"

"Just your naked body snuggled against mine."

Gabby smiled. "I just might even fix *you* breakfast in the morning."

"This just keeps getting better."

Reese was right. The sex had been amazing, but having his strong arms around her in the dead of the night was nothing short of heavenly. She felt warm, secure . . . content. But most of all loved. And while she was usually a light sleeper, Gabby fell into a deep delicious slumber.

* * *

Gabby stirred and her eyelids fluttered, letting in a slice of light. She sighed, wanting to slip back into the dream that she'd made sweet, amazing love to Reese, and then she smiled. It wasn't a dream. With another sigh of contentment she reached for him . . . and came up empty. Opening her eyes wide, she then blinked at the pillow and looked at the floor for his clothes. Gone. Gabby felt a pang of sadness wash over her. After a trip to the bathroom she looked at her mussed hair and slightly puffy lips. Had he snuck out in the middle of the night or did he wait until morning?

Gabby frowned at her reflection, wondering what to do next. Call him? Cry? She swallowed hard and padded on bare feet into the kitchen. Surely he at least left a note.

No note. Only silence. Confusion.

Gabby inhaled a deep but shaky breath wondering why Reese would have left so abruptly. It was still too early for him to have to be at work. Anger sliced into her sadness and she started getting coffee ready, clanging things around. When the coffee started sputtering and dripping, she folded her arms across her nightshirt and frowned. "That's it, I'm calling him and giving him a piece of my mind," Gabby grumbled. But when she picked up her cell phone her fingers trembled. She put her fingers on her lips and shook her head. Was Reese another one of those love-'em-and-leave-'em men her mother warned her about?

"I guess so," Gabby whispered. It saddened her that her mother had gone through these horrible feelings of rejection, and now she realized why she'd been warned over and over. "Now I know. This just sucks." She watched the coffee turn into a steady stream without really seeing it or smelling the aroma she enjoyed every morning.

Gabby went up on tiptoe to reach for a coffee mug, but the sound of her kitchen door opening had her spinning around so fast that it turned into a ballerina dance move. "Reese!" After she stopped spinning she fisted her hands on her hips and glared.

He tilted his dark head sideways. "I take it you're not a morning person?" He nodded toward the coffeepot. "Does it get better after coffee?" he asked with a grin.

Gabby didn't grin back.

"Wow . . . I sure hope so." He put down the package he carried and bent over to give her a quick kiss.

"Where were you?" She kept her tone light, trying to get her emotions under control.

Reese raised his eyebrows. "You didn't have anything for breakfast and I wanted our first morning together to be special, so I jogged over to my place and got supplies to make a breakfast pizza." He reached past her to turn the oven on.

"Oh. . . ." Her heart skipped a beat. "You . . . you could have let me know or something."

"You were sleeping so soundly . . . and looking like an angel, I might add." He suddenly frowned. "Gabby, I was only gone for maybe twenty minutes. Wait. You thought I just . . . *left*?"

"Um, you did leave."

The light in his eyes dimmed. "But you thought I bailed. That I wasn't coming back."

Gabby raised her hands in the air. "What was I supposed to think?"

"Not the worst," Reese responded quietly. He took a step backward and leaned against the sink. Emotions played across his face. "So you thought everything I said to you last night was a crock? That making love to you meant so little?"

Gabby hated the hurt that filled his dark eyes. "No . . . I . . ."

"Yes, you did, Gabby." He shoved his fingers through his hair. "Wow. . . ." He looked up at the ceiling and then back at her. "Will you ever see me for anything other than the troubled kid I was back in the trailer park?"

"I do. . . . It's just . . ."

"Just what? Maybe if I were the mayor of Cricket Creek with short hair and a suit and tie, you'd look at me differently." He sighed and pointed to his head. "This is who I am, Gabby."

"I know who you are! Reese, you're making more out of this than you need to."

Reese shook his head. "I don't think so. Do you think I'll skip out on you like my father did? Are you afraid that I got the leaving gene?" He folded his arms across his chest and gave her a sad, level look.

Gabby felt moisture clog her throat. He was mostly right and she needed to admit it, but she was afraid that if she did he really would leave without giving her a chance. She turned around and went up on tiptoe to get the mugs more from wanting something to do rather than the coffee. Of course she couldn't reach them and with a groan of frustration grabbed the edge of the countertop and felt tears well up in her eyes. This wasn't the way this was supposed to go . . . or end. This was supposed to be the beginning of something wonderful.

"Let me help," Reese said, but instead of reaching up for the mugs he gently turned her around and wrapped his arms around her.

Gabby leaned into his embrace and hugged him around his waist. He felt so warm and solid. She closed her eyes, loving the feel of his strong arms, the scent of his shirt. "I'm sorry," she said against his chest.

"Ah . . . Gabby." He hugged her harder and then reached down and tilted her chin up so she had to look at him. "Baby, I don't want your apology. I want your trust and for you to believe in me."

"If you had just left a note . . ."

Reese rubbed his thumb gently over her chin. "Agreed, I should have left a note. But that's not really the issue." When she glanced away he leaned down and kissed the tip of her nose. "Hey, you can't get rid of me that easily," he added, but his grin looked a little bit forced.

"I don't want to get rid of you. I was upset that you were gone, remember?" She gave him a playful shove and tried to smile, but it wobbled just a little bit.

"Ah, Gabby . . . damn," he said, and lowered his head and captured her trembling mouth with a tender kiss. Gabby fisted her hands in his shirt, pulling him closer. He groaned, deepened the kiss, scooped her up in his arms, and then lifted her up onto the counter. They tugged at each other's clothing, desperate to have skin on skin. . . .

"Baby, put your legs over my shoulders and hold on to the edge of the cabinets." When Reese dipped his head and captured a taut nipple in his mouth, Gabby's breath caught. He licked and nibbled, sending a hot tingle zinging through her blood. And then his mouth was everywhere, hot, hungry. Gabby wanted him, needed him, his mouth, his hands . . . all of him. Grabbing her ankles, he pulled her to the edge of the counter, slid his hands beneath her ass, and held her captive while he drove her wild with his mouth. She arched her back and held on to the bottom of the cabinet, urging him on, until her world exploded.

She was dimly aware of him rolling on a condom. Before she could begin to recover, he threaded his fingers with hers, pushed her arms over her head, and entered her wet heat with one sure, hard stroke. With a soft cry Gabby wrapped her legs around his waist, matching the fast, hard lovemaking. She lost herself in the wild beauty of it, giving herself to him gladly . . . freely.

Her release rolled over her like a tidal wave, the exquisite pleasure almost painful in the intensity. She felt his muscles stiffen and when he thrust deep she clamped her legs around him, never wanting to let him go.

Reese released her fingers and when he would have moved she kept her legs around him, loving the weight of him, the feel of him surrounding her. She ran her hands down his back, feeling the sheen of sweat, loving the rapid beat of his heart so close to hers. He lifted his head and kissed her with another long, hot, passionate kiss, rolling to the side but holding her close.

"You drive me completely crazy."

"You mean that in a good way, right?"

He chuckled. "Mostly."

"I'll take it."

"I could never, *ever* get enough of you."

Gabby kissed the warm skin on his chest. "I know exactly how you feel." She rested her head on his shoulder him but fell silent. She could get so used to having the strength, the comfort, and the security of having his arms around her. Falling in love with him was a heady, wonderful feeling. But could something this intense and powerful be her strong and steady . . . could it last?

Did she have the courage to follow her heart to find out?

As if reading her mind, something Reese was doing a lot of lately, he remained silent but kissed the top of her head. She hoped he had the patience to allow her to ease her way into this slowly, surely, erasing all doubts and fears along the way.

16

Hot and Spicy

TRISH LADLED MORE FRAGRANT CHILI INTO THE PLASTIC container and then snapped the lid in place. After putting it in a tote, she added a small bag of shredded cheddar cheese and a box of oyster crackers and spaghetti. She picked the package up with the intention of taking lunch over to Anthony but then lost her nerve. She'd seen him limp across the lawn earlier still using crutches and assumed he was finally staying home from the restaurant.

Craving Cincinnati-style chili, something she couldn't get in Cricket Creek, she decided to make a pot of her own. Taking some over to Anthony was the neighborly thing to do . . . right? Plus, she wanted to make sure he saw the new article she'd written about River Row Pizza and Pasta. She looked at the canvas tote in her hand and sighed. No big deal.

So why wouldn't her feet move?

Because seeing the man made her heart beat fast and butterflies flutter around in her stomach. That's why! But she really wanted him to read the article and make him say something nice to her for a change. Trish arched an eyebrow and grinned slightly. If he thought the cannoli he'd handed her yesterday with a mumbled apology for being such an ass the other night was enough, he was wrong.

Trish inhaled a deep breath and squared her shoulders but then remembered she was wearing sweatpants and a Cincinnati Bengals T-shirt. Damn, she should change into something more flattering and take her hair out of the sloppy bun.

"What?" she questioned through gritted teeth. She had no desire to impress the man, she thought darkly. She only wanted to do the right thing and take lunch to her injured tenant. Besides, being nice meant that he'd lease his half of the house longer. This was smart business too, Trish told herself, and then looked down at her orange flip-flops. She planned on killing the man with kindness. "Move!" she ordered.

A minute later Trish stood holding the bag in front of Anthony's door. She thought maybe she'd just hang the lunch on the doorknob, knock, and then hightail it back to safety, but of course Digger started making a fuss and before she could take off, Anthony opened the door.

Digger greeted her with enthusiasm. Anthony scowled.

"I made chili and thought you might like some." She thrust the bag at him, trying very hard to ignore that he wore lounging pants low on his hips and no shirt. Did the man ever wear a shirt? His thick wavy hair was mussed as if he'd been lying down, and of course that thought had Trish imagining him in bed. God . . .

"Should I critique it?"

"If you want to. It's Cincinnati-style, sort of an acquired taste."

"What's that supposed to mean?"

"You put it over spaghetti, top it with the cheddar cheese and crackers. It's called a three-way," she said.

He finally grinned. "A three-way, huh? Hmmm, haven't had one of those in a while."

Trish felt her cheeks grow warm. "You are impossible," she sputtered, and started to turn on her heel.

"Would you like to join me?"

Trish wasn't sure if he was still trying to get her goat with the three-way thing or if he was serious, so she said, "No!"

"Ah, afraid that I won't like your cooking, huh? So you can dish it out but you can't take it? Um, if you'll pardon the pun."

"I won't dignify that with an answer."

"Thought so."

Trish glared at him and then, putting a hand on his chest, she pushed past him into the kitchen. Her traitorous fingers tingled from touching his warm bare skin. Digger seemed confused at what was going on and whined to go out, most likely to get away from their squabbling. Except it didn't feel like squabbling but something else entirely.

"Don't go far and don't chase rabbits."

Trish put a saucepan on the stove to reheat the chili and then filled another pan with water to boil spaghetti. As she added a dash of salt she could feel his eyes on her and tried to act as if it didn't make her nervous.

"Make yourself at home," he said, and then added, "Oh, right, you've already done that."

"I told you I never came inside your home, Anthony. I know where everything is because I furnished this place," she said. After tapping the spoon on the side of the metal pan, she turned to face him. "I felt sorry for Digger. Can you blame me?"

"I can try."

Trish let out an exasperated sigh. She thought about leaving until she saw the slight grimace of pain that he failed to hide. She pointed to the chair. "Sit." To her surprise, he did. She walked, or rather stomped, into the living room and grabbed a pillow from the sofa. After returning to the kitchen she pulled out another chair from the dinette table and put the pillow on it. "Prop your foot up."

"You're pretty good at giving orders."

"And you're pretty good at not following them."

"Hey, you've gotta be good at something."

Trish bent down and lifted his leg up and gently looked at his swollen ankle. "You've got stubborn down pat. Do you have any plastic bags? You need some ice on your ankle."

"Top drawer."

Nodding, Trish walked over to the stove and stirred the chili and then added the pasta to the water, all the while trying not to be intimidated that she was cooking for a chef. After filling the bag with ice, she walked back over and gently placed it over his ankle.

"Damn, that's cold."

"That's the idea. Have you taken an anti-inflammatory?"

"Yes, this morning." He gave her a salute. "It's driving me nuts that I can't run."

Trish nodded. "So, what threats were used to get you to leave the restaurant?"

"Tessa threatened to whack me over the head with a spoon. And since I couldn't run . . ."

Trish laughed. "I like your sister."

Anthony's features softened. "She enjoyed hanging out with you guys. It would be great if you did that more often. She sure needs it."

"I'll remember that," Trish agreed.

"And will you do me another favor?" he asked, and waited for her to answer.

"I'm not going to agree until you tell me what you want," she said suspiciously.

And then he smiled.

Not just any smile but a genuine oh so sexy smile that made her toes curl. His smile was a lethal weapon. Trish knew she could never, *ever* give him an inkling of how it made her want to go over there and slide onto his lap. So instead she frowned back at him. "So, what do you want?"

He arched an eyebrow and the damned smile remained. "That's a loaded question. A couple of things, actually. First, don't overcook the pasta. I prefer it al dente."

"Okay. . . ."

"And call me Tony. The only person who calls me Anthony is my mother, and that's only when she's pissed."

"Then she probably calls you that a lot, Anthony."

"Tony."

He laughed again, disarming her even more. Flustered, she walked back in to the stove and checked the spaghetti for doneness. She turned the burner off.

"Where's your strainer?"

"You mean you don't know?" he asked, and then pushed up to his feet, knocking the ice bag to the floor.

Trish fisted her hands on her hips. "What do you think you're doing? Sit back down!"

"I think we already covered that I don't mind very well. Besides, it's above the fridge. You won't be able to reach it."

"Sit down, I can do it." She turned toward the fridge. At five foot eight, Trish rarely had trouble reaching things, but he was right. The cabinets above the fridge were tucked back too far. He came up behind her, and at well over six feet tall he easily reached over her head. Dear God . . . she could feel the heat from his body so very close to hers. Her heart hammered in her chest. "What's taking you so long?" she tried to ask in a testy tone, but of course it came out breathless.

"I thought it was up here," he said, but Trish could tell by the slight amusement in his voice that he was lying. "Maybe not," he admitted, and then she remembered she'd put the damned thing in the cabinet over the stove, easily within reach.

"Are you enjoying making me uncomfortable?"

"Immensely."

"Back up or I'll stomp on your sore foot."

"No, you won't. Why does having me standing so close make you uncomfortable?"

"You're invading my personal space." *And it makes*

me long to turn around and wrap myself around you. Tilt my head up for a long, hot kiss.

"It that it?" he asked. But she was surprised to hear his tone wasn't teasing anymore. Surely he knew how sexy he was even with the constant scowl? When she didn't answer he abruptly stepped back, reached over the stove, and started draining the pasta in the sink. It occurred to Trish that he was divorced. Hurt. Had his confidence been shattered as well? "You can stop glaring at me now. I'm sorry. I don't know what gets into me sometimes," he said quietly.

"I'm not glaring at you, Tony," Trish admitted softly. She wanted to touch him, to explain, but didn't know where to begin. Trish used to feel so embarrassed to admit that her ex had cheated on her as if it were somehow her fault. Steve had a knack for making her feel as if every bad thing fell on her shoulders. Those days were done. "Not in the least."

Tony went very still and then slowly turned around.

"Look, I don't know your story, but here's mine in a nutshell. My ex-husband cheated on me with his secretary, a woman half my age. To add insult to injury he got her pregnant." She swallowed hard. "And I had always wanted a child . . . children, but he didn't. He . . . he told me that he turned to Heather because I'd let myself . . . go."

"What a flaming idiot," Tony said so hotly that Trish smiled.

"Thank you. Steve pretty much shattered what was left of the confidence he'd chipped away at for years."

"I'd like to punch him in the face."

Trish laughed. "I have to admit that I'd love that." But then her smile faded. "So I get it. You start to wonder what is so unappealing about yourself."

A muscle jumped in his jaw, but he didn't look away or make a wisecrack.

"So, I'm about to tell you something and if you use it against me I really will stomp on your injured foot."

"Go ahead."

Trish felt heat creep into her cheeks, but she took a deep breath and said, "Anthony Marino, you are one sexy man. I would think that surely you must know that, but from the haunted look in your eyes I'm guessing you might have your doubts just like I do. You were testing the water with me, standing close, shirtless, no less, to see how I would react. So let me make it clear to you. You are superhot."

Tony looked at her for a long moment. "So, what are you going to do about it?"

"Nothing."

"Then why tell me?"

"I'm not coming on to you. Just being honest." Trish tilted her head to the side. "Because I know how self-doubt feels. And . . . you might be kind of a jackass, but I can read people pretty well—it makes me a good writer—and if I had to guess, you were the injured party and I don't mean your ankle. Look, Tony, I know that you stepped up with your nephew and that you care about your sister very much. So whatever happened in your marriage isn't any of my business, but I think you were hurt. I'm sorry for that."

When he glanced away Trish knew she was right. Her heart went out to him and that's when she knew she had to end where this might lead. Finding him sexy was one thing. Getting emotionally involved was another. She was just starting to find herself and she needed to not get lost in anyone else. Right? That's what her towering stack of self-help books preached. Rediscover yourself first, get centered . . . find a hobby! She'd been buying in to that whole scenario until Anthony moved in, turning her resolve upside down. Damn the man! Trish suppressed a sigh. Getting her groove back was one thing, but was she ready to put her heart on the line?

"Let's eat lunch," she suggested, determined to change the topic. "Oh, and would you please put on a shirt? I'll even go get it."

17

Just One More Thing

SHE THOUGHT HE WAS SEXY. SHE UNDERSTOOD HIM AND what he was going through. And above all else Trish seemed to care.

Knowing he shouldn't but unable to stop himself, Tony reached out and snagged Trish around the waist, pulling her into his arms. Her mouth parted in surprise before he dipped his head and kissed her. Tony told himself that he was just getting caught up in the moment, allowing himself to get just a taste of what he really wanted. It also didn't help that he'd already read the excellent article she'd penned about restaurant reviews in general and giving a second chance after a bad experience. She wrote with humor and insight because she possessed both. And hearing Trish's story made Tony realize that he didn't own getting hurt.

But Tony wasn't even remotely prepared for the sensation of capturing those lips of hers or of having her lush body pressed against his chest. He knew this was doing a one-eighty in the whole staying-away-from-her plan, but damn if it didn't feel so good to have her in his arms. To his delight she reached up and wound her arms around his neck and when he slanted his mouth and deepened the kiss her fingers slid up into his hair. When their tongues met, dipped, played, a jolt of pure heat shot south. Deep longing unfurled in his gut, more intense than he could remember in such a long time. It made him feel alive, wanted, desired.

And he loved it.

Tony cupped her ass and pushed her closer so she could feel how much he wanted her . . . what she was doing to him. Her breath hitched and she moved seductively against him.

If this had been part of a plan to push her away, it backfired big-time.

She was driving him nuts.

The distant sound of Digger scratching at the door brought Tony out of his lust-induced fog. He pulled his mouth from hers slowly, but his heart raced as if he'd just run five miles uphill. She bent her head and leaned her forehead against his chest. Was she pissed? Embarrassed? Or God help him if she wanted more. . . .

"What was that all about?" she finally whispered. Her hands were still locked around his neck, and he understood. His legs were a little bit wobbly too.

Tony inhaled a deep breath, trying to slow his heartbeat. "The grand plan was to keep my distance from you. Apparently, I suck at grand plans."

"Or maybe the plan wasn't so grand," she suggested with a light breathless laugh. "Perhaps you should switch it up."

"Are you going to elaborate?"

Trish unlocked her fingers and then let her hands slide down his chest, lingering as if it might be the last time she did it. "Oh boy . . ." She took a step backward but kept her focus on the floor.

"Trish?"

She swallowed, shoved her hair from her eyes, and then raised her gaze to look him in the eye. "I'll give it to you straight. I haven't felt like . . . like *that* in a very long time. And it scared the hell out of me. So I'm going to walk out the door and keep away from you." She took a deep breath. "So in a roundabout way your plan actually worked."

"I'm thinking maybe you're right and it was a dumb-ass plan to begin with. Maybe . . ." Tony trailed off, not knowing what to say. He tried to tell himself that the timing was all off and that he didn't want love in his life again, but he wasn't buying his own bullshit. He already cared about Trish. It was too late.

She shook her head.

"Is there anything I can do to stop you?"

"Oh yeah. Kiss me like that again. And trust me, I'd be powerless to stop you. But please. Don't."

Tony shoved his fingers through his hair. "Well, doesn't this just suck?"

"Yeah, it was much better when I just ogled you and thought you were an ass."

"Better?"

"Easier."

Tony wanted to gather her in his arms. He understood completely. "This is scary shit, isn't it?"

Trish nodded. "Yeah, I'm not ready. I may never be ready."

"Me neither." Or was he?

"Okay, then . . ."

She nodded and when she brushed at a tear, it was almost his undoing. He more than cared about her. He liked her. And he just knew they would burn up the sheets with some superhot sex. "So now what?"

"I walk out the door and go back to not liking you."

"And just how does that work?"

"It's simple. I'll pretend. I'm pretty good at pretending. Or at least I used to be."

Tony watched her open the door but then pause to reach down and scratch Digger behind the ears. He gave her a sad, "Why are you leaving?" whine that Tony completely understood. He felt the same damned way.

* * *

After Trish left, Tony felt alone. A sense of acute loss washed over him, draining him of energy and joy, leaving only emptiness. Digger looked up at him as if asking why he didn't go after her. "Damned if I know, Digger. I know I'm being a dumb-ass, but I'm just such damaged goods. She's amazing. Deserves much better than my brokenhearted ass."

He looked at the chili but suddenly lacked an appetite, cursing Gloria for doing this to him and then cursing himself for allowing it. Tony scrubbed a hand down his face and sighed, wondering if he could ever heal enough to try again.

But Trish had awakened in him something that he thought had died with Gloria's betrayal. Maybe, just maybe, it was a beginning.

He propped his leg up and lounged on the sofa, but Tony felt anything but relaxed no matter how hard he tried. As the day wore on, it just about drove him crazy to know he could have had Trish warm and willing in his bed. She said that all he needed to do was kiss her and she would be powerless to stop him. But what was even worse was that he knew she was upset. Emotional. Probably feeling a lot of the same shit he was going through all afternoon. God, seeing her tears made his gut churn. For the millionth time he thought about hobbling over there and checking on her but shook his head. "No, damn it. . . . No, no, no!" Tony grumbled, causing Digger to hang his head. "Aw, Dig, not you," he said, and patted him on top of the head.

Tony's stomach rumbled and even though he knew he needed to eat, the thought of food still didn't appeal. He'd stored the chili away and decided that he might try some heated up in the microwave. Just when he'd started to hobble toward the kitchen, a knock at the back door had his heart kicking it up a notch. Digger beat him to the door just as Reese came walking in.

"Hey there, Digger," Reese said with a big grin. He knelt down and gave the happy dog a belly rub.

"You can let him out for a few minutes," Tony said. "Let me guess. Tessa sent you over here to check up on me?"

"Yeah, the dining room is closed and I had a delivery over at My Way Recording Studio, so she suggested that I stop by. How's the ankle?"

"Actually getting a little bit better. I hate to admit she was right, but my stubborn ass just needs to stay off it for a few days."

"Sit down and I'll get you a beer," Reese offered, and then opened up the fridge.

Tony plopped down and propped his leg up. "Hey, shouldn't you get back?"

Reese shrugged. "Everything is ready for tomorrow. Mom was just cleaning up and making lists for everything." He handed him a beer and then shook his head. "Dude, you need to ice that monster."

"I've been icing it all damned day. I think my ankle is permanently frozen."

"Uncle Tony . . ."

"Okay, toss me a bag of ice. It's in the freezer."

"You eat anything all day?"

"Not hungry."

"What was that stuff in the fridge? It smells kinda different but good."

"Cincinnati chili."

"Cincinnati . . . oh, the neighbor writer chick." Reese arched an eyebrow. "You have a weird look on your face."

"It's because my damned ankle is a Popsicle. You'd have a funny look on your face too."

"You suck at lying. Care to spill? I won't tell Mom."

Tony sighed. He and Reese had gotten through some tough times together, and now that he was an adult, and an amazing one at that, they'd become more like brothers. "I made a huge mistake. I kissed Trish."

Reese sat up straighter. "Aw, man, how was it?"

"Amazing."

"So . . . are you gonna start something with her?"

"Hell no."

"Why?"

"You know why. I'm still a hot mess. I have a restaurant to run and . . . and . . ."

"You're scared shitless."

"Yeah, that."

"Well, man up."

Tony took a slug of beer. "If only it were that easy."

"It is."

"Shut up."

Reese sighed and looked up at the ceiling.

"Look, I know what you're gonna tell me again. Like a damned broken record. That I'm giving Gloria the power to keep me down."

"Do you still have feelings for her, Uncle Tony? Is that what this is all about?"

"No, oh, hell no! Catching her screwing another guy lifted those blinders off for good. But why would I invite the possibility to have the same damned thing happen to me again? I mean, obviously I believed in her and didn't see the writing on the wall. How could I not have seen right through her from the beginning? Am I that stupid?"

"No! You're an honest, hardworking, all-around great guy. You see the good in people. Gloria played you. Hey, we all liked her in the beginning. She had us all fooled."

"So what's to say I won't get fooled again?"

Reese looked at him with serious eyes. "I had a similar conversation with Mom about moving on. You're both good people and deserve a shot at happiness."

Tony twirled his beer bottle around. "I think Tessa still loves your dad, Reese. I also think she has this wild-ass hope that he's gonna waltz back into town with some grand explanation and set things straight."

"Then she's living in la-la land. And I can't seem to do a damned thing about it." Reese shook his head. "Hey, but listen, we're talking about you, remember?"

"No, I'm boring. I wanna know about you and sweet little Gabby Goodwin. How's that movin' along?" Tony asked, and watched the play of emotion cross over Reese's face.

"I'm in love with her, Uncle Tony."

"Oh, Reese, man, I'm so happy for you. At least one of us should be lucky in love. Why do I hear a great big *but* in there somewhere?"

"But sometimes I think she still looks at me like I'm that wild kid from back in high school and that she's fighting her feelings for me instead of embracing them. It's pretty frustrating."

"Yeah, I get that, but you gotta remember that that kid is the last memory she has of you, Reese. And, dude, you were a handful."

"Yeah, and look at me. I'm still not a suit and tie. Never will be. So if that's what Gabby wants . . . well, I guess I'm screwed."

"You think she wants someone like Drew?"

Reese lifted one shoulder. "I think he represents stability to Gabby. Something she hasn't had the luxury to have in her life. I'm just going to take it slow. But damn it, it's hard not to tell her how much I really care about her."

Tony sighed. "Yeah, well, take it from me. You gotta have trust or you got nothin'."

"I hear ya."

"So, what the hell are you doin' here? Head on over there with one of those sweet-ass desserts you make. If that Italian cream cake doesn't melt her heart, nothin' will."

Reese pointed at Tony. "Excellent idea."

"I have my moments." He waved at Reese. "Now get outta here!"

Reese scooted the chair back and stood up. "Okay, but if you need anything just give me a call. And hey, don't worry about tomorrow. We're fully staffed and I've got Ryan making a pretty mean pizza, leaving me open to do other things. Mom is making chicken piccata and I'm making meatballs, so we have a couple of main courses to write on the chalkboard. The menu will just have to be a bit limited until you're back in action." Reese clamped a hand on Tony's shoulder. "Just get better, okay?"

"I will." When Reese opened the door, Digger bounded inside. "Hey, Reese?"

He turned around.

"I'm so proud of you, ya know?"

Reese smiled back at him. "Yeah, I know."

Tony watched his nephew leave and felt a lump of emotion get lodged in his throat. Funny how he'd helped Reese through a tough time and now the kid was doing the same thing for him. He had family. A growing business. "Life could be worse," he said to Digger.

But then the image of Trish filled his head. "And a whole lot better, huh, Dig?"

18

What Matters Most

WHEN REESE ARRIVED BACK AT RIVER ROW PIZZA AND Pasta, he was surprised to see Gabby and his mother sitting at a table deep in conversation. Even more surprising was the bottle of Wild Turkey and two glasses sitting on the checkered tablecloth. To his knowledge, neither his mother nor Gabby was a big drinker, especially the hard stuff. His mother cradled her glass in her hands and after a second took a sip without making a face or flinching. Neither of them even noticed his entry into the room. *What the hell?*

A big bouquet of red roses sat on a small table next to them. At first Reese felt a flash of alarm, thinking that the flowers might be for Gabby from Drew, but why would she bring them here? That left his mother. Her mascara was smudged as if she'd been crying. Gabby's eyes were also filled with tears. Reese swallowed hard and walked their way. "Mom? What's wrong?" he asked gently, prepared for the worst. His legs suddenly felt as if they were made of rubber and he had to grab the back of a chair for support. "Who sent the flowers?" he asked.

"Your . . . your father," she answered brokenly, and swiped at her cheek.

Reese bit back an oath before sitting down. He looked over at Gabby, who seemed at a loss for words. The Wild Turkey suddenly held a hell of a lot of appeal.

"It's our twenty-eighth wedding anniversary." She sounded so tired, so sad that it clawed at Reese's heart.

"Was there a note?" Reese asked. "I mean, are you sure it was from . . ." He couldn't say the word *dad*. ". . . him?"

A tear slid down her cheek and she nodded.

"Tessa? Is it okay to show Reese the note?" Gabby asked.

She closed her eyes and nodded again.

Gabby handed him the small white envelope. Reese tried but couldn't keep his fingers from trembling when he slid the card out. The note read *I don't blame you if you never forgive me, but I will love you always. I think of you every day but especially today*. Reese wanted to rip the note to shreds and throw the damned flowers in the trash. Something of what he was thinking must have shown on his face, because his mother was now looking at him with a ravaged expression.

"I know there's a reason for your father leaving, Reese."

"Mom," Reese said gently. "What reason could there possibly be for a husband and father to leave his family? Are you forgetting that he cleaned out your bank account first? You're acting like he went off to war and is missing in action. He's just missing."

"He *must* have had a good reason. Reese, we loved each other so much. He loved you. Adored you. We'd been saving for the down payment on a house. I . . ." She faltered and took another sip of her bourbon. "I wish I knew."

Reese stood up so fast that his chair toppled over and hit the floor. After righting it he stomped over and got a glass from behind the counter and came back over to the table. With a shaking hand he poured a generous shot and tossed it back, letting the bourbon burn down his throat and splash into his churning stomach. "I'm gonna find him," Reese said flatly. "Track him down and make him give you some answers."

"No," Tessa said. "If he's in hiding, there has to be a reason. Maybe he's in some kind of danger?"

Reese gave his mother's hand a gentle pat. He understood. For a long time he had conjured up some pretty elaborate reasons that his father might have disappeared, most of them sounding more like a movie than real life. After a while he had given up and faced reality. "Like I said, you deserve to know. It's high time we found out once and for all." He gave her hand a firm squeeze.

Reese looked at Gabby. "Where did the order come from?"

"The order came from my Web page and was paid through PayPal. I didn't put two and two together at first."

Reese would have asked more questions about a billing address, but Gabby looked uncomfortable and in truth he didn't know if he wanted his mother to have that information until he knew more. "Yeah, he's hiding because he's ashamed," he ground out. "And he should be. He needs to man up and face the music." He glanced at Gabby, whose eyes were big and round. He hated that she was witness to this and his anger. God, she had to feel it radiating from every pore in his body. So much for her thinking he was stable. He shoved fingers through his hair. Maybe he wasn't. "Do you want me to call Uncle Tony and get him over here?"

"No, he needs to stay off that ankle. I'll be fine. This is just a shock. I haven't heard from Mike in such a long time. I was worried. I was . . ." She stopped and shrugged.

Gabby tilted her head as if unsure whether she should speak up. "I knew this was going to be hard. I usually love delivering flowers, but I dreaded bringing the roses to you."

"Oh, Gabby, you are such a sweetheart. No, it's fine, really. Look, why don't you two get out of here and do something fun? Relax and watch a movie or something. It's still early for kids your age, right?"

"Mom, I'm not leaving you," Reese insisted. He looked at Gabby, trying to get a bead on how she was taking this. As much as he'd been looking forward to seeing Gabby, he needed to make sure his mom was okay.

"Oh, honey, it's nearly my bedtime. Truly, I'll be just fine," she insisted, and Reese wished he could believe her. Her words might be firm, but the haunted look in her eyes told another story.

"Why don't you walk your mom home, Reese? If it's not too late you can drop by my place later. I'll be up for a while."

Reese looked at his mother.

"Sounds like a good plan." Tessa smiled, but her bottom lip trembled a little bit. When Gabby stood up she did the same and gave her a hug. "Thanks for hanging out with me for a little bit. And erase that worry from your pretty face. This is just . . . life."

Gabby nodded, but Reese noticed that she pressed her lips together hard as if warding off tears. He walked over and gave her a hug too. "Thanks. I'll stop by later for sure." He squeezed her shoulders and then placed a light kiss on her cheek.

"No hurry," Gabby whispered in his ear. "Take care of your mama."

Reese nodded and then walked her to the door. "I'll see you soon."

"Hey, stay with her if she needs you, okay?"

"I will," Reese promised, falling even more in love with her.

After locking up the restaurant, Reese walked his mother down the sidewalk along the banks of the river. Decorative streetlamps illuminated the way, casting a soft glow that sliced through the muted darkness. "Are you really okay, Mom? Be honest with me."

When they paused she set the vase down on the sidewalk and stood facing the water, watching the tiny waves lazily lap against the shore.

"If you want me to I can chuck those into the water." He picked up a rock and tossed it to demonstrate. "I've still got a pretty good arm."

Tessa glanced down at the roses and sighed. "A big part of me wants you to."

"Or I could give you the honors."

She reached down and pulled one long-stemmed rose from the bouquet, lifted it to her nose, and inhaled it. "I've just always felt as if there's more to the story than we know."

"If you believe that, why have you resisted trying to find him? Contact him? Nowadays it's pretty easy to track somebody down, Mom. Unless they've gone into some serious hiding."

"Oh, I don't know." She hesitated and then gave Reese a sideways glance. "I guess I was afraid of being proven wrong. Clinging to hope even if it was a false sense of hope was easier in a lot of ways. Or at least I thought so."

"You know that's not healthy, right?"

"Yeah," she answered quietly. "I know. But why do you think he sent the flowers? Why now?"

Reese felt a flash of anger and had to pause and toss another rock into the water to calm down. "I don't have a clue. But seriously, Mom, how could you even entertain the thought of taking him back if he would have the nerve to show up?"

She ran a fingertip down the rose petal. "I don't really know that I could. But the hard part for me is that there wasn't any argument before he left. Nothing leading up to it or any clue that when Mike left for work that morning he would never come back." She inhaled a deep breath. "I know it must sound crazy, but that last kiss on the cheek that he gave me is frozen in time . . . along with my feelings."

"And that's the reason you deserve to know why. I really think it's the only way for you to have closure and to move on. And I deserve to know too. Just say the word and we'll track him down."

She nodded. "I'm getting there. Let me process this and then we'll go from there."

Reese picked up her hand and squeezed it. This was a start. He wasn't going to push it. Getting the damned flowers might even turn out to be a good thing if it led her in the right direction. "You let me know. Ready to head home?"

She nodded.

The walk was a short one, up the hill just to the edge of town. The cute little brick bungalow suited his mother, and he knew she was so proud to be a home owner. She'd come such a long way on her own with only occasional help from her parents. Since she carried the damned flowers, Reese held open the white wooden gate.

"I know you don't want to, but you'll have to hold these while I fish around in my purse for my keys."

"You're a better person than me. You know how I feel. I would have chucked these things in the Ohio River," he admitted.

Tessa slipped the key in the lock and opened the door adorned with a grapevine wreath. "A smarter person would, I suppose."

"You're far from stupid, Mom." He handed her the flowers.

She flicked on the kitchen light. "I'm so glad that we talked about this tonight. As hard as it was to do." She rubbed a petal between her fingers. "Oh, Reese, so many years have gone by. I don't spend my days depressed any longer, and having you and Tony back here really helps."

"I'm glad to be living close to you." He'd loved his time in Brooklyn, but Cricket Creek felt like home in a way the big city never had.

"I know in my head that I should be so angry, but none of the pieces fit. Like I said, we were just so . . . happy. We were looking at land to build a house and Mike was going to try to buy Fred's shop when he retired."

"But, Mom, I want you to move forward." He swept a hand toward the flowers. "Come on, he had to know sending these would upset you. How the hell does he know where to find you still, anyway?"

"I'm listed in the phone book."

"But the flowers came to the restaurant," Reese commented, but then shook his head. There really was no rhyme or reason for his father's actions, and Reese thought that sending the flowers was pretty damned cruel. But after what he did, Reese supposed he was capable of doing anything. Reese refused to feel any emotion other than anger. He'd given up hope a long-ass time ago.

"Listen, honey, I'm fine. Really. I think I'll take a long bath and try to get a good night's rest. You need to take what little is left of the evening and spend it with Gabby. You don't get to see her nearly enough. She was just so sweet to me today."

"Are you absolutely sure you're okay?"

"There are worse things than getting flowers," she tried to joke. "Seriously, a hot bubble bath is calling my name."

"All right, but call me if you need anything even if it's just to talk. Promise?"

"I promise. You are a good son, Reese." She kissed him on the cheek. "Now go!" She shooed him with her fingertips.

Reese shoved his hands in his pockets, deep in thought, as he walked back to Gabby's. He tried to tamp his anger down, but really, what kind of game was his father playing? Tomorrow he was going to talk to Uncle Tony about it and see if he wanted to help him track him down. He wasn't about to witness his mother being jacked around. It was high time that they did something, and the flowers were the last damned straw.

As Reese approached Gabby's door he felt a nervous flutter hit him in the gut. After what just happened, how would she react? Gabby's own mother had been on the receiving end of a man leaving. Would this spook Gabby? Remind her of the pain her mother had gone through as well?

Reese inhaled a deep breath, paused, and then knocked. He was in the middle of rehearsing a little speech about how he wasn't like those asshats when the door swung open. Just when his brain started to register how cute she looked in pink cotton shorts and a white tank, Gabby launched herself into his arms. Surprised, Reese laughed and when he lifted her up he shook his head. "What's this all about?"

"I thought you liked it when I threw myself at you. You gave me an open invitation to do so, remember?"

"I don't like it, Gabby, I love it and the invitation is always open, day or night, rain or shine," Reese assured her before capturing her mouth in a much needed long, hot kiss. He knew part of this was to give him comfort, make him forget, and be his soft place to land. It occurred to him that this was what people who loved each other did.... Why, no, *how* could he ever leave something as wonderful as this?

"Make love to me," she whispered in his ear.

"Gladly." Reese carried her back to her bedroom. Two fat vanilla-scented candles flickered on her nightstand, making shadows dance on the wall. Soft music played from her laptop, and the bed was turned down. Reese gave her a soft smile.

She caught her bottom lip between her teeth. "I was hoping..." Her shy admission was the sexiest thing ever. The fact that she was thinking about him, *wanting him*, filled Reese with confidence. Gabby was opening up to him, letting down her guard, and hopefully falling as much in love with him as he was with her. The last time they made love had been wild . . . intense, but the music, the candles set the mood for slow and easy. That was fine with him. He wanted to touch, to taste every inch of her and savor every minute in her arms.

Reese made quick work of shedding his shirt and jeans, needing to feel his body sliding against hers. She watched him and he loved the admiration in her eyes. "I could never get tired of looking at you," she said. When he sat down on the bed she surprised him by straddling him, taking control. "Or touching you," she added, and then started running her hands over his shoulders before exploring his chest. "I know you've been on your feet all day. Would you like me to give you a massage?"

"I would like that a lot," he said with a low chuckle.

"Just promise you won't fall asleep on me."

"There's not even a remote chance of that."

"Just wanted to make that clear," she said with a slow smile filled with promise. She swung her leg over and knelt on the bed. "Now lie facedown for me and I'll get started."

This sexy side of Gabby mixed with her sweet demeanor blew Reese away. And the anticipation of having her hands kneading his muscles had Reese groaning before Gabby even touched him.

"Oh, I'd better take these clothes off so I don't get oil on them," she warned, and he heard the soft *whoosh* when her clothes hit the floor. Knowing she was naked and not being able to see her was killing him. But when he started to turn over, she put a restraining hand on his back. "Oh no, you don't. Just use your imagination."

"But the real thing is so much better," Reese protested.

Gabby answered with a low chuckle, and when her hands started massaging his calves, he forgot everything else but her hands on his body. Her fingers were surprising strong and in no time Reese became putty in her hands. He moaned when she dripped warm oil onto his thighs and went to work.

"Too hard?" she asked.

"Yes, I am," he said with a laugh.

"I mean my hands. . . ."

"No . . . ah . . . that feels amazing. If you ever decide to stop selling flowers, you could make a fortune doing this," Reese said, but the sudden thought of Gabby's hands on someone else didn't sit well. "Forget I said that," he mumbled, and she laughed. Her hands worked magic. "Seriously, where did you learn how to do this?"

"I thought about medical massage for a little while before going forward with my degree in horticulture."

"Mmmm . . ." was all he could muster when her hands moved up to his back. He felt the mattress shift and realized that she was straddling his thighs. The image had him moaning for another reason. God . . . this was so relaxing and such a super turn-on at the same time that his brain didn't know how to react. The flickering candles, the soft music, the scent of vanilla, and the feeling of Gabby massaging warm oil into his skin was putting him on sensory overload.

It was quite simply . . . awesome.

Her hands massaged deeply into his muscles and pretty soon every last shred of tension left his body. He felt his eyelids grow heavy, but when Gabby leaned forward to work his shoulders he felt her breasts graze his back and he suddenly became wide-awake. She moved upward and straddled his hips . . . and if he rolled over . . .

"Dear God," he groaned.

"Feel good?" she asked next to his ear.

"Nothing has ever felt this good," he answered in a weak tone that had her chuckling. "No . . . seriously. This is the best thing, ever. Well . . . second best."

"Glad to hear it." She chuckled again and then slid her body against his, kissing his neck. And that was Reese's undoing. He had to see her.

He had to make love to her.

"Baby, I have to turn over. Do you need to put something on the bed to soak up the oil?"

"I have a towel," she said, and as soon as he heard her put it on the bed, he rolled over. And damn, she took his breath away.

The candles flickered, making the sheen of oil on her skin take on a golden glow. And her half-lidded eyes told Reese that she wanted him as much as he wanted her. It wasn't just her physical beauty but her kindness, her sweetness. In that moment Reese knew he would do anything to make her happy . . . anything to protect her, keep her safe. He was completely and totally in love with Gabby Goodwin.

Reese wanted to tell her so badly, but he held back, wanting the bond between them to strengthen and for her to trust him without hesitation. He needed to prove he wasn't like either of their fathers. It wasn't fair, but he knew he had to take away any of her doubts. He would never leave her, but he didn't want to tell her. Reese wanted Gabby to know it, to feel it.

But what he could do was love her with his body, show her without words how much she meant to him. Scooting up to a half-sitting position against the pillows, Reese pulled her in for a kiss. She grabbed his shoulders and kissed him back, leaning into him, moving against his body, driving him wild. He didn't know it was possible to be this aroused. "Ride me, Gabby," he said in her ear. Cupping her sweet ass, he guided her upward and she sank down onto his almost painfully hard cock.

With a little cry she came up to her knees and with his hands spanning her waist he guided her while she gripped his shoulders and rode his upward thrusts. Her nipples grazed his chest, slick and oiled. He wanted to hold back and wait for her, but he simply couldn't and, grabbing her waist, he trust upward deeply and felt a powerful rush of pleasure explode.

Dimly, he heard her breath hitch followed by a throaty

cry, and her sweet heat clamped around him, wringing every last ounce of pleasure from his body. While he was still buried deep inside her, he wrapped his arms around her and kissed her over and over as his heart pounded in his chest.

He loved her and right now that was all he could think about and all that mattered.

19

I Think I Love You

GABBY WOKE UP IN STAGES. FIRST, A SMALL MOVEMENT, A soft sigh, but she kept her eyes shut, not wanting to begin her day just yet. Well, at least not get out of bed. Lying with her cheek against Reese's biceps, her arm looped over his chest and her leg resting over his thigh, just felt too warm and wonderful to even consider getting up.

"Are you awake?" Reese's voice sounded deliciously sleep-laden and oh so sexy.

"How did you know?" Her reply sounded equally lazy.

"Your breathing changed."

"So you've been awake for a while?" She started tracing random patterns on his chest with her fingertip. The sheet was tangled somewhere around his hips, leaving lots of skin to explore.

"Yeah, but I didn't want to move and wake you. It's so cute when you snore."

Gabby snatched her hand away and came up on her elbow. "I do not snore!"

"How would you know? You're sleeping."

"I . . . I just know!" she exclaimed, but then nibbled on the corner of her bottom lip. "Do I?"

Reese chuckled. "No, babe, you don't snore. But I'd still love you if you did," he added lightly, but Gabby's heart did a little tap dance in her chest.

Was he still joking around or did he just profess his . . . *love*? Should she ignore it? Ask if he meant it?

Tell him she loved him too?

She did. Love him. Gabby knew it with all of her heart. But the words stuck on her tongue. It was as if telling him that she loved him gave him the powers of the universe . . . well, of her universe. Gabby had seen her mother love freely, with her whole being, and had also seen it tossed back in her face as if she meant nothing.

"I'm sorry."

Gabby looked down at him, not realizing she'd been staring across the room. She tilted her head at him. "What for?"

"I didn't mean to say . . . *that*."

"You didn't mean it?"

Reese came up on his elbow to face her. "Oh no, I *meant* it, Gabby. I've been lying here wondering since the sun came up if I should tell you. Last night I wanted to say it but held back."

"Reese—"

He silenced her with a fingertip to her lips. "Gabby, I've loved you for a long time. First, with the innocence of a little kid. And then with the fierceness of a teenager."

"But . . . but you always had a different girl on your arm," she protested against his finger. "I didn't see you much."

"You avoided me. But I always thought about you. I tried to keep an eye on you."

"You did?"

"Yeah, all I ever wanted was you." He closed his eyes and sighed. "I'm not a little boy or a mad-at-the-world teenager. I'm a grown man and my feelings for you are real." He opened his eyes and looked at her. "But I wanted to wait to tell you how I feel. I wanted to gain your trust and show you I'm not that messed-up kid any longer. I also wanted to wait until the restaurant was on firm ground." He swallowed and then shook his head. "But seeing my mother wait . . . and wait? Wasting her time?"

"But that's way different."

"Yes and no. Confronting your feelings, letting the past go. All ways to heal. Uncle Tony is going through some of the same kind of heartache. We've all been through a lot of stuff, but we all deserve to be happy. And I'm happiest when I'm with you. It's pretty simple. I love you."

"I wasn't expecting—"

He cupped her chin. "I *know*. Gabby, the fact that I love you slipped out, but you know what? I'm glad that it did. Waiting is only wasting time, and while I sit back and wait someone else might swoop in."

Gabby knew he was talking about Drew, who used any excuse to stop by Flower Power. While she was flattered by the attention, Drew didn't make her heart skip a beat when he walked into the room. Only Reese did that. She wished she had the courage to open up and tell him.

"So in other words, I'm asking for us to be exclusive. I know this sounds kinda like we're in the eighth grade, but there's no other way to put it. I want you to be my girlfriend."

Gabby blinked at him, but when she opened her mouth he shook his head.

"Hey, I don't expect you to say that you love me. That's something that should come freely and not feel forced. But I want you to be my girl. We haven't really addressed that. And it's not because we slept together. I don't want you to feel as if you have to agree because of that . . . and damn, I can't seem to shut the hell up!" His chuckle sounded nervous and he shook his head. "Am I complicating things? Pushing? This is exactly what I didn't want to do."

Gabby put her palm against his cheek. "No. Reese, you have a right to know where you stand. I don't want to be with anyone but you." She wanted to tell him that she loved him, but stupid fear held her back from taking that leap.

"I'm sorry that I rambled. I was just thinking of all those things while you slept. You know me, I'm not a talker. This is nuts."

Gabby smiled. "I think that your rambling was super-sweet and absolutely adorable."

"God . . ." He ran a hand down his face and gave her a lopsided grin but then looked at her with those dark sincere eyes. "But I really am glad that I told you. And no matter whatever happens with us, I want you know that I will always be here for you. All you have to do is call and I'll be on my way." He reached up and ran a fingertip down her cheek. "I mean that."

Gabby swallowed hard. She loved him. She truly did. But when she started to say it, her heart pounded and the words wouldn't come out. People leave. *Die*. Loving someone hurts. Her breath caught and she started to look away so he wouldn't see her desperate fear. But he did.

"Ah, Gabby," he said, and pulled her into his arms. For a few minutes he simply held her.

It blew Gabby away that this tough-as-nails man could be so gentle, so understanding. "Just give me time."

"I'm a patient man. I'm not going anywhere." He kissed the top of her head and gave her a hard squeeze. "I wish we could stay in bed all day, but I have to make some desserts and get the dough rising."

"I have to get downstairs too."

"Can I see you tonight?"

Gabby nodded. "Absolutely."

"I'll bring lunch over for you and Joy."

She pushed up and looked at him. "Salads please! I

love your pizza, but, well, soon my booty is going to be as big as the side of a barn."

Reese laughed and then arched an eyebrow. "We'll just have to find a way to work off some calories."

Gabby laughed with him, glad that the serious moment had passed. She knew that it was unfair to keep from him what he deserved to hear. She would tell him. Soon.

"Hey, and if you could get the girls together again and invite my mom out, that would be great. She needs to have some laughs and forget about . . . you know."

"Joy told me that there's a pig roast and concert coming up soon at Sully's. It's the CD launch party for Jeff Greenfield. Would she like to go?"

"I'm sure she'd love it."

"But can you spare her on a Saturday night?"

Reese nodded. "We're fully staffed now, so things are running a lot smoother. We've got Ryan making pizza and we're going to hire a few more employees over the next couple of weeks. Mom will put up a fight, but she needs a Saturday night off." He wrapped his arms around her. "And that will mean I can sneak away more often too. Especially when Uncle Tony's ankle is better." He gave her a light kiss and said, "In fact, I'd like to do something special soon. To celebrate."

"Celebrate?"

Reese grinned. "To celebrate that you're officially my girlfriend."

Gabby leaned in and kissed his chest. "What shall we do?"

"I'll surprise you," he promised, and sucked in a breath when she continued to kiss his chest. When she nuzzled his neck he groaned. "You're making it really hard to leave."

"Mmmm, just something for you to think about all day long."

"Oh, don't worry. I will."

Gabby watched him put on his clothes, wishing that

they could both play hooky and spend a lazy day doing nothing. He looked up and nodded.

"I know. It's hard to leave you. I want to make you a huge breakfast and then get right back into bed." He leaned over and gave her a lingering kiss. "But I'll have to settle for bringing you lunch."

"Remember, a salad. And no dessert."

Reese chuckled. "I might have to tempt you with a little something."

Gabby laughed and then felt a sense of loss when he left. She hugged the pillow that smelled faintly of his aftershave and sighed. "His girlfriend," she whispered. A warm, giddy sense of happiness washed over her. She hadn't felt this much joy since before her mother died. For a long time she'd felt guilty when she laughed, but she knew her mother was looking down and smiling. She would want her to find love and live a happy life. When a little stab of fear nudged against her brain, she shoved it away and headed for the shower to get ready for work.

"Well, now, someone sure is glowing today," Joy observed, and wiggled her eyebrows. "Does it have something to do with a certain hot young Italian?"

Gabby sat down at the craft table and cradled her mug of coffee in her hands. "It might."

"Oh, give a girl more than that," Joy protested while snipping off a length of red ribbon for the Get Well Soon flower arrangement she'd been working on.

"Reese asked if we could be exclusive."

"And?"

Gabby smiled. "I said yes."

"Well . . . duh." Joy tapped her smiley face coffee mug to Gabby's. "Congratulations! I think it's lovely that you have somebody special in your life. You've certainly got a lot to offer."

"Thank you, Joy. By the way, I love the arrangement you're doing. Daisies are such simple but cheerful flowers, don't you think? They're my favorite."

"Yes, and I also think that you're changing the subject awfully quickly. Care to tell me what's hovering in the back of your mind?"

"I don't know what you mean."

"You are a terrible liar."

Gabby shrugged.

"Let me guess. You're a little bit scared." She held her thumb and index finger an inch apart.

Gabby blew out a sigh. "How stupid is that?"

"Ah, sweetie . . ." Joy poked a fern into the bouquet. "Not stupid at all, Gabby. You're afraid that allowing yourself to feel happiness is opening the door for it to be snatched away from you." Joy's green eyes suddenly clouded over.

"Sounds like you're speaking from experience," Gabby gently inquired.

Joy nodded slowly and her hands trembled so much that the daisies shook as if in a sudden breeze. "My handsome young Eddie was taken from me in the war. I kissed him good-bye at the train station . . ." She put the flowers down. "And he never came back, even though, of course, he promised me he would."

Gabby's heart squeezed in sympathy. "Oh, Joy, I'm so sorry. Were you . . . were you married?"

Joy inhaled a shaky breath. "He was going to propose when he came home on leave for Christmas. My father told me he'd asked for my hand in marriage. You see, my birthday is Christmas Day. That's why my mother named me Joy." She smiled but her lips trembled. "Eddie wanted to propose on Christmas Day, but he never got the chance." She shook her head. "Let's just say I'm not a big fan of the holiday season or my damned birthday. Turned my name into a bit of a mockery," she added with a sad chuckle. "And to this day the sight of a train makes my heart lurch."

"Oh . . ." Gabby felt tears well up in her eyes. "I'm so sorry."

"And I've been afraid to love like that ever since."

She raised her hands skyward. "And now I'm an old lady. Such a waste, wouldn't you say?"

Gabby reached over and took Joy's hand, turned it over, and put her fingers on her wrist.

"What are you doing, child?"

"Checking for a pulse. Yep, you're alive. You still have time to find love. And you have somebody very interested in making you happy."

Joy gave her a watery chuckle. "You're a sassy one today. Where did you learn that from?"

"I'm looking at her."

Joy laughed while wiping at tears and Gabby did the same thing. "Would you just look at us? Just a pair of fraidy cats." She placed her palms on the table and gave Gabby a serious look. "I say we need to . . . *grow a couple*."

Gabby tossed her head back and laughed and then showed Joy her knuckles. "Fist bump."

Joy tapped her fist to Gabby's.

"Hey, I'm going to ask Tessa and some of the girls to go to Jeff Greenfield's CD release party at Sully's. Do you want to go too?"

"Sure. I'll even wear my red cowboy hat."

"Great, let's close up early so we can walk down there and get a good seat. I'm sure most of Cricket Creek will be there to hear their hometown boy country star. Luckily we don't have any weddings to prepare for this weekend."

"I think you're right. It will be packed."

"But hey, if Clyde happens to ask you to go, then I want you to go with him, though, okay?"

Joy closed her eyes and inhaled deeply. "Okay."

"Thank you, Joy."

"For what, sweetie?"

"For letting me know that I'm not the only one with fear holding me back. Talking about it sure does help."

"Fear is a powerful emotion," Joy agreed.

"But so is love," Gabby said, thinking about how sincere Reese had been when he told her he'd do anything to make her happy. Including waiting.

Joy made a show of dusting her hands together. "Well, now that we got that settled we'd better get to work on these orders."

Gabby smiled. "You're right. Let's crank up the music and bust these orders out."

"Oh, and I forgot to tell you that we just got an additional order from Lee Ann Daugherty, who just opened Tea for Two up on Main Street."

"Oh, right, next to the toy store and candy shop?"

Joy nodded. "Lee Ann is such a lovely lady. I hope that her new shop does really well. She's wanted to do this for a long time now. I think she's also going to serve light lunches."

"Well, we will have to go sometime soon. We'll wear dresses and big floppy hats," Gabby added with a smile. "Speaking of lunch, Reese is bringing us some food later. I made him promise to bring salads."

"Bless your heart! I've been doing my water aerobics class with Savannah at Whisper's Edge, but that pizza is just too doggone good to pass up when he brings it here. He's such a good boy, Gabby. I'm happy for you. Now, if his handsome devil uncle would come to his senses and go after Trish, all of our love lives will be on the upswing." But then she put a hand on her chest. "Oh, how did Tessa take it when she got the roses from her husband?"

Gabby shook her head sadly. "It was hard for her and for Reese too. I've always been confused over why in the world he deserted them like that. I remember thinking they had such a nice family and wishing my mother would find somebody as good as Mike Parker. It blows my mind when I think of it."

"It would be a good thing for them to get some answers." Joy shook her head. "But I don't know how he could begin to show his face in this town after what he did. People in Cricket Creek have long memories. He's not likely to be well received if he ever did decide to come back."

Gabby nodded, remembering the anguish on Reese's face when he came in and saw the flowers. "You're right about that," she agreed as she went over and turned on some music. But for now she was going to think happy thoughts. Gabby smiled. She had a boyfriend. She was loved. And it felt amazing. Lunch could not come soon enough even if it was just a salad.

20

Beginning Again

TONY THUMBED THROUGH THE *COOKING LIGHT* MAGAzine absently, dog-earing a few recipes that he thought had promise. He wasn't much on changing authentic Italian dishes, but Tessa insisted that they should have a least a few lighter selections to offer to those trying to watch their weight and eat healthy. Tony sighed as he absently flipped through the pages. Being laid up like this threatened to bore him out of his skull. He picked up his phone and considered texting Tessa once more about how things were going, but she'd already said if he texted her one more time she was coming over to whack him in the head with a spoon.

Tony's brain kept drifting in the direction of Trish. He tried to tell himself it was because he was bored, but he knew better. God, the kiss had been amazing. He groaned, drawing a head lift from Digger, who was in as much need of exercise as he was.

"This just sucks." Tony tossed the magazine down and picked up the remote, hoping to find something of interest. And then he heard it. A woman's scream. "Trish? What the hell?"

Digger scrambled to his feet and gave Tony a "what are you waiting for?" look before running toward the back door. When another scream split the air, Tony's heart started pounding. Like Digger, he scrambled to his feet, knocking the damned ice bag to the floor. He hobbled as fast as he could while grimacing in pain, but the scream of distress had him moving pretty damned fast.

Tony immediately spotted Trish with her back plastered to the side of the garage. Judging from the small spade she clutched in her hand, it appeared as if she'd been gardening but something had obviously scared the daylights out of her. When she pointed the spade in a threatening manner, Tony ran toward her, ignoring the stab of pain each time his injured ankle felt the impact of the ground. And then he saw it. A long black snake suddenly reared its head upward, hissing at Trish.

This time her scream became more of a whimper as if she thought if she screamed the snake would strike. Tony knew the ugly thing was harmless, but he could see the stark terror on her face and so he hurried forward. She finally tore her gaze from the snake and looked over at Tony and Digger.

"Trish, it's okay. It's more scared of you than you are of it," he told her calmly, but she only gave him a terrified shake of her head.

"It . . . its tongue is out," she squeaked. "I think it's going to bite me!"

"Stay put. I'll get it."

"Don't *touch* it!" she pleaded, and when he moved closer she pushed herself so hard against the garage that Tony would have chuckled if he didn't feel so sorry for her. "It might bite you. And keep Digger away!"

Tony moved forward as fast as he could and even though he wasn't fond of snakes and pretty damned scared, he wasn't about to let her know it. Looking around, he spotted a stick. After picking it up he ignored his thumping heart and quickly slid the stick under the middle of the snake and gave it a hefty toss toward the open field leading to the woods. Digger ran out to investigate and Tony hobbled over toward Trish. He tossed the stick aside. "You okay?"

She nodded, but he noticed that when she reached up to push a blond curl from her cheek that her fingers trembled. "I just loathe snakes. I mean I'm simply terrified." She gave him a sheepish look and tried to smile. "Thanks for coming to the rescue. Again."

"Raccoons, snakes? What next? Sasquatch?" When her eyes rounded he chuckled and realized that he liked coming to her rescue.

"Hopefully, not a spider." She shuddered. "Or a rodent."

"Well, you're near the woods and the river. There's bound to be spiders and snakes. Surely you figured that?"

Trish slid to the ground and put her elbows on her knees. She inhaled a shaky breath. "I didn't think past getting out of Cincinnati." She shook her head. "Funny, but I always thought of myself as being a rather outdoorsy person. I guess this is a bit more rural than the suburbs."

"Yeah, animals generally love being near the water. But seriously, most are harmless."

She flicked a glance at him. "You must think I'm such a dingbat."

Tony laughed, really laughed, and thought she was so damned cute. "I haven't heard that term in a while. I don't consider you a dingbat."

"A dork, then?" she muttered.

Tony lifted one shoulder and then sat down next to her. "Maybe a dork. . . ."

"You weren't supposed to agree with me." She gave him a shove and then pointed the spade at him.

Tony was happy to see her sass return. For a minute she looked close to tears and he really didn't know what he'd do if she started crying. "Okay, a cute dork, though."

"Weren't you afraid of the snake? I mean, the thing was several feet long!"

"Nah . . . ," he lied, thinking he needed to beat his fists against his chest. "I'm sorry the damned thing scared you."

"I guess I'm scared of a lot of things. What are you scared of, Anthony?"

He looked at her for a moment. *Falling for you,* he thought but shrugged again and tugged at a long blade of grass. "I guess my biggest fear right now is not making a success of the restaurant."

She nodded. "Understandable."

"You?" Tony asked casually but watched her closely.

"Ha." She picked up a pebble and tossed it. "You might be here a long time if I answered that. You should have asked what I'm not afraid of," Trish replied in a joking tone, but Tony sensed some truth and it bothered him much more than he wanted it to. He should really get up and hobble back into the house. This was getting personal again and she'd made it clear that she wasn't ready for personal. He should respect her wishes, but damn if it wasn't getting more and more difficult to do so. When his arm brushed against her shoulder, he felt a sharp zing of awareness. Her long legs, tanned and bare, made him swallow hard. Her flip-flops exposed a French manicure and a toe ring glinted in the sunshine. He wanted to run his hands down her legs and see if her skin felt as smooth and soft as it looked.

Tony knew he should go and yet he found himself asking, "Why don't you start with your biggest fear? Other than snakes."

Trish inhaled a deep breath and at first Tony didn't think she was going to respond. "Loneliness," she answered softly. "I mean, don't get me wrong, I love this little town and when I moved here it was such a relief to get away from . . . everything." She tossed another pebble. "But loneliness can be . . . suffocating."

He surprised himself by answering, "Believe me, I can relate."

"You have family here. That has to help."

"Yeah, but it's not the same as . . . well . . . you know."

"Yeah. I know."

Tony looked down and his damned hand took on a life of its own and he reached over and picked up her hand. It was as if he couldn't control his actions around her.

Or maybe it was that he didn't want to.

Tony brought her hand to his lips and kissed it briefly but held on. He understood. They sat there for a couple of minutes, silent, thinking, knowing they were moving into dangerous territory. "So, what's you next biggest fear?"

"Oh no, it's your turn."

"I thought I was doing this interview," he replied, rubbing the top of her hand with his thumb. Feeling her skin, sitting this close and getting a whiff of her perfume danced through his brain and skittered south.

Trish surprised him by answering, "Number two is a strange combination of being afraid of falling in love again . . . and then *not ever* falling in love again."

Tony didn't laugh because he understood once again. Completely.

"I mean, I hope it will happen again." But then she shrugged. "I guess."

Tony nodded. "Oh, I get it. After having my heart ripped out of my chest and then used for batting practice, it's pretty damned scary to step back up to the plate."

When she nodded glumly Tony had a moment of clarity.

"And that's bullshit," he said fiercely.

Trish turned to face him and raised her eyebrows, he guessed at the harsh tone and his admission. "How so?"

"Well, look at you. You're smart, gorgeous . . . damn, and caring." He grinned. "And funny, even though you're not always trying to be," he added, and got another shove. "Anybody who had you on his arm, in his life, would be one lucky S.O.B. and your ex is a complete dumb-ass. I'm just sayin'."

"I gave a similar speech to you, Tony. Did she cheat on you?"

He nodded. She'd opened up so much. It was his turn now. "Yeah, she turned on me when the recession hit and the restaurant started to struggle. We would have gotten through it, but she hated not getting to spend like crazy. I responded by working longer, harder. Maybe if—"

"Don't!" she said firmly.

"Don't what?"

"Blame yourself for her cheating. I've been down that road and it's a dead end. There's never, *ever* an excuse for infidelity."

"For a long time that's all I could think about. What I did wrong that pushed her into the arms of another man."

"No!" Trish squeezed his hand. "Look, I'm well aware that there's two sides to every story and no one is perfect." She pointed at herself. "I'm not perfect. But I do know one thing for sure. There's *nothing* we did or didn't do that gave her or my ex that right. Nothing."

Tony nodded and had to fight back emotion. After clearing his throat he said, "Thank you for that."

"Are you still in love with her?" Trish asked softly.

Tony shook his head. "No. I know now that the person I was in love with never really existed. I waited so long to get married, determined to find the right woman to share my life with. It's so hard to get over all of those lost years. Giving everything I had to someone who didn't deserve it. Trish, how do you ever get over it? Get rid of the anger and the fear of having the same damned thing happen all over again?"

Trish leaned her head against his arm and sighed. "I sure wish I knew the answer to that question."

Tony looped his arm over her shoulders. For a long time they sat there in silence. Finally, he said, "I think this is the beginning."

He felt her head nod against his shoulder and she finally said, "Yeah, me too."

"So, should we take baby steps? Or one great big flying leap?"

21

A Leap of Faith

"WOULD YOU BE OFFENDED IF I TOLD YOU TO TAKE A flying leap?" Trish asked. She grinned when she felt him shake with laughter.

"Not at all."

"Although leaping might still remain a little bit painful," he told her.

"Oh, I forgot!" Trish scrambled away from him and looked down at his ankle. "And you ran out here when I was screaming like a goofball! Oh, does it hurt? I hope this didn't set you back." She put her hand on her mouth and gingerly examined his ankle. "My goodness, all I do is cause you trouble."

"Maybe you're the kind of trouble I need," he said, causing Trish to look up at him. "Hey, I freely admit that it felt good to come to the rescue. It was worth the little bit of pain it caused to make sure you were okay."

"I owe you one, then," Trish answered slowly. She wondered how frayed gray gym shorts and a worn New York Mets T-shirt could look so supersexy. Maybe because she knew what he looked like without the shirt?

The dark stubble shading his jaw and the dark wavy hair just shy of needing a trim only added to the appeal.

"One . . . what?" He arched a suggestive eyebrow. "Do I get to choose?"

"I . . . uh . . ." The soft breeze that blew across the field did nothing to cool Trish off. She wanted to scoot up there, straddle his lap, and kiss the man senseless.

"Let me fill in the blank for you: a kiss."

"A . . . kiss?"

Tony tilted his head to the side. "Too much to ask?"

"S-sounds like a reasonable request," she tried to say lightly but sounded a bit breathless instead.

"Nice. So, when can I collect?" Tony asked, and the look he gave her made a hot shiver slide down her spine.

Right this minute got stuck on the tip of Trish's tongue.

"How about now?"

Was the man seriously reading her mind? Trish searched his face, trying to read him. The spontaneous kiss they'd shared was one thing. And he did the kissing. Trish couldn't even remember when she had taken the lead and kissed a man. "I . . ."

"Take a flying leap, Trish," he challenged, but didn't laugh this time. Instead, he gave her a serious yet seductive look that had her slowly moving toward him. At first she didn't even realize what she was doing and then suddenly she found herself straddling his legs and looking into his deep brown eyes. "Do it," he softly encouraged, but his hands remained at his sides. "Kiss me."

Trish blinked and then dropped her gaze to his mouth. After licking her lips to moisten them, she leaned just slightly closer. She placed her hands on his shoulders, feeling the solid strength, the warmth, and leaned closer still. Although he remained silent Trish could tell by the rise and fall of his chest that he was anticipating this as much as she was. She looked in his eyes, seeing golden flecks and molten desire.

Desire for her.

She touched the tip of her tongue to his bottom lip,

teasing, nipping, and then with a soft sigh molded her mouth to his . . . and kissed him. He opened his mouth for her and she took full advantage, dipping her tongue in gently, shyly, savoring the taste, the texture, and the silky heat. Her hands slid up to his head and she threaded her fingers through his soft hair.

With a low groan Tony put his hands on her waist, pulling her closer. Trish moved against him and the sensation of his hard body against her softness sent a jolt of desire through her that took her breath away. She sucked in much-needed air and melted against him, needing to get closer still.

Tony's hands were suddenly beneath her shirt touching her bare skin and she loved it. He had big palms, slightly callused fingers, and the slight abrasion made her tingle.

This felt wanton. Wicked.

It felt fantastic.

She didn't think she'd ever wanted a man more than she wanted Tony right now. But just when Trish was about to tug Tony's shirt until he got the message about removing it, Digger came bounding toward them with his ball.

"Well, that was bad timing," Tony said with a pained laugh. "No doggie treats for a week."

Trish leaned her forehead against his chest, suddenly a little bit embarrassed. "Maybe he has more sense than us," she said with a nervous laugh. "What are we, anyway? Teenagers?"

Tony reached down and tilted her chin up. "It sure feels like it," he told her. "I don't think I've been this turned on since I was about seventeen."

Trish felt heat creep into her cheeks. "We're outside," she whispered as if someone might hear. "And I was about to strip you half naked!"

"I know. It's awesome," he said with a grin. "Well, except for the half-naked part. I'd rather be totally naked."

Trish laughed weakly. "I don't know whether to be proud or embarrassed."

His grin faded and he gave her a serious look. "I haven't felt this alive in a long time, Trish. Damn, that felt good." He rubbed his thumb over her chin. "But I want to make love to you in my bed where I can take my time." He dipped his head and kissed her with such tender sweetness that she wrapped her arms around his neck and held him tightly.

After pulling back he said, "Let me cook you dinner tonight. I'll fix whatever you want."

"No!"

His face fell. "Why not?"

"Because you have to stay off your ankle. I'll fix dinner for you."

"You're a bossy little thing."

"So you keep telling me." She arched an eyebrow. "Are you going to follow orders?"

"I think you could get me to do whatever you wanted," he told her.

"Really, now?" Trish had some suggestions that had her feeling more like a college student than a divorcee. She arched an eyebrow. "That's good to know."

"Yeah. So . . . what do you want?"

Trish tilted her head to the side and tapped her cheek with her finger. "I think I'll make a list."

"Like a honey-do list?"

"No, more like a honey-do-me list," she whispered in his ear. "But first I have to do some shopping."

"For groceries?"

"No . . . lingerie." She drew out the word.

Tony's eyes widened and he scrubbed a hand down his face. "Dear God, am I going to wake up on my couch with an ice pack on my ankle and a ball game on the television? Was this all a dream?"

Trish put a hand on her hip and tilted her head. "Yeah, but when you do I'll be in your kitchen cooking you dinner. But you'd better get in there and rest up," she said, and then turned on her heel. With her head held high she started walking toward her back door. Trish could feel his eyes on her and she grinned, wishing she could turn around and see the stunned look that must be on his face, but it would ruin her exit.

Embarrassment vanished. She felt bold and beautiful. After living a life of restraint, trying to please instead of being herself, this felt even better than a flying leap. This felt airless, like soaring.

Tonight could not come soon enough.

22

The Things We Do for Love

AFTER DROPPING LUNCH OFF FOR GABBY AND JOY, REESE decided to stop in Designs by Diamante on his way back to the restaurant. He wanted something special for Gabby, and his mother had told him that the jewelry in the store was all handcrafted and one-of-a-kind items.

After entering the shop he stood there feeling a little bit lost, but the soft music and cinnamon-scented air put him at ease. Reese was also relieved to see a pretty woman about Gabby's age standing behind the counter. Hopefully, she'd be able to help him pick out something special. Shopping for jewelry wasn't something he did frequently . . . or well, ever. Candy necklaces hardly counted.

The clerk flipped her long dark hair over her shoulder and gave Reese a big smile. "Thank you!"

"I haven't bought anything yet," Reese responded with a grin.

"Yes, but I'm from Chicago, home of amazing pizza that I've dearly missed until now. You're one of the owners of our new Italian place—am I right?"

"Yeah," Reese replied, and felt a little surge of pride. "So you like our pizza?"

"Absolutely! Your pizza is delicious, so thank you!" She stuck out her hand. "I'm Bella Diamante. My mother owns this shop."

Reese shook her hand. "Nice to meet you, Bella. *My* mother suggested your shop for a gift for my girlfriend."

"Gabby Goodwin, right?"

"How did you know?"

"Small town." Bella laughed and then shrugged. "Took me a while to get used to it after growing up in Chicago, believe me, but I love it here."

Reese nodded. "I've been away for a few years. I've forgotten that news travels fast in Cricket Creek."

"Well, welcome back! And again, thank you for the pizza. Now, let me help you find something special for Gabby."

"Do you know her?" He wasn't surprised in the least that Gabby had so many friends who cared for her.

Bella smiled. "She's doing the flowers for my wedding. Addison is my wedding planner. I'm having a huge barn wedding out on the Greenfield Farm."

"Oh, congratulations!"

"Thanks! My fiancé is a pro baseball player, so I've had to do most of the planning myself. Gabby is such a sweetheart! You're a lucky guy."

"Well, I know that I'm lucky she goes for a guy like me," he said in a joking tone, but Bella frowned.

"I don't get it? What do you mean, a guy like you?"

"I kinda stand out in this town." He pointed to his tattoo and winced. "And I was kind of a screwup back in high school."

Bella chuckled. "Oh, I hear ya. I wasn't a saint in high school either. Gave my single mom some gray hair, for sure."

Reese chuckled.

"But listen." Bella nibbled on the inside of her lip for a second and then continued. "I get where you're coming from. Three years ago I showed up for a party at Sully's dressed in stilettos and a cocktail dress. I didn't know that casual attire meant jeans and T-shirts." She rolled her eyes. "The parking lot was pretty much filled with pickup trucks. I didn't think I'd fit in either." She raised her palms upward. "I was ready to turn around and leave, but that night I met my fiancé. Ironic, huh?"

"Love at first sight?"

Bella tipped her head back and laughed. "Hardly. Logan and I butted heads for a long time before we realized how we really felt about each other. In case you haven't noticed, I have a strong personality and pretty much speak my mind."

"Nothing wrong with that," Reese said.

"Good, then I'll go a step further and tell you that Cricket Creek was struggling pretty hard-core when I moved here. But after the baseball stadium was built, the local economy improved and things have continued to get better. They just all kind of banded together and wouldn't give up hope."

"Tell me about it. None of this was even here. This was just a hillside where we rode dirt bikes when I was a kid."

Bella nodded. "Well, the reason I'm butting my nose in and telling you this is that in my experience, although there are most definitely some small-town values remaining, Cricket Creek is pretty accepting and progressive. I don't think you need to worry about what you did way back in high school."

Reese thought that over. "You're probably right," he said. In truth, everyone who'd come into the restaurant had been supportive and he knew the town had taken care of his mother the years he'd been in Brooklyn. Honestly, though, other than his family the only one he really cared about believing in him was Gabby.

"Now, let's pick out something pretty for Gabby. My mother does custom work when time allows, but if you want something right now we can do that too. Something really fun is a charm bracelet. You can customize one that suits Gabby's personality. And you can keep adding charms to it while you build memories together."

"I think that's a really cool idea."

Bella led him over to a glass display case. "Sweet. Let's get to work."

"I want to do the charm bracelet for tonight, but there is something kind of different that I'd like for your mother to make for me if at all possible," Reese said when he was hit with sudden inspiration.

"Shoot. Mom is on vacation with her husband, but let me know what you have in mind. I'll take some notes and ask her."

Reese told Bella the story of the candy necklace and by the end she had to swipe at a tear. "That's the sweetest thing ever. Seriously."

Reese grinned. "So, do you think she could make something like that?"

"Mom can do just about anything and she loves a challenge. I'll run this by her and get back to you on it. In the meantime let's get the charm bracelet going. I'm thinking something with a flower on it, right?"

"Wildflowers are her favorite."

Bella brought out a tray filled with charms. After searching she came up with a daisy. "How about this?"

"I like it."

"Ah! Here's a slice of pizza. Do you want to add that to kind of represent you?"

Reese grinned. "This is fun. I know Gabby is going to love this."

Fifteen minutes later Reese walked out of the shop with the bracelet in a beautifully wrapped package. As he walked past the quaint shops he caught his reflection in a picture window and shook his head. He was grinning from ear to ear once again and didn't even realize it.

The grin remained when he walked into the restaurant. With the lunch-hour rush over, the main restaurant was almost empty, but they'd be busy later, so he hurried into the kitchen.

"Where've you been, sweetie?" Tessa asked. "I was starting to get worried."

"It's kind of hard to get mugged in Cricket Creek, Mom. And if you look I did send you a text message."

"Oh." She glanced around the room. "I never know where I put the doggone thing. Ah, over by the sink. Sorry. I didn't look."

"Would have kept you from worrying."

Tessa shrugged. "I'm a mom. I worry. It's my job," she said while stirring a pot of sauce. "Oh, what do you have in the package? Something for Gabby?" She tapped the spoon on the metal pot and smiled.

"A charm bracelet from the jewelry store you told me about. I figured we'd be dead, so I stopped while I had the chance."

"It's a cute store."

"You've been in it?"

"Eh, once when they had open house a while back. You know me. I'm not much on jewelry," she said, but something flickered in her eyes when she said it. Reese remembered his dad would bring her unexpected gifts, most often jewelry. Nothing fancy but it always made his mother happy. It really didn't take much to make his mother smile, well, back then, anyway. She wiped her hands on a towel. "I wish I could see it," she said. "Gorgeous wrapping."

"Bella did it. She's a cool chick. Loves our pizza, by the way, and that's saying something since she's from Chicago."

"We've had a lot of folks move here from the Windy City in the past few years. Her stepdaddy is the bigwig who built these River Row shops. We've got a lot of movers and shakers who moved to this little town."

"I'm a mover and a shaker," Reese said, and demonstrated by wiggling his ass. He was rewarded when his mother laughed.

"Um, I don't know what you're doing, but it needs to stop," Tony said from the doorway.

"Just what are you doing here?" Tessa demanded.

Tony put his palms in the air. "Whoa, just hold on. I'm just here to pick up some dessert."

"And to check on things," Reese added.

"That too."

Tessa tilted her head. "Wait. Dessert? Give your sister more information than that."

"What, a guy can't stop in for some cake? You know I have a sweet tooth."

Tessa narrowed her eyes.

"You might as well answer her," Reese said with a grin.

"Okay, well, I sort of rescued Trish from a snake and she's cooking me dinner."

"Ohhhh," Tessa said, and wiggled her eyebrows.

"As a thank-you and to keep me off my foot. Nothing more." At least not until nightfall.

"If you say so," Tessa said. "But . . . if it were something more, you should stop by Gabby's and pick up some flowers."

"You need to quit playing matchmaker." Tony glowered at her, but Reese noticed something different about his uncle's demeanor. He just seemed more . . . relaxed. The brackets of tension around his mouth were gone even when he was trying to frown.

"That's how we do things in Cricket Creek. Get used to it," Tessa shot back, completely unfazed. They both knew that his uncle was a softie beneath his tough-guy demeanor.

"I have red velvet cake in the fridge." Reese angled his head toward the stainless steel refrigerator.

"That will do quite nicely," Tony replied, but when he started to hobble over there, Tessa waved him off.

"Would you just sit down, for Pete's sake? I'll wrap up a couple of slices for ya."

"What is it with women ordering me around?" Tony grumbled, but he suddenly noticed the wrapped package and looked at Reese. "For Gabby?"

"Just a little somethin'." He shrugged but couldn't hold back a slight grin.

"You should take lessons from your nephew," Tessa

said. "He knows how to woo a girl." She placed the wrapped dessert in front of him.

"Hey, Mom, come on. My red velvet cake should do the trick."

Tony shook his head. "I'm not wooing anybody. I just thought it would be a nice gesture to bring dessert. That's all! *Capisce*?"

Reese exchanged a look with his mother.

"Right . . . ," Tessa said in a tone that conveyed that she wasn't buying it.

Finally, Tony sighed. "Okay . . . okay, I might be a little bit fond of her. And I'm probably out of my ever-lovin' mind for ever going there at all. You'd think I'd learned my lesson."

Tessa put a hand on his shoulder. "Wrong. You're out of your ever-lovin' mind if you don't."

"Speaking of— " Tony began, but the timer on the oven buzzed.

"I'll get it," Tessa said quickly. "The pizza is for Maggie McMillan. I'll deliver it since when she called she said she wanted to talk to me."

"You thinkin' about buying some property?" Tony asked.

"No, I love my house. I think it might have something to do with going to the Jeff Greenfield concert."

"Oh, well, if you want to hang out for a while, I'll man the phones."

"Just stay off the ankle and ice it, okay?"

"Gotcha," he said, and gave Tessa a salute, but after she left he turned to Reese. "Well, Tessa dodged that bullet, but we need to talk to her about Mike."

"I agree," Reese answered. "Mom's put on a pretty good front, but ever since those damned flowers came, I've felt an underlying sense of sadness that's worse than before. We need to get to the bottom of this and help her to move forward once and for all."

Tony nodded. "Moving forward isn't easy, but it's the only healthy way to live."

Reese leaned his hip against the sink and looked at his uncle. "So, you're gettin' along with Trish?"

"Ah, Reese, I tried to keep my distance, but it's pretty damned difficult when she lives in the same house." He grinned. "And keeps gettin' herself in trouble. When that snake came at her while she was in her garden she freaked." His grin widened. "Then I had to pretend I wasn't scared shitless of the damned thing when I picked it up with a stick."

"The things we do for love," Reese agreed.

"You really love this girl, Reese?"

"Yeah, she's pretty special."

"You told her yet?"

Reese nodded and then looked away.

"Ah, so she didn't say it back?"

Reese shrugged. "I said it too soon." He scrubbed his hand down his face. "I shoulda waited but it just slipped out. Man, I'm trying to go slow, but it's not easy when you feel so strongly. She's just still kind of fragile and you were right. I still think she sees me like I was sometimes and it scares her. So going slow is key, I guess."

"Ah, Reese, the best things in life are the hardest, the scariest. Love, marriage . . . owning your own business. But honestly, I think being burned and betrayed and bouncing back from that is the hardest thing of all."

"I thought about that. I mean, how do people even do that? Why? I just don't get cheaters."

"Beats me. It wouldn't even begin to occur to me to cheat on someone. I mean, that's just basic. But hey, we're Marinos. We're loyal to a fault. Your mom won't even look at another man, and Mike's been gone nearly ten years."

Reese shook his head. "I still don't get it."

"Hey, I'm sorry to bring it up again."

"We have to, Uncle Tony. We've danced around it long enough. I don't want Gabby to think I'm a flight risk like my . . . like *him*. I want to get to the bottom of it once and for all."

"I know a P.I. back in Brooklyn. Just say the word and I'll give him a call."

"I'll talk to Mom about it tomorrow. I've waited for her approval to do this, but I need this as much as she does. I'll try to get her to agree first, because I think she's close, but if she says no . . . we'll do this anyway. Not behind her back. I'd never do that, but I'll just tell her that the time has come."

Tony nodded. "I agree with you. But hey, tonight just enjoy being with Gabby. I should be able to get back in here tomorrow so you can have a much deserved day off."

"Thanks, Uncle Tony. Now you'd better get out of here before Mom comes back to interrogate you some more."

"Good point," Tony said, and gave Reese a wave as he headed out the door.

23

Mean Girls

WHILE TAPPING HER FEET TO THE MUSIC, GABBY PUT THE finishing touches on the giant bouquet and then looked across the shop to where Joy busied herself sweeping the floor. She had to giggle when Joy paused and used the end of the broomstick as a microphone and stated belting out "It's Raining Men."

"Hallelujah!"

After Joy brought the song home, Gabby called over to her, "Hey, I've got to deliver this big bouquet to Jessica at Wine and Diner. Do you want to go with me and we'll stay and eat dinner?"

Joy walked her way. "Aren't you seeing Reese tonight?"

"Not until he gets off work. Are you going to see Clyde later?"

"Ha! No way. I saw him flirting with Millie Thompson yesterday."

"Maybe it was the other way around," Gabby suggested.

Joy lifted her chin defiantly. "Even so, he sure didn't seem to mind one little ol' bit. I've decided to give him the cold shoulder."

"Or perhaps he was simply trying to make you jealous again to get your attention."

"Humph, well, if that was his intention it worked and now I'm pissed." She fisted her hands on her hips. "Silly man. Chocolate would have worked much better."

Gabby laughed. "Well, his loss is my gain! Do you want to grab some dinner with me?"

"That sounds nice. I've actually wanted to try Jessica's new summer menu. A big salad sounds refreshing." Her eye moved to Gabby's delivery. "Wow, Gabby, that bouquet is lovely. Those irises will last a long time too."

"It's from Ty McKenna. Apparently, the Cougars have been on the road a lot lately and he's missing her." Gabby smiled. "Isn't that just the sweetest thing? This is when I just love this business. Flowers just bring a smile, comfort . . ."

"Or say I messed up big-time," Joy added with a chuckle. "When's our next wedding?"

"I met with Bella Diamante last week. She and Logan are finally tying the knot in the fall after baseball season."

"Oh, I remember that hotshot pitcher. He made it to the big leagues! You know, we should take in a Cougars game sometime soon. I haven't been to a baseball game yet this season and it's going by so fast."

"It sure is."

She patted Gabby's hand. "I really enjoy working with you. I know you could have hired someone younger and you took me on as a favor to Miss Patty."

"Nonsense," Gabby said. "Granted, Miss Patty suggested it, but you got the job on merit. And you're a . . . *joy* to have around," she added with a giggle.

"Dear me, I really do think I'm rubbing off on you," Joy said.

"Well, I feel comfortable around you and can tell you anything. It's . . ." She pressed her lips together for a second. "It's kind of like having the grandmother I never knew and a good friend all wrapped into one amazing, feisty package."

"Oh, Gabby, you've been so good for me too. In truth I was getting to be kind of a fussy old worrywart in my old age and I feel young again. Well, younger, anyway. What was that song we were singing the other day . . . oh yeah, you brought my sexy back." She did a little butt wiggle.

Gabby laughed. "Well, maybe *grandmother* was a stretch," she said.

"Hey, grannies can be sexy."

Gabby nodded. "I agree! But seriously, I know it's a ways away, but this year you and I are going to enjoy Christmas too. It's been a tough holiday for me since I lost my mom, but I want to get the magic back. We're going to have a Flower Power float in the big Cricket Creek parade and do it up right. Are you feelin' me?"

"I'm feelin' ya," Joy answered, and smacked her leg.

A few minutes later they were riding in the Flower Power panel van that Joy referred to as the Scooby Doo van because of its blue and green color and mod orange flowers. "I just wanted it to look like a hippie van to go with the whole Flower Power theme," Gabby said with a laugh. "But I see where you're coming from," she added as they headed up into downtown Cricket Creek. "Good thing we got going before the dinner crowd. Main Street is already buzzing with tourists and locals too."

"I think Cat Carson was performing an afternoon concert over at Sully's and people have filtered downtown. Good for business!"

Gabby agreed and found a parking spot close to the front door since she had the big flower arrangement to carry inside.

"Oh, I can already smell the food," Joy commented. "I didn't know I was this hungry until now."

"Me too," Gabby agreed, and walked inside when Joy held open the door.

"Well, now, would you just look at that," Myra, joint

owner of the diner, said after Gabby approached the counter at the back of the restaurant. "Let me guess. This is for Jessica?"

"Sure is," Gabby said.

"Well, Ty is either in the doghouse or just being a sweetheart," Myra said, but smiled.

"Is Jessica here?" Gabby asked.

Myra nodded. "Yes, and here way too much if you ask me. I might not be able to cook her fancy-pants stuff, but I could hold down the kitchen once in a blue moon. People still like my chicken-fried steak and meat loaf. But, then again, nobody's asking me. I'll go get her."

"Want to sit at the counter?" Joy asked.

"Yes, it's still my favorite place to sit. Brings back memories of my spinning around on the stool until Mom said I was going to get dizzy. We couldn't afford to eat out often, but I think Myra gave us a big discount. Like an *almost free* kind of discount. Mom was too proud to take her up on it unless we had some homegrown vegetables to bring."

"Sounds like a good trade-off. Myra's always been a generous lady. She hardly ever raised her prices, even when times got tough."

"I always liked going to Sully's where Mom waited tables, but she didn't like having me in a tavern and preferred to bring me here. Pete would, of course, send food home with Mom all the time."

"Good old Pete Sully. He does a lot of charity work too. I was so glad when he got back with his wife, Maria. It sure did stun everybody in Cricket Creek when she up and moved to Nashville."

"I guess it just goes to show there's always hope," Gabby agreed. "I didn't have a clue Maria Sully wrote so many big-hit country music songs."

"Good people, those two."

"Yeah, Mom didn't know Pete had been paying for a life insurance policy on her. Pete's the reason I could open Flower Power."

"That's the way of things here in Cricket Creek. Just like when Myra took Jessica in as a pregnant teenager. We take care of each other around here. That's why so many of these big-city folk come here to visit and end up staying."

A couple of minutes later Jessica came out with Myra. "Hi, Gabby! And hey there, Joy! Oh, would you look at the lovely arrangement. Gabby, you sure are so talented. You need to bring a few arrangements to sell in my gift shop and leave some cards."

"Thanks, Jessica! I will do that for sure."

Gabby watched Jessica open the note and then hold it to her chest.

"What's it say?" Myra asked.

"It's private, Aunt Myra," Jessica said, and held it out of reach when Myra grabbed for it.

"Oh . . . hogwash. Gimme that." Myra managed to snatch it from her. "'I love you.' Well, hellfire. That's it? Couldn't he be more creative?" Myra asked, but brushed at the corner of her eye and then gave Jessica a hug.

"I think it's the most romantic thing when a man sends flowers for no reason at all," Gabby said, and then sighed. "He said it was just because he misses you and Ben so much when he's on the road."

"Or he's trying to butter you up for something," Myra said.

"Myra," Joy sputtered, but then laughed behind her hand.

"I'm just kidding. Jeez, can't anybody take a joke anymore?" she asked, and they all laughed.

"So, are you ladies staying for dinner? We have a new summer salad menu." Jessica slid an insert to the main menu toward them. "They're all good, but my favorite is the one called Berry Delicious. You can choose blueberries or strawberries in a bed of mixed greens, tossed with gorgonzola and walnuts and then add grilled beef, chicken, or salmon. I like it with our house vinaigrette, but the lemon poppy seed is good if you choose the fish."

"Oh, sounds lovely," Joy said with a nod. "I'll take mine with strawberries and the chicken."

"I'll have the same but with the salmon and poppy seed, please," Gabby said.

"Care to add a glass of wine? The salads pair well with a Pinot Grigio."

"Oh, of course," Joy said, and Gabby nodded. "Bring the wine right away!"

While they sipped the Pinot they chatted about flowers and upcoming fall arrangements. "I need to take a drive to Lexington or Nashville to the big warehouse center to stock up sometime soon," Gabby said.

"We're running low on some vases too," Joy reminded her, and then nodded toward the front picture window overlooking the street. "I hate to bring this up but Drew stopped in earlier and asked for you. He wanted to know if you've made a decision about joining the beautification committee. He's only asked about a million times. That man doesn't give up easily."

Gabby took a sip of her wine. "I really should do it. Joining the committee would be good public relations for us, but I'm just so busy."

"Is that the only reason?"

Gabby sighed. "No, I don't want to lead Drew on and I really don't want Reese to get upset."

"Well, Mr. Mayor should be professional about the whole thing. And, Gabby, Reese should be understanding and trust you."

"I know . . . but those are both *should be* situations," Gabby said, but paused when Myra brought out their salads. "Oh, this does look *berry* delicious," she commented with a grin. "Thanks, Myra." She took a bite and groaned. "Oh, the dressing is so good. After having the homemade dressing here and at River Row Pizza, it's going to be hard to stomach anything out of a bottle."

"I agree," Joy added. "Perfect for the warmer weather too."

"Enjoy, ladies!" Myra said. "And don't forget we have

some light desserts too. The raspberry sorbet is scrumptious and has very little sugar."

"Oh, we might have to try that," Gabby said to Joy.

"You're changing the subject, dearie," Joy observed as she speared a strawberry with her fork.

"Things are going so well, but I still think that Reese has it in the back of his head that I want someone in a suit and tie. I mean, this is Cricket Creek. Drew is about the only guy who does wear a suit and tie," she tried to joke, but frowned.

"Did he hit the mark just a little bit?" Joy asked gently.

Gabby took a sip of wine. "I have to admit that Drew represents a lot of the respect that was denied to me growing up. The trailer park had a reputation . . . some of it deserved, but a lot of really good people lived there too."

"And it would have been fun walking around on the arm of the mayor."

"Well, yeah, but I'm in—" she started to say, but a couple of girls she'd gone to high school with sashayed into the diner. While chatting and laughing they breezed past Gabby, and if they noticed her they didn't say anything. *Some things never change,* Gabby thought with dark humor. She swiveled her stool so she wouldn't have to look at them when they slid into a booth not far away, and she concentrated on her salad. Joy was distracted when Myra topped off their wineglasses.

"On the house," Myra said with a wink.

Gabby smiled her thanks, but her ears perked up when she heard Reese's name mentioned. She told herself not to listen, but human nature took over and she strained her ears to hear what they said.

"Yeah, Jen, when I got a glimpse of Reese while eating pizza yesterday, I about slid out of my chair. He's even hotter than back in high school. I mean, I had to use my napkin to soak up the drool. I wonder if his kiss is still as amazing as back then."

"I'm guessing even better," Jen answered. "Seriously, Angie, you should find out. He was so into you senior year."

"He's dating that little wallflower," Angie said, and then laughed. "Ha, get it? Wallflower . . . ," she added, and they laughed.

Gabby took a sip of wine and glanced at Joy to see if she had caught on to what was going on.

Joy angled her head toward the booth. "You know them?"

"Mean girls from high school," Gabby whispered. "I was a geek and from the trailer park, so I had two big strikes against me. Those two used to walk by me in the lunchroom like I didn't even exist. Classic, huh?"

"Don't listen to those hussies," Joy said, and normally Gabby would have chuckled at her choice of words, but she got a weird feeling in the pit of her stomach at the thought of Reese kissing another girl.

"Ha, are you kidding me?" Jen said. "He's such a badass. Damn, and those armband tattoos are supersexy. The little Gabby chick won't hold his interest long. But why wait? Go for it."

"It's tempting," Angie said in a singsong voice.

"Just have him deliver a pizza late tonight and answer the door in a teddy," Jen suggested, and they both laughed.

"Gabby!" Joy whispered. "Don't listen. Reese wouldn't give either one of them a second glance."

Gabby nodded and managed a small smile, but her delicious salad suddenly didn't taste quite as good. While Gabby knew that Joy was absolutely right, hearing those girls took her back to a place and time when she had felt insecure and often on the outside looking in.

As if reading her mind, Joy said, "You wouldn't want to be friends with the likes of them back then and even less now. You're too good for them."

"There was a time when I didn't feel good enough," Gabby admitted. Sometimes she still didn't, but she left that part out.

"Well, sugar, we've all had dark times in our life like that, but those days are done. Look at you! College graduate and shop owner and did it all on your own. I know it's hard sometimes, but don't let your past dictate your future."

Gabby raised her eyebrows. "Are you ready to take your own advice?"

"I almost never take my own advice." Joy gripped the stem of her wineglass. "Wait . . . why?"

"Because Clyde Camden just walked in and he's heading right this way."

Two spots of pink blossomed in Joy's cheek, and her eyes widened. "Really?"

"I kid you not."

"Well, there you are, Joy!" Clyde said as he stopped next to her stool. "I've been looking all over for you."

"How did you find me?"

Clyde arched an eyebrow. "Sounds like you were hiding from me," he said smoothly. "Is that true?"

"I don't hide from anyone," Joy informed him with a lift of her chin. "Least of all you," she added, but then frowned. "Wait. I think that last part might not have come out right."

Clyde chuckled and then waved at Gabby. "Mind if I join you?"

"Would it matter if I did?"

"Not in the least. You can't get rid of me that easily," he answered smoothly. When Myra approached he said, "I'll have a glass of what they're having and refill their drinks please."

"Oh, not for me." Gabby raised a palm. "I'm driving. But, Joy, why don't you stay? This salad is huge, so I think I'll have Myra box up the rest for me," she said, and before Joy could protest, Gabby stood up. When she reached for the bill, Clyde beat her to the punch.

"This is on me, pretty ladies."

"You don't have to do that," Joy protested.

"I understand that completely. But I want to. Please

indulge me. I only ask that you keep me company for a while."

"Thank you, Clyde," Gabby said. "You are a true gentleman."

Clyde dipped his head. "It's my pleasure." He gave her a nod and then smiled warmly at Joy.

"Nice to see you, Clyde. Joy, I'll see you on Monday." She squeezed Joy's shoulder and then picked up her boxed salad.

"Thanks for coming in," Myra said to her. "Don't be a stranger."

"I won't," Gabby promised. "Tell Jessica that her salad was delicious. I loved the lemon poppy seed dressing with the salmon. I'll bring some floral arrangements for the gift shop too."

As Gabby walked toward the door, she glanced over to the booth where Jen and Angie chatted away, waving their hands and laughing a little bit too loudly. There was a time when Gabby would have wanted to sit at their table but not anymore. As she drove the Scooby Doo van back to Flower Power, she had to smile. If she had been accepted by the popular girls, she most likely wouldn't have studied nearly as much or spent as much time with her mother before she passed away. Like the Garth Brooks song: thank God for unanswered prayers.

When Gabby pulled into Wedding Row the streetlamps were just beginning to flicker on and as she passed the quaint shops she was suddenly struck by how pretty and cheerful the storefronts appeared, and the sight brought a lump of emotion to her throat. She no longer needed the acceptance of anyone else, because she'd finally found it within herself.

She belonged . . . *here*.

Gabby blinked back tears when she thought back to a time when strangers had helped pay for her and her mother to eat. Her mother's medical bills had been covered by Pete Sully, even though she'd been too sick to work. This was home. And she was so proud of it.

Gabby drove down the street slowly. When she passed Addison's bridal boutique, she stopped. "From This Moment." She read the name on the awning, and confidence seemed to fill her inch by inch until it reached her lips and widened into a smile. Gabby knew that life was going to throw roadblocks on her journey toward happiness, but she'd jump them, knock them down. She was tired of holding back and of being afraid to face another loss. Reese loved her and it was high time that he knew that she loved him too.

And tonight she was going to tell him.

24

Cheeseburger in Paradise

TRISH KNOCKED ON TONY'S DOOR AND TRIED TO IGNORE the nervous flutter in her stomach.

"Come in, it's open," Tony called. Digger barked a greeting and danced around when she entered, nearly knocking her over. "Digger, down!" Tony ordered from where he lay stretched out on the sofa.

"Sorry I'm late," Trish said as she put her dinner ingredients down onto the countertop. "I was on a deadline and needed to finish before I could come over." The article about the popularity of barn weddings on the Greenfield Farm took forever to write because she couldn't keep her mind off Tony.

"You're wearing jeans and a T-shirt," Tony observed glumly. "What happened to the lingerie you promised?"

"I was joking." Trish rolled her eyes at him, but in truth she wore a satin and lace teddy beneath her casual attire and that was another reason she'd arrived so late. She lost her nerve a dozen times before leaving on the silky lingerie. Every movement she made reminded her of the fact. "You didn't take me seriously, now, did you?"

His dark scowl made her laugh until her nervousness

vanished. With the disappointment still written on his face, he scooted to a sitting position and got up from the sofa.

"You're supposed to stay off your feet until dinner is ready." She attempted to sound stern, but his presence filled the small kitchen and so she turned away from him before she ruined her plans and shed her clothing right then and there.

"I will. I just want to watch you cook."

"I don't want you to watch me."

"Why? Afraid that I might critique you?"

Trish didn't turn around, but she could feel the arch of his eyebrow.

"I'm afraid you might drive me crazy."

"I already know I drive you crazy."

"I didn't mean like that!" But it was true.

"What did you mean, then?"

"That you'll tell me what to do. I can cook." She finally risked turning around and made a shooing motion toward the chair. "Sit!"

Digger immediately sat and they both laughed.

"He'll give you his paw too."

"I'm impressed."

"I've been bored. The treats are in the cookie jar."

Trish leaned over and lifted the lid of the jar. "Gimme your paw." When Digger complied she laughed and gave him the treat.

"I'll prop my foot up, but I've had all I can take of the ice pack for today. I'm getting close to being healed, anyway."

"Which is why you don't need another setback," she said sternly. God, he looked good in his shorts, but thank heaven he wore a shirt. "I promise you won't have to come to my rescue again."

"I like coming to your rescue," he said, and came over to stand near her. "So, what's on the menu?"

Me. "Cheeseburgers."

"Cheeseburgers? Aren't you trying to impress me?"

"No! But there is an art to making an excellent burger. You won't be disappointed." She leaned over to turn the oven on to preheat.

"You're going to bake them?"

"No! I'm preheating the oven for the sweet potato fries. I thought we should attempt to be a little bit healthy. And I've chosen lean sirloin mixed with a little bit of chuck for flavor. Of course good buns are key."

"I couldn't agree more," he said, and Trish just knew he was staring at her bum.

"Do you have a one-track mind?"

"Yes."

Trish laughed, becoming both at ease and aroused at the same time. "Oh, I forgot something!"

"Yeah, the sexy lingerie."

Trish turned around and pulled a face. "You wish. No, I'll be right back."

When Trish hurried out the door, Digger followed her. She hefted the heavy cast-iron skillet from the stove where she'd left it. She paused and took a deep breath. "Okay, Trish, get your groove back. Come on . . . Damn, where did that confident woman go running off to?" She looked down at Digger, and as if sensing her distress, he turned his head and licked her hand. She knew she was obsessing. Overthinking. When tears threatened to spill down her cheeks, she put the skillet down, went into the bathroom, reapplied her lipstick, and then glared at her reflection. "You want this. Now go for it."

Trish rubbed her lips together and then inhaled a shaky breath. "Okay, Digger, let's do this."

When she reentered his kitchen Tony put his beer bottle down and angled his head. "I was beginning to wonder if you were coming back."

"Were you worried?"

"Yeah," he answered, lacking the teasing tone. "Well, you know, kinda," he quickly added, and Trish laughed.

Tony nodded toward the skillet. "For cooking or a weapon?"

Trish laughed. "Cooking. At least for now." She carried a cutting board, a sharp knife, and a big sweet potato over to him. "Slice this into french-fry-size pieces, please."

"What am I, your sous-chef?"

"Yes."

"Skin on?"

"I prefer it for the nutrients, but I'll leave it up to you." She brought olive oil, sea salt, and cracked pepper over to him along with a mixing bowl. "Lightly coat the fries and then I'll bake them to crispy perfection. I hope. Sometimes they turn out a soggy mess."

"The trick is to make sure that the fries are dry so that the oil sticks."

"Ah, I'll remember your advice." She tapped her head.

"I have a nice chipotle sauce in the fridge that will be excellent for dipping."

"Did you make it?"

"Of course."

Trish pointed to his beer. "Is there more where that came from?"

"Absolutely," he said, but then pulled a face. "Beer, cheeseburgers. I can't run. I'm going to have to find a way to burn off these calories."

Trish felt heat slide down her spine when some erotic solutions popped into her mind.

Dear God. . . . She opened the fridge, glad for the cool air and the cold beer. After popping off the cap, she took a long, grateful drink before risking another glance his way. His head was bent over his task, and Trish admitted to herself that there wasn't anything about him that didn't turn her on. Thick dark hair curled over his ears, a beacon calling to her fingers to slide right in and tug his face up for a kiss. He'd shaved but already sported a five-o'clock shadow, and her palms itched to cup his jaw and run her palms over the roughness. And the man had a full mouth that was simply made for kissing. But his eyes drew her in more than anything else. Not only were they gorgeous, but they expressed his emotions even when he wanted to hide what he felt. Beneath the hot glances, the twinkle of humor, a lingering hint of fear remained. Trish understood. And tonight she vowed to squash the fear and embrace hope.

But she knew it wasn't going to be easy.

"You don't have to watch me. Actually, I know how to make sweet potato fries. In fact, I'm quite the fan. Chock-full of beta carotene and all that good stuff. There's more to me than Italian cuisine, sweet cheeks."

"Did you just call me *sweet cheeks*?"

"I did. Are you offended?"

"No, thank you for noticing how sweet my cheeks are."

Tony chuckled. "I've known since you took out the trash in nothing but your robe. Now you can quit watching me. I'll get this right. I promise." He deftly sliced through the thick sweet potato to demonstrate.

God, even his voice turned her to mush. His rough-and-tumble Brooklyn accent was beginning to soften with the slower cadence of the South. "Ah, I believe you, but that's not why I'm watching you," Trish softly admitted.

"Then why?" Something flickered in those expressive eyes and she realized she needed to let him know how she felt. Women weren't the only ones who needed validation.

Trish gave him a slow smile. "Because I like to look at you."

Their gazes held for a long delicious moment before Trish turned back to the stove and went to work. She knew she was keeping him off-kilter, wondering what she was going to do next. It was killing her not to go over there and slide onto his lap, but she refrained, knowing that a slow simmer was going to end up being a lot more satisfying in the end . . . if she could stand the wait.

Watching Trish prepare the burgers turned out to be equal parts highly entertaining and slow torture. When she bent over the oven to flip the fries over, her shirt hiked up and either he was dreaming or he caught a glimpse of red satin. Was she wearing a hot red teddy under those casual clothes? He was dying to find out. As much as his stomach rumbled for the burgers, he was hungry for her even more.

"The fries will be about ready in ten minutes. How do you like your burger cooked?"

"Medium."

"Good, me too."

Tony glanced at Digger, who watched Trish with adoring eyes. He grinned at his dog, understanding completely. She brought over condiments and a Kentucky Ale and then presented him with a big juicy burger topped with a thick slab of cheddar cheese and a toasted bakery bun.

After swallowing a bite she shook his head and grumbled, "Damn it."

Trish's eyes widened. "What?"

"This burger is amazing. I was hoping to criticize." He held up a sweet potato fry. "And baked to crispy perfection. I give you five stars and a bonus for having the pleasure of watching you prepare it."

"Why, thank you very much." Trish shrugged. "It's just a burger. I thought surely I couldn't mess it up."

"Are you kidding? You were absolutely right. There is an art to a great burger, and you've mastered it." He took another big bite and nodded. "Obviously I love food, but I'm so busy in the kitchen that I grab a nibble, a bite, rarely getting the opportunity to sit and savor a meal. Add having it prepared for me by a beautiful woman? It doesn't get any better than this," he said, and then feeling a little bit exposed by his speech, he turned to look at Digger. "Right, Dig?"

"Again, thank you." She inclined her head and Tony thought the slight blush in her cheeks was so damned cute. He knew in that moment that there wasn't anything calculating or pretentious about Trish Daniels. She wasn't anything remotely like Gloria, and he needed to remember that fact and simply relax.

Tony finished off the last bite of his dinner and leaned back in his chair. "That was so good."

"I'm glad you enjoyed it. Sit back while I clean up."

"I feel like a slug watching you do all of the work."

"Oh, you're going to owe me a big fat Italian dinner."

"And you'll get it. But just pile the dishes in the sink to soak. I'll get to them later. Whadaya say we sit on the patio with the rest of our beer and toss a ball to Digger?"

"I like that plan."

Five minutes later they were sitting outside on the patio in the waning sunlight. The sky was quickly turning into a glorious palette of deep red and vivid purples with streaks of bright orange. A light breeze kicked up enough to cool the air and bring the sweet scent of summer. Digger was delighted to romp in the field filled with tall grass and cheerful wildflowers.

"I know they're considered weeds, but I just love wildflowers. I know what some of them are, but I need to get a book to identify them like black-eyed Susan, soft yellow foxglove, purple wild onion, goldenrod, and field mint. I bet that Gabby knows them all. She's such a sweet girl. She and Reese make a cute couple."

Tony smiled at her. "They do. Reese has cared about her since they were kids. With his father deserting them like he did, Reese and Tessa sure have been through the mill."

"You seem worried."

Tony shrugged. "After Mike sent the flowers I got this weird feeling in the pit of my stomach that something is going to happen."

"Like him showing up?"

"I don't know how he'd have the nerve, but yeah, maybe. I just hate to have them suffer a setback. It was really hard to see my baby sister suffering when Mike walked out. I took Reese in, but I always wished I could do more."

Tony felt a muscle clench in his jaw. "Seeing someone you love in pain is tough to witness." He cleared his throat and then continued. "Tessa is a damned good person. I just wish I could fix everything, ya know?"

"Hey, everything will be all right," she said firmly. "You have each other and that counts for a lot."

Tony reached over and took her hand. "You have a way of calming me down." He brought her hand to his lips and kissed her knuckles. "Thank you."

"I'm glad."

Tony smiled and held on to her hand, rubbing her thumb over the soft skin. They watched Digger run around while the sun sank lower in the sky. When fireflies started to flicker, Digger chased them, making Trish laugh.

Tony tried to remember when he'd felt this relaxed and at ease with a woman. But touching her stirred his blood, and when the soft evening breeze brought the scent of her perfume his way, he longed to caress much more than her hand. And yet he was loath to break the spell and so he waited.

"It's a beautiful night," Trish commented.

"Yes, it is."

"A full moon, I think."

After a moment he asked, "So . . . are you wearing the teddy?"

Trish looked at him and smiled. "I keep my promises," she responded in a husky tone that felt like a physical caress.

"I don't think you promised me."

"I promised *myself*." She paused and then continued. "I reminded myself that I needed to move forward instead of looking back all the time so good things don't pass me by."

"That's pretty profound."

"I've read a lot of self-help books," she answered with a slight grin. "I've got a lot more where that came from."

"You didn't exactly answer my question."

Trish tossed the ball to Digger, who was getting tired of being ignored. "I don't intend to," she said, and then stood up.

Tony felt a flash of alarm thinking he'd somehow offended her. Was she leaving? His stomach felt as if it dropped to his toes and he scrambled to stand up, nearly knocking over his chair. But instead of heading toward her patio, she opened his door and walked inside. Digger followed at her heels like a lovesick puppy. Tony grinned. He could relate.

Confused, Tony thought Trish might head over to the sink to do the dishes, but she paused by the archway leading upstairs. His heart pounded and he stopped in his tracks.

Trish tilted her head, making her blond curls slide seductively over her shoulder. "Don't you want to find out?"

"Absolutely." After three long slightly limping strides, Tony pulled her into his arms and then pushed her up against the wall. Raising her hands about her head, he threaded his fingers through hers, held her captive, and then kissed her as he'd been dying to do all night long. He moved his mouth to her neck, nibbling, licking, loving the feeling of her hair against his cheek. He felt her breath catch and she moaned softly when he sucked her earlobe into his mouth.

"Let go of my hands. I want to . . . *need to* touch you."

"Not yet," he said, and then kissed her almost roughly, demanding, while pressing his body against hers. She'd been in control all night and now he wanted to turn the tables. He planned on making love to her until she trembled in his arms and cried out his name. "I want you in my bed," he said hotly in her ear, and she nodded.

"Take me there."

Tony released one hand but held on to the other, leading her up the stairs to his bedroom. After turning on one small lamp he turned back to her. "Undress for me, Trish."

She arched an eyebrow. "You first," she said, not willing to give up her hold on him.

Tony nodded and then tugged his shirt over his head. He loved the look of longing in her eyes, and when she reached out and ran her hands over his chest he sucked in a breath. She tugged his shorts down and when she lightly traced a fingertip down his shaft he felt the sensation all the way to his toes.

Taking a step backward, she pulled her shirt over her head and shimmied out of her jeans.

"God . . . ," Tony breathed, and let his gaze travel over her standing there in a red satin teddy edged with black lace. He knew that it took some courage for her to do this, and the knowledge made the moment sexy, seductive, and something that would remain in his memory forever. With her shoulders back, she stood there boldly, proudly but with a slightly vulnerable edge that made him fall in love with her even more. "You take my breath away," Tony said, and meant it. Although toned and firm, Trish had the full curves of a real woman.

She smiled and when she shrugged ever so slightly one delicate strap slid over her shoulder. The move was unintentional and so sexy that Tony stepped closer. He cupped her full breasts in his hands, rubbing his thumbs over her nipples until they pebbled through the satin. Dipping his head, he replaced his hands with his mouth. She sucked in a breath and sank backward onto the bed as if her legs could no longer hold her. Tony understood. He felt the same way.

Tony paused for a moment, drinking in the sight of her propped up against the pillows in the red teddy. Her golden curls tumbled in sexy disarray. She looked up at him with wide eyes and then gave him a slightly shy but come-get-me grin.

"What are you waiting for?"

"I just wanted to look at you. File this picture of you in my brain for future reference."

She laughed, throaty and smoky, before peeling the teddy off and tossing it to the side.

"Ah . . . and this sight is even better." He paused to roll on protection and then slid his body against hers. The feeling of skin on skin had him groaning before he lowered his head for a long, hot kiss. "I want to touch you, taste you everywhere," he said before starting a trail of moist kisses down her body. He gave his attention to her breasts, licking, sucking, and nibbling until she arched her back and fisted her hands in the sheet. Tony traveled lower, easing her thighs apart so he could taste her intimately.

"God . . . Tony . . . no. Oh!" She threaded her fingers in his hair and arched upward. Her breath became shallow delicate pants. "This is, oh . . . too much. . . . I . . . ," she pleaded, but he wasn't about to stop. For him, pleasing a woman was almost as satisfying as being buried deep inside her. "Please . . . I want . . ."

"This?" Knowing she was close to climaxing, Tony scooted up, lifted her hips, and thrust inside her wet heat.

"Yes!" She hooked her long legs around him while he made love to her deeply, savoring each thrust, each stroke. When she pressed her shoulders into the pillows and arched upward, he felt her body open and then clench, and hearing her throaty cry of his name sent Tony over the edge with her.

Pleasure erupted, gripping and intense, and then tumbled downward, wrapping around him slowly, sweetly. With a satisfied groan he rolled to the side and pulled Trish close. He buried his face in her hair, inhaling the scent before tenderly kissing her shoulder.

"That was—" she began, but he kissed her neck and caressed her breast.

"Wonderful?"

"Yeah, that."

"We're just getting started, you know," he promised in her ear.

"Bring it on," she challenged with a low giggle, and

then rolled around to face him. She gave him a slow, sultry kiss and then laid her head on his chest.

Tony rubbed his hand up her back and then kissed the top of her head, feeling protective. "Stay with me tonight."

She nodded, kissed his chest but didn't speak. She didn't have to say a word. He understood.

25

Facing the Music

REESE SPREAD THE LAST OF THE FUDGE ICING ONTO THE chocolate layer cake and then turned and flicked a worried glance over at his mother. She'd been exceptionally quiet all afternoon and evening. While he was anxious to head over to see Gabby, he wasn't about to leave until he got to the bottom of what was bothering her. When she came over to gather up his dirty dishes, Reese asked, "Hey, Mom, everything okay?"

"Sure," she said, but turned swiftly toward the sink and started rinsing the big metal bowl. "You should get on over to Gabby's. There's nothing left to do," she added over her shoulder.

"Mom, I'm not leaving until we talk about whatever's on your mind. Gabby will understand. Let's go out into the dining room and have a seat."

She dried the bowl and then wiped her hands on a towel before tossing it into the dirty laundry pile that she'd wash at home. She piddled around doing everything but looking at him.

"I mean it, Mom," he told her gently. "I won't leave."

"Okay." She nodded and followed him into the dining room. Reese sat down, but when she started straightening things on the table instead of talking, he knew something was definitely wrong.

Reese hoped she was going to tell him that she'd finally made the decision to file for divorce. He knew how difficult it must be to voice the words and he opened his mouth to get the conversation started, but she spoke up first.

"Your father bought Fred's Garage."

Reese sat up straighter and felt his heart lurch. "What?"

"Maggie broke the news to me. I didn't even hear it from your father."

"So . . . is he in town?" Reese tried to wrap his brain around this information. "Moving back here?"

She shrugged but then nodded. "Apparently, he's bought a house too. Maggie didn't realize until recently that Mike owns a company called M.P. Properties LLC. When she put two and two together she wanted to give me a heads-up."

"Mom . . . but he . . . he hasn't contacted you?"

"No. Not unless you count the flowers."

Reese felt a flash of excitement, a warm rush of hope, but then anger doused it like a cold splash of water.

"But I imagine he will."

Reese suddenly wanted to shout and throw things, but he knew he had to keep it together for his mother's sake. "So, how do you feel about this?"

"Stunned. I imagine you are too."

All Reese could do was nod. He didn't know how he was supposed to feel. How he could feel. "When he contacts you, calls you, or whatever I want to go with you. You don't have to face this on your own. Maybe Uncle Tony should go too."

"No, I've already thought of that. I know Tony will always be there for us, but we need to face this together. You and me."

Reese reached over and took his mother's hand. Her

eyes brimmed with unshed tears, but she squeezed his fingers.

"Listen, I'm strong. Stronger than ever. We've built a nice life here in Cricket Creek and I won't let anyone destroy what we've rebuilt. Especially not your father. But we'll hear him out because you're right. We deserve an explanation. It's just that a little heads-up would have been nice."

"We didn't get one when he left. Frankly, I'm not surprised that he didn't warn us. But I am floored that he has the damned nerve to return to Cricket Creek," Reese added darkly. He had the urge to pound his fists on the table but refrained for his mother's sake.

"We both knew that something was up, Reese. I had that feeling after the roses and I know you did too."

Reese sighed. "Now what?"

She lifted one shoulder and Reese hated the haunted look in her eyes. "I guess we wait," she said.

"No." Reese shook his head. "We've waited long enough. We're going to track his sorry ass down and get some answers. And I'm going home with you. I'm not going to risk him coming to you while you're home alone."

"Reese, no! You need to head on over to Gabby's. We'll revisit this in the morning."

"I wouldn't be good company for Gabby tonight, Mom. She would want me to stay with you, and in truth I would never be able to be completely there for her until this was resolved anyway." Reese knew that now. The emotion churning around in his gut was gnawing at his happiness, bringing up old feelings of anger. He and his mother needed to meet this head-on. Together. "Now let's lock up and I'll take you home or you can stay upstairs at my place if you prefer. The choice is yours, but I'm not letting you out of my sight. I don't want him to show up on your doorstep and me not be there."

She sighed. "You're a stubborn young man."

"I'm a Marino. I come by it naturally."

She finally smiled. "I'll lock the front door and sleep on your sofa."

"You'll sleep in my bed and I'll take the sofa," he insisted. He was about to stand up when the front door opened.

And his father walked in.

Reese heard his mother's audible intake of breath and glanced her way. She'd gone white as a slice of provolone. Seeing the stark emotion on his mother's face had Reese rising to his feet. He wasn't a kid; he was an adult, and his father was going to have to face him man-to-man.

Reese had perfected the dark scowl during his rebellious years, and he gave one to his father now. But to his credit, Mike Parker's stride never faltered as he walked forward. Reese felt a tremble in his hands and balled them into fists at his side. His mother remained sitting, most likely because her legs felt as weak and unsteady as Reese's did. Not that he'd let him see one little bit of this emotion or a shred of weakness. Reese lifted his chin and waited for Mike Parker to speak.

"Hello, Reese, Tessa," Mike said in a soft but steady voice.

"Mike . . . ," Tessa responded, but Reese remained stony and silent. How was he supposed to address the man, anyway? The term *father* hardly fit. He wore khaki slacks and a light blue golf shirt so different from his dark blue mechanic's uniform that remained in Reese's memory. His sandy brown hair was neatly trimmed but threaded with silver. He was a tall man, but Reese had him by a good three inches and he was glad that his father had to look up at him. Fine lines around his eyes showed the passing years, and a thin scar that Reese didn't remember sliced across his chin, but he looked fit and strong.

But the twinkle, the ever-present amusement in his light blue eyes, was absent, replaced by wariness, sadness. The father Reese remembered had once been a teasing, funny, happy man, but there wasn't even a trace of that personality now. Reese felt a stab of something akin to sympathy, but he steeled his spine, refusing to feel anything but resentment and disdain.

Mike stood there for a long awkward moment and then cleared his throat as if trying to find his voice again. "I had this whole speech ready, but now I'm having trouble remembering where to begin," he admitted gruffly.

"Why you left us would be an excellent place to start," Reese suggested tightly.

He closed his eyes and inhaled a deep breath. "Uh, mind if I sit down?"

Reese did, but his mother gestured toward a chair. "Can I get you something to drink?" she asked in a not quite steady voice.

"Water, maybe? Please?" Mike replied, but when his mother made a move to stand up, Reese waved her off, not wanting her to have to walk on unsteady legs. Taking angry strides, he went to grab a bottle of water from the fridge, barely resisting the urge to hurl the bottle at him. Instead, he put it on the table with more force than necessary.

"Thank you," Mike said, and unscrewed the cap.

Reese handed a bottle to his mother as well and then sat down, crossed his arms over his chest, and waited.

Mike took a swig from the bottle and then cleared his throat once more. "First let me say that I'm sorry. I am deeply, regrettably sorry from the bottom of my heart. I let down the two people in the world that I love the most."

Reese heard his mother's shaky intake of breath but somehow remained silent when he wanted to yell and curse, unleash all of the pent-up anger.

"What started out innocently as my Wednesday night poker game with my friends turned into a gambling habit that got out of hand." He frowned and inhaled a deep breath. "We didn't play for much, but I started winning and suddenly I was putting a couple, three hundred dollars into our savings every month. Then I got the harebrained idea that I needed to head to the gambling boats once or twice a month since I had convinced myself I was a good poker player. And I kept winning. Encouraged, I gambled more . . . and then more, getting into betting on sports. Soon, I'd started piling up enough money that we were going to be able to build our house sooner. I let Fred know that I wanted to buy the garage as soon as he was ready to retire. He'd already promised I'd get first shot at it, anyway." He paused and closed his eyes. "And then my luck took a bad turn. I hit a losing streak that cleaned out our savings. Desperate, I borrowed money from the wrong people thinking I'd hit it big and make everything right. But I didn't. When I couldn't pay back the loan I was beaten within an inch of my life," he said flatly.

Tessa inhaled sharply, put a hand on her mouth. "Were you in the hospital? Why wasn't I called?"

"Fred took me to his fishing camp. I recovered there. Tessa, they . . ." He paused again and swallowed hard. ". . . threatened that they'd . . . they'd hurt you. I was terrified. Fred helped me out and I eventually paid them off, but I wasn't about to put you and Reese in danger and so I left. I was so ashamed and I was determined not to return until I could replace the money I'd lost and pay Fred back. I made him swear that he wouldn't tell you what happened."

"And so you think you can waltz back here and pick up where you left off?" Reese asked harshly. "After ten years of no explanation, almost no contact?"

"No. Reese, I never expected for it to take so long. I worked endless hours, lived as cheaply as I could, scrimping, saving, and then started investing rather than gambling. It worked until the recession hit and I lost nearly all I'd gained and had to basically begin again."

Tessa finally spoke up. "But why didn't you just come home? Explain? We were a family. We would have gotten through this together. You should have just come home. Explained everything."

"I thought I'd already lost both of you and . . . and I couldn't face that or face you. I'd let down my wife and son in every way possible. I was deeply ashamed. But I thought if I'd become successful, wealthy, then I'd have something to offer besides an apology."

"And so now you own Fred's Garage?" Tessa asked softly. "And a house?"

"On the ridge overlooking the river where we planned our dream home," he said. "I bought up property in Cricket Creek when the value plummeted. I made some good investments, including the old trailer park."

"Tristan McMillan and his mother are developing it into single-family homes," Tessa said.

"They bought it from me . . . my company."

Reese blinked at him. "And you think this makes everything right? We didn't need money! We needed you. Or at least the man I once loved and respected."

He shook his head. "No . . . no. I don't deserve your forgiveness, but you deserve an apology. And anything else you need."

"I don't want a damned dime from you. You can't buy back what you lost," Reese told him.

"I know that. I don't expect anything. I don't deserve anything. I wouldn't blame you if you turned your back on me for the rest of your life. I didn't mean for one year to blend into the next and the next. Fred, bless that man, kept me informed about you as much as he could."

"So Fred told you about Tony and Reese opening the pizza parlor?"

He nodded. "I sold this land to Mitch Monroe about three years ago. It was just a rocky hillside at the time and I bought for practically nothing."

"Since when did you know anything about real estate?" Reese demanded.

"I read, studied, *everything* I could get my hands on

about investing and making money. I'd been investing in Cricket Creek . . . I suppose, to stay close to you."

Reese looked at him, still trying to get a handle on his emotions and wrap his brain around the fact that his father was sitting just a few feet away from him. His heart thudded. His stomach twisted. He couldn't even imagine what his mother must be feeling.

"Of course, Tessa, we're still . . . married, so—"

"I don't care about money either, Mike," she interrupted. In fact, the mere mention of it seemed to give her strength. "I was content to save our pennies until we could afford our dream house, and if that never happened I was happy in the trailer park. I had all I ever needed."

"I wanted more for you and Reese. . . ."

She nodded and then surprised Reese when she stood up. "I appreciate you coming and finally giving us the explanation we've been wondering about for ten years. Now if you'll excuse me, we were just closing up for the night." She gave him a level look, then turned her back and walked toward the kitchen.

Wow. Reese's mother was stronger than he gave her credit for. And he needed to remember that.

When Mike took a step toward her as if to give her a hug, Reese shook his head. "Don't. You don't have that right."

"No, I guess I don't." Mike nodded slowly.

"You put her through hell. After you disappeared I started to get into trouble. Mom couldn't handle me and sent me to live with Uncle Tony even though it about killed her to send me away. He straightened me out and was a father to me. More of a father than you became. That's why I go by Reese Marino now."

His father blanched, visibly shaken. "I'm so sorry. If only—"

"Just stop. *If only* means nothing to me. You left. Period."

"Okay." He nodded again. "Thank you for listening, Reese. I'd give anything to turn back the clock, but I can't, so . . ."

"So you should go."

He scrubbed a hand down his face. "I'm sorry, Reese. I should have come back and faced the music. I was a coward. And Tessa's right. No amount of money or success can bring back those lost years. We weren't rich, but I had it all and was too stupid to know it. I gambled with more than just money . . . I gambled my life away. I want to have you back in my life more than anything, but I don't blame you one bit if you don't want that." He swallowed hard and then turned to go.

And Reese stood there and watched his father walk out the door.

Reese walked on wooden legs over to lock the door and then headed into the kitchen. His mother sat on the stool next to the phone where she took pizza orders. Her feet were resting on the top rung and she leaned her elbows on her knees. He braced himself to see her crying, but she wasn't.

Reese walked over and hugged her. "You are the strongest woman I know."

"Well, you know what they say: What doesn't kill you makes you stronger." She gave him a rather sad smile. "I always knew there was something crazy that happened to him." She patted her chest. "I felt it. But I never would have guessed gambling. That was shocking." She sighed. "He looked so tired, so sad."

"Mom—"

"Oh, don't worry. I'm not going to throw myself into his arms," Tessa promised firmly, but when she reached up to brush a lock of hair aside, her fingers trembled. "But it does feel good to finally have some answers." She attempted a smile. "I'll take you up on spending the night. I can't fathom being alone after this and I know you have to be shook-up too."

"At least," he began, but then shook his head.

"Tell me. Please."

"At least . . . he didn't leave because of me."

"Oh, Reese!" Her eyes widened. "Why would you think such a thing?"

"Because nothing else made sense. I figured it had to be me." He shrugged. "It's classic. Kids always think that it's their fault."

"I didn't know. . . ." Her voice shook.

"I shouldn't have mentioned it."

"No!" She put a hand on his arm. "I want to know how you feel about everything. We're in this together."

Reese nodded. "I wasn't about to let you be by yourself. Let's go upstairs."

"I'm sure it's neat as a pin, right?"

Reese chuckled. She was so good at changing the subject, lightening the mood if only a little bit. "Of course!" When she slid down from the stool, he looped his arm around her and squeezed. "I love you, Mom."

She looked up and gave him a trembling smile and a tear slid down her cheek. "I love you too and I'm so very proud of you. And I always will be. Now let's head upstairs. I'm dead on my feet."

After finding a new toothbrush and a big shirt for his mom to sleep in, he got her tucked into bed. "I know it's going to be hard, but I hope you sleep well."

"I'm exhausted, so I don't think it's going to be an issue," she said with a small smile. "Quite an eventful day, huh?"

"Yeah, hey, I'll even fix you smiley face pancakes in the morning. Although mine might not turn out as good as the ones you used to make. Sound good?"

She gave him a tired laugh, but a laugh nonetheless. "You betcha."

Reese got some blankets out of the linen closet and headed for the sofa. He'd wanted to call Gabby, but when he got settled beneath the covers he was surprised when his phone said it was well after midnight. "Damn," he whispered when he noticed he'd missed a couple of text messages from her. He sent a text asking if she was up but didn't get a response. Reese hoped she was sleeping and not angry, but he wanted to tell her about the unexpected appearance of his father, not send such stunning information in a text message. He waited, staring at his phone, but she didn't respond. Reese sighed. Just hearing her voice would have made him feel so much better, and God, he really wanted to be in her arms right now.

Having that thought made him realize the heartache his mother must have suffered all those years, yearning, longing, and missing her husband. She'd confessed it to him already, but even if she hadn't he could see the love for him in her eyes. But could love, no matter how strong, heal ten years of pain?

Surprisingly, Reese wasn't feeling the acute anger he'd expected to consume his thoughts. Only sadness remained. Reese suddenly thought about how much he loved Gabby. Losing her wasn't something he thought he could bear and so he understood his father's regret, his acute sorrow.

Reese inhaled a deep breath and rolled over to his side. A deep ache settled in his chest, and the wound that had healed suddenly felt ripped open, raw, and exposed. Granted, he'd heard the sincerity in his father's voice, seen the stark sadness in eyes. But could he ever forgive him? Much less allow him back into his life? But Cricket Creek was a small town, so it would be hard to avoid seeing him.

Knowing he needed sleep, Reese turned his thoughts back to Gabby. When her sweet face drifted across his mind he smiled and relaxed, thinking that he couldn't wait to have her in his arms once again.

But sleep eluded him and although he fought against it like an ice pick anger started chipping away at his hard-won peace. He knew he had to hold it together for his mother's sake and for his relationship with Gabby. He hoped and prayed he could dig deep and find the strength to do it.

26

Just Remember I Love You

AFTER A RESTLESS NIGHT OF TOSSING AND TURNING, Gabby woke up lying nearly sideways with her feet tangled in the sheet so much so that she had to work like an escape artist to get free. She grabbed the spare pillow, hugging the middle, while memories of strange disjointed dreams danced around in her head. She hoped that the dreams were random and didn't possess any meaning. She yawned, frowned, and then with a long moan she shut her eyes against the fingers of sunlight reaching through her window.

A glance at her cell phone told her it was way too early to be up on her day off and she shut her eyes, but after failing to fall back asleep she groaned again and then threw the covers back. As soon as her feet hit the floor, her stomach rumbled. She remembered she'd skipped the late dinner she'd planned when Reese failed to show up last night, and her body felt the need to protest.

"Right . . . ," Gabby mumbled, and then let out a little yelp when she saw her reflection in the mirror. Her short, layered hair looked as if it had been styled with an egg beater. "I seriously need some really strong coffee."

But after she padded barefoot into her kitchen, she couldn't muster up the energy to start coffee, and the oatmeal she'd planned on eating suddenly held no appeal.

Gabby snapped her fingers. "I need a sticky bun from Grammar's." But then she remembered it was Sunday and the bakery would be closed. She thought about walking up to Wine and Diner for breakfast, but the prospect of talking to people had her sighing. Last night Gabby planned to tell Reese that she loved him and now she felt so damned confused. A million questions went through her head and she closed her eyes, fighting off tears.

When her phone beeped, Gabby's heart started beating faster. Reese? She thought back to the message he had sent late last night saying that they needed to talk. *We need to talk*. In her experience those four little words never led to anything pleasant.

With trembling fingers Gabby picked up her phone. The text message was from Joy reminding Gabby about the charity pancake breakfast at Whisper's Edge. Gabby smiled sadly. She didn't think she would go, but it helped to know that she now had people in her life that cared about her. After putting the phone down on the counter, she went ahead and made coffee, not even thinking about the task as she did it, so much so that she felt mildly surprised when the scent of coffee filled the air.

The machine sputtered and gurgled as if it were any ordinary morning. But it wasn't. Gabby's ordinary had become Reese slipping his arms around her about now, kissing her neck, and saying something sweet or sexy. Feeling loved, protected, and wanted had become ordinary, so this sudden shaky fear of impending we-need-to-talk doom took her off guard. But Gabby had learned through experience that life went on no matter what horrific event occurred. Lost in her thoughts, she suddenly realized that someone was tapping on her door.

"Addison!" Gabby said in the most cheerful voice she could muster.

"Hey there, Gabby!"

"Come on in."

"I come bearing gifts!" Addison breezed into the kitchen and put a plastic container on the table. "I had some leftover wedding cake. . . . Well, these are actually cupcakes, what so many brides are doing these days. Anyway, I had some samples from Grammar's and I thought you might like a few. I know it's early, so if you weren't up I was going to leave them on your doorstep." She grinned. "Like the cupcake fairy."

Gabby gave Addison a hug. "I was just wishing I had a pastry. A cupcake will do nicely. I just brewed some coffee. Care to join me?"

Addison shook her head. "I'm going for a jog along the river before the day gets too hot. Having those cupcakes around is going straight to my bum." She turned around and pointed. "Reid is working on the farm today, so after my run I'm going to do some inventory." She tilted her head and frowned. "Hey, are you okay?"

"Yeah." She waved a dismissive hand. "I just didn't sleep well last night." She pointed to her spiky hair. "I've got some serious bed-head going on. I think it has something to do with the odd dreams I had. One involved being chased by a giant frog." She shrugged and attempted a chuckle. "Go figure."

"Yeah, insomnia sure sucks." Addison nodded but didn't look as if she quite bought it. "Well, I'll be around most of the day if you want to pop in the shop and shoot the breeze. I might head out to the farm and do some hiking in the woods or take a ride on a quad if you want to join me. I can actually drive one now, although I go much slower than Reid. Sara's adding a fire pit to the patio next to the barn for fall weddings."

"Oh, that's a great idea."

"Yeah, I wanted to see the progress. Give me a call if you're interested in going with me."

"Thanks, I'll remember that," Gabby said lightly, but suddenly struggled to keep it together.

Addison eyed her closely. "Listen, if you're having guy trouble, stress with the shop, I totally get it, so please come over and talk later if you want to, okay?"

"I promise." Gabby nodded and gave her another quick hug. "And thanks for the cupcakes. I need to start jogging too!"

"You can join me whenever you want to. Trust me, I don't push too hard. I use the term *jog* or *run* loosely. I mostly power-walk." She pumped her arms, demonstrating. "Or just walk," she whispered behind her hand. "But taking the route along the river is relaxing and makes me feel as if I'm working out."

"I'll remember that too."

"Okay, well, catch ya later."

After Addison left, Gabby poured coffee into a big mug. She peeked at the fancy cupcakes, but the cloying scent of sugar didn't sit well with her stomach and she opted to sip her coffee instead. Hopefully, she'd hear from Reese soon and her runaway mind would settle back down.

After a few minutes passed, Gabby considered calling Reese but then dismissed the notion. Reese needed to contact *her* and give *her* an explanation for standing her up.

After forcing herself to eat some strawberry-flavored oatmeal, Gabby showered and pulled on a pair of worn denim shorts and a Cricket Creek Cougars T-shirt. She went through the motions of making the bed, smiling at the beauty of the patchwork quilt handcrafted by Reid Greenfield's mother. When she'd tried to purchase the quilt at Addison's bridal shop, her friend insisted on giving it to her. Gabby sat down and ran her hand over the soft cotton, thinking that she really did need to get out of the apartment and take a break from thinking about Reese.

Gabby thought about Addison's offer to hang out and Joy's invitation to the pancake breakfast and then wondered if there might be a Cougars baseball game to attend? Or maybe she'd walk up to Sully's Tavern for lunch and get a much-needed bear hug from Pete. All of the options made her smile. She had people who cared about her. Friends she could count on. But Gabby suddenly knew just where she needed to spend her afternoon. She inhaled deeply, thinking she might pack a picnic lunch to take along, and then heard knocking at her door.

Just when Gabby had given up on the hope that it would be Reese standing on her doorstep, there he was, making her heart kick into high gear. She hurried over and opened the door, wondering if she should hug him, but instead she stepped aside and motioned for him to enter. "Hey there," she said softly, hating the uncertainty in her voice.

"Hey, yourself," Reese said, and gave her a hug that should have put Gabby at ease, but she could feel the tension in his embrace.

"Can I get you something to drink?" she asked.

"Water would be great," Reese answered, appearing so serious that Gabby felt another jolt of uneasiness. She grabbed two bottles of cold water from the fridge and handed Reese one before sitting down across from him at the small table.

"So, what's on your mind?" Nervous, Gabby toyed with the label on the bottle and waited.

"My father is back in Cricket Creek."

"Oh my goodness." Gabby put a hand on her chest. "So . . . so you've seen him?"

Reese nodded. "Just when we were about to close, he walked into the dining room." He shook his head. "Mom was floored."

"I can imagine." She waited for him to continue.

"He had a gambling problem, Gabby. Owed money to the wrong people, dangerous people, and so he left."

Gabby reached across the table and put her hand over his. "Oh, Reese, I'm so sorry. At least now you know the reason."

"Reason? I view it as an excuse. He said he didn't want to return until he could make things right. But he was a coward. He messed up and his damned pride kept him away. Now he's back armed with piles of money and he somehow thinks that makes it all okay."

"I doubt that he thinks that," Gabby responded gently, but Reese pulled his hand away.

"Really? Well, he can go to hell for all I care."

"Reese, I understand your anger, but—"

"No, you don't." He took a swig of water. "I prayed for so many years for him to return, and now that he has I wish he'd just stayed the hell away. Mom could have divorced his sorry ass and we could have all moved on. We were doing so well and now he's come back and fucked it all up. Mom is a mess. Uncle Tony is mad as hell."

"And so are you."

"Yeah. I'm trying really hard not to be, and at first all I felt was sadness. But anger is gripping me, Gabby, and I'm having a hard time shaking it off." He closed his eyes and sighed. "I'm so sorry to put you through all of this."

"Reese, I'm here for you," Gabby assured him, but the stark look in his eyes worried her. "I don't blame you for being angry. Who wouldn't be?" She was about to tell him that she loved him, but he scooted back and folded his arms across his chest and stared down at the floor. She could feel him erecting a wall and she needed to tear it down before it gained strength. "I'm not going away. I want to help you through this. That's what people who love each other do."

He glanced up. "But you never told me you loved me, remember?"

"I do. I love you, Reese." It felt wonderfully freeing to finally voice her feelings.

"Ah . . . Gabby." He shook his head. "You're saying that because you think you have to. I want you to say it because you feel it," he said, and unfolded his arms to tap his chest. "In here."

"You're wrong. I wouldn't say it if I didn't feel it, Reese. I should have said it sooner. I was . . . afraid. I was going to tell you last night. And then . . ."

"And then my . . . father showed up and ruined everything."

"Everything isn't ruined."

Something flickered in his eyes, but he remained silent. Gabby understood. Anger was a defense Reese used to mask hurt and to combat his own fear. But she didn't want to see him slip into that dark place.

"Reese, I realize this is hard, but— "

"Gabby, you can't possibly realize how I feel, so don't even try. The man gambled away my family's hard-earned money and then left for ten years. Now he thinks he can come waltzing back into our lives." He snapped his fingers. "Just like that. Well, my mother might trust him enough to let him back in her life, but I won't." He shoved his fingers through his hair. "I tried to hold it together. But I was up most of the night thinking about the whole damned thing and I just got more and more pissed off. I didn't let my mother know, but damn, I just . . ." He shook his head, looking up at the ceiling.

"I really do understand your anger."

"No, you don't. You couldn't possibly."

"Really, Reese?" Gabby pushed away from the table and stood up. "I was angry at my mother for dying. She smoked. It killed her. I was angry beyond all reason. I asked her so many times to stop, but she didn't. And she died." Gabby blinked back tears. "But I forgave her because she was my *mother*." Her chest rose and fell. "And I would give anything to have another day . . . damn, another hour with her. Look, I know it will be a process. A long road. But your father is back. You have that chance. Don't blow it for the same reason he failed to come back. Pride. Foolish, selfish pride. It cost him ten years and put you and your mother through hell. Don't do the same damned thing!" Her voice shook, but she stood her ground. "Why waste another minute?" she asked, and then leaned forward. "Do you know where I was headed?"

Reese shook his head.

"To the field of wildflowers where I scattered my mother's ashes. I used to go there on a regular basis, but I've been so busy with the shop and . . ." She shrugged. "It's hard. Emotional. But I need to go more often. I miss her so . . . *so much.*" She swiped at a tear. "And when I'm in that field with the wildflowers swaying in the wind, I feel like she's there. With me." She closed her eyes and then opened them and looked directly at Reese. "I don't have a second chance. I won't see my mother, feel her hug, and hear her voice until I'm on the other side with her. But you have the chance. Take it! If it doesn't work out; if he disappoints you again, well, you can't do anything about that. It's on him. But take the chance you've been given."

Reese looked at her for a long, emotional moment and then stood up. "I just don't think I can. I don't want to give him the power to hurt me again." He inhaled a long breath and blew it out. "I can tell by the look in your eyes that I'm disappointing you. I'm pretty damned good at disappointing people. I should go."

Gabby nodded. "You shouldn't go, but I won't stop you." As much as she wanted to pull him into her arms, she could feel his resistance, his anger. As hard as it was not to run after him, she knew he needed space and time to think, get his head wrapped around his father being back in Cricket Creek.

When his hand hesitated on the doorknob her heart thudded, but he turned and walked away. She stood there for a long, lonely moment and then inhaled a bracing breath. She needed to pay a long-overdue visit to the field of flowers where her mother's soul smiled upon her, bringing Gabby strength and serenity.

27

The Eye of the Storm

TRISH LOOKED UP FROM HER LAPTOP WHEN SHE HEARD the rumble of thunder. Cloud cover meant cooler temperatures so she could sit on her patio to write instead of being cooped up in the air-conditioning. There'd been a threat of storms all afternoon, but so far it had remained rumbling in the distance. "I don't know how much longer our luck is going to hold out, Digger. I might have to take you inside soon."

Digger looked up from where he lay chewing on a rawhide stick. Trish thought he looked funny with the stick held between his paws and so she picked up her phone and took a quick picture. But he too seemed increasingly leery of the darkening skies and rolling thunder. If lightning cracked across the horizon, she would hightail it inside. Trish had been terrified of thunderstorms ever since she was a little kid. A tornado had touched down in her neighborhood, uprooting a tree that crashed onto her house above her bedroom window just moments after she'd run into her parents' bedroom to climb into bed with them. High winds and strong storms brought back that fear.

Trish typed another paragraph of her review of the local high school's adaptation of *The Music Man*. She smiled, thinking that although the play hadn't been stellar, the students were earnest in their effort and she'd enjoyed every minute. Just when she started humming "Seventy-Six Trombones," lightning flashed across the sky followed by a loud clap of thunder that had her just about jump out of her skin. When Trish shrieked, Digger hurried over to her side.

"It's just a thunderstorm," said a deep voice, making Trish jump again, nearly knocking her computer off her lap.

"Doggone it, Tony, do you have to sneak up on me? For an awkward moment I thought it was Digger talking like that dog in the baked beans commercial."

He jammed his thumb over his head. "I pulled into the driveway and even locked my door. Didn't you hear the horn beep?"

"I was too busy being concerned by the thunder and lightning."

"So you're scared of storms too?"

Her chin came up. "A little."

"Well, this is likely to be a doozy. Make sure you have a flashlight and candles ready. I closed up early. No one is likely to come out in the storm, and I didn't want kids delivering in dangerous weather."

"Good call," Trish said, trying not to feel disappointed that he didn't offer to have her stay at his place during the storm. But then again she'd seen very little of Tony over the past couple of days. Of course Trish knew about Mike Parker returning to Cricket Creek. News like that travels fast in a small town.

Although Tony hadn't volunteered any information, Trish didn't want to pry, but she felt him distancing himself from her and she suddenly felt as gloomy as the weather. But Trish understood. Emotions had to be running high, reminding her that relationships could cause such pain and sorrow.

She felt that pain right now. And she didn't like it.

"Well, I'm going to head inside. Like I said, I don't enjoy storms." She raised her eyes skyward. "And this is getting too close for comfort."

Tony glanced at the sky and then back at her. "Thanks for watching after Digger."

"No problem. We're buds. I enjoy his company," Trish responded in a breezy tone that she didn't feel.

Tony nodded. "Well, again, thanks. I've been really tied up with work and . . . family stuff. It's been a rough few days." He rolled his head to his shoulders as if trying to get rid of tension.

"I can only imagine."

"Yeah." Tony's eyes met hers and held briefly as if he were making a decision, but then his gaze flicked away.

Trish felt his need but also his reluctance and she totally got it. This family matter was deeply personal, and letting her in, confiding in her, meant taking their relationship to a level that went beyond physical or even emotional because the foundation would become complete trust. Trish understood his turmoil. Once you were on the receiving end of betrayal, it was pretty difficult to learn to trust again.

"Well, I'm going to head inside and grab a cold beer followed by a hot shower."

"Sounds like a plan," Trish said lightly, wishing she had the nerve to tell him something sexy like that she'd wash his back. She tried to channel the sex kitten that had spent the night with him not long ago, but the wary look in Tony's eyes gave her pause. Trish closed her laptop, deciding that she would stand up and at least give him a hug. Perhaps physical contact would remind Tony what they already shared and could build on. But as soon as she stood up, a loud clap of thunder had her flinching. She glanced upward in time to see lightning slash across the sky. The wind kicked up, blowing her hair across her face. She could smell the rain in the air and felt a little flash of fear.

"You'd better get inside," Tony said. "You don't want your laptop to get wet."

"Good point," she agreed, and with a pat on Digger's head she turned toward her door. She could feel his gaze on her and had to fight the urge to turn around.

But Tony Marino didn't own getting hurt. Trish had done everything in her power to make her marriage work and had been rewarded with being cheated on with a young woman who had his baby. With Tony she'd stepped outside her comfort zone, taking a leap of faith they'd talked about in an effort to please him.

Well, damn it, she was done doing all of the giving, the pleasing.

Trish stepped inside her kitchen and closed the door without looking back. If Tony wanted her, then he would have to come and get her. "If not . . . well, it was his damned loss," she muttered.

Trish stomped her foot, but her eyes rounded when she heard the wind whistling through the trees. She hurried over to the television and turned on the weather channel. With her hand to her mouth she looked at the radar map knowing that the deep red color heading her way wasn't a good sign. She read the message scrolling at the bottom of the screen and sure enough, there was a tornado watch in effect until midnight. "Okay, at least it's not a warning," she assured herself, hoping the storm would simply blow over.

With a heavy sigh Trish hurried to the kitchen and opened the pantry door. A moment later she located the box with her storm emergency kit. Hugging it to her chest, she suddenly wished that her house had a basement rather than being built on a slab. A lot of people she knew shrugged off the threat of a tornado. After being on the receiving end of one, Trish knew to take violent weather seriously and decided to charge her laptop and cell phone just in case they lost power. Then she uncorked a bottle of wine, grabbed a paperback novel, and kept the weather channel on in the background. She wasn't about to take any chances.

"Stop looking at me like that," Tony said to Digger. "Trish will be fine. It's just a damned thunderstorm." He tried to ignore the guilt that he hadn't invited her over at least until the weather passed. The frightened look on her face had him sighing. He ran his fingers through his wet hair and flipped on the television to watch the Cincinnati Reds play but decided to check the weather channel just to see the radar map. "See . . . only a tornado *watch*, not a warning. It looks worse than it is," he added when Digger gave him that sad doggie look before flopping down onto the hardwood floor, resting his head on his paws.

"I've got too much shit going on to get seriously involved with her," he said. "Why would I want to put even more on my already full plate? Huh?" Tony closed his eyes and shook his head. These past few days had been killer. He hated to see Tessa and Reese going through such an emotional upheaval. He didn't even begin to know how to handle the situation. Did Mike deserve a second chance with his wife and son? Tony sure as hell didn't think so. He wanted to punch the jackass in the face. But in the end it wasn't his place to decide or even give advice. All he could do was be there for both of them. But after witnessing Tessa going through hell, Tony knew he didn't want to put himself in that position ever again. For, like, a hot minute he thought he did with Trish, but this past week had knocked some sense back into him. The risk just wasn't worth it. He needed to keep his ass on his side of the two-family house.

And then he heard sirens.

Tony rushed over to the window to see tree branches bending in the stiff wind. Fear for Trish slammed him in the gut. "Come on, Digger!" he yelled, opened the door, and ran in the rain over to Trish's place. He banged on the door, cringing when thunder boomed and lightning cracked way too close for comfort. He banged harder, nearly blinded by the sudden pouring rain. Digger barked in protest. Thankfully, a moment later, Trish opened the door.

"What are you doing? Are you crazy?" she asked when they all but tumbled into the kitchen.

"The answer to that would be hell yeah."

"What were you doing out in this mess? There's a tornado warning!"

"Coming to your rescue." He slicked his hair back, soaked to the skin, dripping water everywhere. Digger did the dog shake, making his wet fur stand on end and water fly everywhere.

"I don't want you to come to my rescue," Trish shouted, and pointed to the door, but the storm picked up the pace.

"Well, too bad, because here I am!" Tony patted his wet chest hard, sending a spray of water droplets her way. "But if you want me to go I will," he said, knowing full well she wouldn't send him back out there.

"Fine, but Digger stays. I don't want him to get struck by lightning." She turned on her heel.

"Where the hell are you going?"

"To the bathroom, the safest place in the house if a tornado strikes," she said, and stomped down the hallway.

"Are you serious?" he asked, and sloshed after her.

Trish stopped in her tracks, making him nearly run into her. "My neighborhood was hit by a tornado when I was a little kid. The Cincinnati area had had some pretty nasty run-ins with tornados. A huge tree came crashing into my bedroom. Had I not just run to my parents' room, I would have been injured or maybe even died. Yeah, I'm not just scared. I take tornado warnings seriously," she explained tightly, and then went into the bathroom and shut the door.

Tony stared at the door for a full ten seconds, but when the lights flickered and went out he opened the door and joined her. She sat huddled in the bathtub. A small Coleman lamp sat on the toilet lid. She looked up at him and glared.

"I'm sorry. I should have offered to stay with you earlier."

"I told you I don't need you to come to my rescue."

"What if I want to?" he tried with a slight shrug.

"Apparently, you don't. Digger most likely guilted you into coming over here." She looked around Tony to where Digger lounged on the floor as far away from the shouting as possible. "Look, it doesn't matter." She shrugged, but Tony could see the pain in her eyes.

But it did matter. Tony didn't have a clue how much until that very moment. "It does matter." Seeing Trish huddled in the bathtub with a hurt expression on her pretty face hit Tony hard. "You matter."

Trish remained silent.

"Can I join you?"

"No, you're sopping wet," she said, but the bite in her tone had lessened. It was a step in the right direction.

"I can remedy that." Tony started peeling off his wet clothes.

"What do you think you're doing?"

"What you asked me to do."

"I didn't ask you to strip!"

Tony shrugged and when he was naked took a step toward the tub.

"Don't you dare!" she sputtered.

"Isn't it safest in there?"

"Yes, but—"

"Then here I come."

"No! At least grab a towel." When she scrambled to her feet he pushed her up against the tile wall, and with his hands on either side of her head he kissed her. She pushed at his chest and Tony did the right thing and took a step back. Forcing anything, even a kiss, wasn't something he would ever do.

"Trish, I—" he began, but the words died in his throat when she started taking off her clothes.

"Don't get the wrong idea."

"Oh, I think I'm getting the right idea."

"I just need to take my mind off the storm."

He tilted his head. "Ah, so I'm just a distraction."

"Correct. So don't get the impression that this means I like you or anything." She tossed her clothes to the side.

"I don't like you either," he shot back, but reached over to cup her breasts.

"Good. It's mutual."

"Yeah," he growled, rubbing his thumbs over her nipples. "It's mutual.

"I more than like you," he continued in the same tone. "I'm falling in love with you. So get used to it."

"It's mutual," she snapped back, and then pulled his head down for a hot, demanding kiss.

God, she tasted like wine and woman and he couldn't get enough. He trailed kisses down her jaw to her neck, licking, tasting, and then feasted on her gorgeous breasts. She sucked in a breath, bracing her hands on his shoulders when he slid his hand between her thighs, loving how hot, how wet she was for him. He caressed her core, and when he eased two fingers inside her, she gasped. Sliding down to his knees, Tony lifted one leg over his shoulder and replaced his fingers with his mouth.

With a moan she held on to him, moving sensually, while he licked faster and faster until she dug her fingers into his shoulders and cried out. He felt her tremble and, coming to his feet, he held her tightly.

Tony kissed her while she came down from her orgasm. "Baby, I don't have protection . . . is it okay?"

"Yes." When Trish nodded he thrust upward. She clung to him, wrapped her legs around him. He could hear the rain pounding on the roof, the wind whipping through the trees, and branches tapping against the window. But Trish was the eye of his storm, the calm, the strength he needed . . . wanted.

There was no use fighting it. He loved her. And that truly was all that mattered.

28

Don't Stop Believin'

"HEY, REESE, YOU'VE BEEN IN THIS PIZZA JOINT NONSTOP all week long. Why don't you get out of here and go hang out with Gabby?"

Reese looked up from dusting three dozen cream puffs with confectioners' sugar. "I'm taking a break from seeing Gabby."

Tony crossed his arms over his chest. "Taking a break?"

"Until I can get my shit together."

"Until you get your shit together?"

Reese put the sugar shaker down. "Are you gonna repeat everything I say back to me?"

"Yeah, so you know how damned dumb it sounds."

"How is getting my shit together dumb? Uncle Tony, I'm still dealing with my father coming back to Cricket Creek."

Tony grabbed a cream puff. "I'm having trouble seeing how one relates to the other."

Reese shot him a look. "You gotta be kiddin' me."

Tony swallowed a bite of the cream puff. "Wow, these are amazing. No, I'm not kiddin' you."

"Look, Gabby has it in her head that I should give

this thing with my father a chance. He fucking *left*. And now we know why and it's not pretty."

Tony set the cream puff down and licked his thumb. "Life often isn't pretty, Reese. We all have our crosses to bear, our baggage. It isn't the hand you were dealt but how you play it."

"You got any more bullshit clichés to shovel my way?"

"Yeah, plenty. You wanna hear 'em?"

"No."

Tony sighed. "Wow, you still do that scowl pretty damned well. Hey, go back to that dark, angry place you were ten years ago. Carry around the chip on your shoulder and see where it gets ya." He angled his head toward the door. "In the meantime you're gonna lose the love of a wonderful young woman who makes you happy."

Reese scrubbed a hand down his face.

"Look, let Tessa and Mike work out their problems, Reese. If they reconcile or get a divorce, it's their decision and you have to respect that. The way I see it, if they do make it, well, their love was unstoppable. Tessa is a strong, amazing woman. If anyone has the capacity to forgive, it's her."

"I realize now just how strong Mom really is and has been all of my life." Reese gave him a level look. "But I don't think I can forgive what my father did."

Tony reached over and clamped a hand on his shoulder. "You don't have to do it right this minute . . . or *ever* if that's your decision. Just keep an open mind and look inside your heart."

Reese nodded slowly.

"Do you love Gabby?"

"I do."

"Then don't screw it up. Hey, you don't want her to date dipshit Drew, do ya?"

"Did you have to go there?"

Tony chuckled. "Sorry, but yeah. You gotta think about how it would feel if you saw her with someone else. Go on, picture it."

"No!" Reese didn't want to have that image in his brain. "Yeah, but what if—"

"No what-ifs! Now go. Get outta here. Go grab your girl and take her dancing at Sully's or somethin'. Have some fun."

Reese took his apron off and tossed it at Tony. "You'll clean up?"

"No problem. And don't show up here tomorrow or I'll kick your ass."

"Ha, like you could do that."

Tony put up his fists and jabbed the air. "Wanna go?" He pulled Reese in for a bear hug. "Man, I love you so damned much," he said gruffly. "Rips my heart out to see you sad. You love Gabby and I can tell she feels the same way. Grab her and hold on tight. She's the real deal and they're hard to come by." Tony swiped at his eyes. "Damned onions makin' my eyes water."

Reese laughed. "Yeah, me too. I put a lot of onions in those cream puffs."

Tony chuckled. "So that was the secret ingredient."

"Yeah, don't tell." Reese gave his uncle a high five and then headed up to his apartment to shower and change. After tugging on a blue polo and his favorite Lucky jeans, he headed out the door feeling better than he'd felt in days.

Reese took his time walking past the shops, pausing in front of From This Moment to gaze at the wedding dress in the window. He suddenly imagined Gabby in that dress standing in a field of wildflowers . . . and he suddenly knew what he wanted to do.

He hurried to Designs by Diamante but slapped his leg with he saw the closed sign on the window. Disappointed, Reese turned to leave, but someone opened the door.

"Hi, Reese, I thought that was you. I'm glad I caught you."

"Bella, hey, what's up?"

"I've tried to call you couple of times this past week, but you didn't pick up."

"Sorry. It's been a crazy week," he explained, thinking that was the understatement of the year.

Bella angled her head toward the shop. "I'm here helping Mom. Come on inside. I've got something pretty cool to show you."

Reese followed Bella into the jewelry shop. An older version of Bella walked out from behind the counter. She extended her hand. "Hi, you must be Reese. I'm Nicolina, Bella's mom."

"Nice to meet you, Nicolina."

"Thanks for bringing fantastic pizza and pasta to Cricket Creek."

Reese chuckled. "Bella already thanked me."

"It deserves another thank-you. We love Italian food. Can you imagine that? Your chicken piccata is divine. Just the right amount of lemon."

"Thank you. We make everything from scratch."

"It shows! Come on, follow me over to a display case." She pointed. "I call the collection the Sweetest Thing. I was inspired by your request for the candy necklace and the sweet story behind it."

"Wow," Reese said while looking beneath the glass. "All of the jewelry looks like candy." He looked up. "But it's real?"

Nicolina nodded. "Mostly made out of semiprecious stones to keep the price down, but yes, real. Calorie free!"

"Sweet, huh?" Bella asked, and laughed. "Sorry. Had to."

Nicolina chuckled and raised her palms in the air. "After I made the candy necklace I couldn't stop making pieces that look like candy."

"She became obsessed." Bella rolled her eyes.

"It was just so much fun!" Nicolina picked up earrings that looked like purple gumdrops. "Isn't it adorable? The necklace that looks like gumballs are actually hand-dyed pearls. There's a candy corn bracelet perfect for Halloween."

"Wow, that necklace looks just like rock candy." Reese pointed and grinned.

"There are earrings to match," Bella chimed in. She picked up a classic ring pop and slid it onto her finger. "This is my favorite. They've been selling like crazy."

Nicolina nodded. "Not that some of this kind of jewelry hasn't already been done, but I've never tried it. It's just so whimsical and cute. And I have you to thank."

"You're welcome."

Nicolina arched a dark eyebrow. "And I have your candy necklace if you still want it."

Reese nodded. "Absolutely!"

"That's what I was calling about," Bella explained.

Nicolina reached behind the counter and then showed him a necklace that looked just like the candy version, but the pastel colors were a bit deeper in tint and glazed, picking up the light.

"Wow, it's really beautiful. Gabby is going to just love it."

Nicolina beamed at him. "She is such a lovely girl. I've provided the jewelry for wedding parties, so we've met through Addison. Of course, as you know we all try to support each other here on Wedding Row. Is there anything else I can get you? Another charm for her bracelet, perhaps?"

"Mmmm, maybe. But I also had something else in mind." Reese took a deep breath and then glanced over at the ring case.

Bella's eyes widened. "Reese?"

Reese gave her a grin. "I . . . I want to take a look at engagement rings."

"I knew it!" Bella jumped and did a little jig. "Wonderful! This is so awesome! You two are such a supercute couple."

Reese laughed and felt a surge of joy. He looked from Bella to Nicolina. "Any suggestions?"

Nicolina tapped a fingernail to her cheek. "Come on over to the engagement rings. There is a classic daisy diamond ring that I think you might like."

"Really? There is such a thing?"

"Yes." Nicolina nodded. "I have a really pretty one that has yellow sapphires for the petals and a cluster of diamonds in the center." She picked it up and showed it to him.

Reese took the delicate ring and looked at it. He felt emotion gather in his throat and nodded. "I don't have to look at anything else. It's perfect. I'll take it."

"I do think it suits Gabby." Nicolina smiled at him warmly. "I'll even give you a nice discount to thank you for the candy jewelry inspiration.

"Do you know her ring size?"

Reese shook his head. "No."

"Well, if this doesn't fit we can fix that. Just have her stop in."

Reese grinned. "Assuming she says yes."

"I don't think you have to worry about that," Bella said. "But we'll cross our fingers for you." She held up her hands to demonstrate.

Each step that Reese took toward Gabby's felt as if he were walking toward his future while leaving the past behind. Gabby had been right all along. He needed to find the strength to reconcile with his father and find true peace. And as Uncle Tony said, he didn't have to get there all at once. It would be a journey, a process, but one he needed to take.

Reese stopped in front of Flower Power for a minute, rehearsing his proposal in his head. Part of him wanted to hold off and plan a special dinner and do something memorable like putting the ring in the dessert or something, but he knew he wouldn't be able to wait.

Just as Reese started to turn toward the alley leading

to Gabby's apartment, he heard some commotion behind him. He turned around to see several teenagers shouting at one another. Reese could smell a fight a mile away and so he started walking their way, hoping to diffuse things before it got out of hand.

"You guys need to knock it off," Reese said sharply.

"Dude, mind your own business," one of them shouted, and actually started coming toward him.

"I mean it," Reese continued firmly. "You don't want me to call the cops."

"How about I just shut you up?" the kid boasted, but before the kid could take a swing at Reese, one of the other teens sucker punched the kid in the face. A moment later all hell broke loose. Knowing someone could get seriously hurt, Reese dialed 911. "Hey, there's a bunch of kids fighting out on Wedding Row in front of Flower Power," he said. "You'd better get here quick," he managed to say before he backed away from the fray.

Knowing he shouldn't get in the position where he might have to defend himself against a minor, Reese stayed put, but when the fight between two of them started to get brutal, he placed his phone and package out of the line of fire and stepped forward. "Knock it off," he shouted, but his words fell on deaf ears. Reese cringed when he heard the sound of a fist connecting with a nose. Not willing to witness anyone get seriously injured, he pulled on the shirt of the attacker and tugged hard.

With an enraged growl the kid turned and took a swing at Reese, connecting with his jaw. Pain exploded in his head and he tasted blood. Reese staggered sideways and hit the ground with a bone-jarring *thud* just as a police cruiser screeched to a halt in front of Flower Power. The teens scattered, but the officers managed to detain a few of them. Out of the corner of his eye Reese spotted Gabby coming around the corner of the building. When she saw the cruiser her eyes widened, and then she turned and spotted Reese.

"Ohmigod." She hurried over and knelt down beside him. "Reese! You're bleeding. Are you okay?"

Reese touched his sore bottom lip with his tongue and cringed. "I'll live," he tried to joke, but he watched her swallow hard and frown.

"You . . . you were in a fight? I'm sorry, but I called the police. . . . What . . . what were you thinking?"

Reese felt his heart start to thud. He scooted the package behind his back. "I was *breaking up* a fight," he answered quietly. He chuckled without humor. "Really, Gabby? You think so little of me?"

She put her fingertips on her mouth. "No . . . I mean, it looked—"

"Save it," he interrupted sadly. "I guess you'll always think that, now that my father is back in town, this is how I'm going to handle my anger."

"No . . . Reese. I'm sorry. I was sleeping and—"

"Gabby . . ." Reese shook his head. "You're in your pajamas. The police are going to ask me for a statement. Go on back inside so you don't have to be a part of this." He picked up his phone and showed her the call to 911. "Just so you believe me. I beat you to the call."

"Of course I believe you."

"Maybe, but I need for you to believe *in me*. There's a big difference."

She reached over and cupped his chin. "Reese, I'm truly sorry. I made a mistake. Please come up and let me get some ice for your lip when you're finished down here, okay?"

Reese nodded, but his mood shifted, saddened. After giving his account to the police, he couldn't bring himself to go up and face Gabby. So she wouldn't worry he sent her a text message telling her he was heading home. When she responded that he should come up, he replied that he needed some time to sort things out.

For the past week his emotions had been on a roller-coaster ride and he decided he needed time to think. He knew one thing for sure. Well, he knew two things. He loved Gabby. But proposing to someone who didn't believe in him wasn't a good idea.

"Reese, what don't you understand about me kicking your ass if you showed up here? You deserve a day off to spend with Gabby."

Reese stopped chopping onions and shrugged.

"Wait. Didn't it go well with her last night?"

Reese shook his head and then relayed the fight incident. "Uncle Tony, I'm beginning to wonder if Gabby will ever fully forget who I was and believe in who I am now."

"Reese, I think you're taking this too hard. You said she'd just woken up and come out to see you bloody and the cops there.... Well, maybe you should give her a break."

"Really? Would you have immediately thought I'd been in the fight?"

Tony started gathering ingredients for a fresh pot of marinara. "I would have assumed that if you were in the fight it would have been for a damned good reason. But ya gotta remember that women are weird when it comes to fights. They never think there's a good reason to throw a punch. I beg to differ."

"So you think I'm overreacting?"

"Yeah, I do. You're overreacting and overthinking. Would ya stop being such a girl?"

"I just thought of a good reason to throw a punch."

Tony chuckled. "Good. That means you've got some fight left in ya."

Tessa pushed through the double doors. "Are you two at it again?"

"Of course," Reese said, and looked at his mother closely. The brackets of tension around her mouth were gone and she seemed more at ease.

"Over what?" Tessa asked, looking from Tony to Reese and back again.

"Get her opinion," Tony suggested.

Reese hesitated but then explained the events of last night. "So, Mom, do you think I overreacted?"

"Yes." She walked over and looked up at his swollen lip.

"See!" Tony slapped his leg.

"Well, guess I was a little emotional because I was going to ask Gabby to marry me," he said. "And then all hell broke loose."

Tessa stepped back and looked at him with a sense of wonder. "To marry you?" She put her hands on her cheeks and did a little wiggle.

"Wow," Tony said. "Of course I'll be your best man."

"You're forgetting I didn't ask her," Reese reminded him.

"Well, then, go do it," Tony urged him.

"Do you have a ring?" Tessa asked.

Reese nodded and then reached down into his pocket. "Want to see it?"

"Of course!" she said, and Tony rushed over as well.

"A diamond daisy! Oh, very art deco. It's lovely. Perfect for Gabby!" She looked up at Reese with tears shining in her eyes.

"It is pretty sweet," Tony said. "Now go ask her."

"No!" Tessa said. "You have to plan something special."

Reese shook his head. "I don't think either of you get it. I'm worried that Gabby doesn't believe in me."

"That's silly," Tessa said. "Of course she does."

Reese stood there looking at them.

"You're being ridiculous," Tony added.

Reese blew out a big breath. "I guess I'm making something simple into something complicated."

"Not really," Tessa answered. "Life is hard, unpredictable, and yes, complicated. I think the trick is to pare it down and try to make it simple. You love her and love doesn't conquer all. . . ." She put her hands on his cheeks. "But it conquers most things. Now think of something special. Memorable. At the scoreboard at the baseball game?"

Reese shook his head. "Too public."

"In her dessert at dinner?" Tony suggested.

"I thought about that one. But then I kind of imagined her swallowing it, so I scrapped that idea."

"Skywriting?" Tessa asked.

"No, didn't you see that commercial where the couple can't catch up to the airplane?" Reese asked, and then snapped his fingers. "I got it."

"What?" they asked in unison.

"I'll deliver it in a pizza box."

"Perfect!" Tessa shouted, and Uncle Tony nodded his agreement.

Reese picked up an empty box and then with sudden inspiration snagged a white paper bag as well.

"I want a full account tomorrow," Tessa said, and gave him a hug.

29

Special Delivery

GABBY ARRANGED LONG-STEMMED ROSES IN A TALL VASE and then slid it over to Joy to add sprigs of baby's breath. There wasn't anything that could cheer Gabby up, not even the latest Bruno Mars song that Joy got up and danced along with.

"Come on, Gabby, shake your groove thing," Joy urged.

Gabby shook her head. "I don't feel like dancing."

Joy stopped and put her hands on her hips. "You need to march down to that pizza parlor and confront Reese. What he's thinking is just silly. You made a little mistake. So what?"

"Yeah, but add this to the fact that he'd stayed away from me for days before that. I just don't get it."

"Sweetie, he was sorting through his feelings. Having his father show up like that had to be hard."

"I know that." Gabby tapped her chest. "But I want to be here for him. That's what couples do for each other."

"Ah, but the mistake is *not* giving the other person space. He needed space, Gabby. And he obviously figured it all out."

Gabby groaned. "And then I jumped to conclusions and messed up."

"We all mess up. Listen, the boy was on the ground bleeding. The police showed up. Cut yourself some slack, for pity's sake."

"I just don't know why it upset him to the point where he didn't even come up to talk to me about it."

"You need to ask him that question. Go on down there."

"I can't just waltz right in."

"Order dinner! It's a restaurant." Joy lifted her chin a notch. "Do you want me to go with you?"

Gabby felt herself smiling. "No, but I love you for asking."

"Oh, Gabby, I do love you to pieces too. I miss your lovely smile and bright laughter. You're one of those people that can just light up a room. I want that light shining again."

"I'll figure it out. But hey, it's getting late and we're all but finished here. I'll sweep up. Is Clyde picking you up?"

"Yes, we're having dinner at Wine and Diner with Miss Patty and Clovis. But I'll cancel if you want company or if you'd like to join us."

"That's sweet of you, Joy, but I'm fine. Well, I'm not fine, but I will be."

"Call or shoot me a text if you need anything at all. Okay?"

"I promise." Gabby smiled. After Joy left, though, she suddenly felt tears fill her eyes, but she blinked them away. Well, almost. One fat tear slid down her face. She sighed as she swept. Maybe Joy was right. Maybe she should just show up and order pizza and see what happened.

Gabby dumped the leaves and stems into the trash and was heading over to lock the front door when she looked up and saw Reese enter the shop.

"Here's your pizza. Pepperoni, mushrooms, and extra cheese."

"I didn't order pizza," Gabby said, but felt breathless at the mere sight of him. She wondered if that feeling would ever go away and then knew the answer. It wouldn't.

"You didn't?" He raised his eyebrows and blinked at her.

"You're a terrible actor." She wanted to smile but wondered just what he was up to.

"Well, I brought it, so you might as well dig in." He walked closer and put the box down on the counter. "It's on the house." He lifted a white bag. "And so is the cannoli." He handed her the bag. "In fact, why don't you eat dessert first?"

Gabby's heart started beating wildly. Something was going on here. "Sure, why not?" She opened the bag, but instead of cannoli, there was a square box wrapped in pretty paper. "Since when do you gift-wrap dessert?"

"When it's for you." He leaned over and kissed her cheek but then stepped back and shoved his fingers through his hair. "I'm sorry about this past week, Gabby. I was working through some stuff. I shouldn't have taken your assumption so seriously. Sometimes that chip on my shoulder is hard to shake."

"No, it's fine. I respect that you needed to sort things out. I hope I didn't overstep my bounds when I gave you advice about your father."

Her reached over and cupped her chin. "There are no bounds for you to overstep, Gabby. There never will be."

She smiled but it trembled.

"Open it."

She nodded and untied the pink ribbon. When she lifted the lid she gasped and then took the necklace out of the box. "It looks like the candy necklace. . . . Oh my, but it's real! Reese, it's simply gorgeous and oh, the meaning behind it."

"It will last forever. Just like my love for you," he said in a husky tone, but then grinned. "And this one won't get sticky on your neck."

Gabby laughed and had to get his help with the clasp because her fingers were shaking. "Thank you so much." She reached up and touched it. "I'll treasure this always." She went up on tiptoe and hugged him. "Reese, I love you so much. Being without you . . ."

He hugged her harder. "Isn't gonna happen anymore. I know we both have our businesses, but hey, I'll even attempt flower arrangements to be with you if you can't break away."

She stepped back and grinned. "And I'll make cannoli. Toss pizza dough in the air. I've always wanted to do that, actually."

Reese chuckled. "Good, now that we have that figured out," he said, and then nodded toward the pizza box. "Are you ready for the main course?"

"Sure," she said, but then suddenly realized that she didn't even get a whiff of pizza. She looked up and met his eyes.

"Open it," he urged softly.

Gabby nodded and opened the lid. She put a hand on her chest when she saw the ring box. "Reese?"

Reese smiled. "I want to do this right." He picked up the ring box and then got down on one knee. "Gabby Goodwin, will you marry me?"

Gabby felt happiness well up in her throat and burst forth with a joyous, decisive "Yes! Reese, I will marry you." When he opened the box she gasped. "Oh . . . oh, it's a daisy. Oh, Reese, I just love it. It's simply gorgeous."

Reese took the ring out of the box and slipped it on her finger. It touched her heart that his fingers also trembled. "Does it fit?"

"Yes. Perfectly!" She raised her hand to show him. A tear slid down her face and then another.

"Happy tears?" He wiped them away with the pad of his thumb.

"Yes, you make me very, *very* happy." She smiled, laughed. "Okay, step back."

He did.

She wiggled her fingers for him go farther and then paused to admire her ring. "Are you ready?"

Reese grinned, knowing what she was going to do. She ran at him, launching herself so hard that when he caught her he stumbled backward. "Still throwing yourself at me, huh?"

"You'd better get used to it."

"I'll never get used to it or take you for granted," Reese promised, and then dipped his head and kissed her while holding her tightly.

Gabby wrapped herself around Reese and melted into his embrace. She felt safe and secure, surrounded by his love. The little boy with the big heart had grown into an amazing man. And in that moment Gabby knew without a doubt that she'd kept her promise to her mother. Reese Marino was her Mr. Strong and Steady and always would be.

Reese rubbed his thumb over her bottom lip. "When do you want to get married, Gabby? Please don't make me wait too long."

Gabby smiled softly. "In the late spring when the scent of the earth is in the air and gardens are being planted. I want to feel the warmth of the sun on my face while we stand in a field of wildflowers and say our vows." She closed her eyes and sighed.

"Ah, a wildflower wedding." Reese captured her mouth in a tender kiss. "Perfect."

Epilogue

Holes in the Floor of Heaven

Nine months later

GABBY STOOD AT THE ENTRANCE TO THE BIG, BEAUTIFUL red barn and everything about her smiled . . . her face, her heart, and her soul. She felt like a fairy-tale princess in her vintage-inspired wedding gown of sheer ivory crinkle chiffon overlaying peach crepe silk. The tiered, ruffled hem, ethereal angel sleeves, and delicate lace edging added a touch of sweet romance. As soon as Addison had seen the dress, she sprinted over to Flower Power and grabbed Gabby for a fitting, knowing the dress was perfect.

Addison and Sara had transformed the rustic interior of the barn into understated elegance. The sheer beauty of it all washed over Gabby, making her glow with happiness. The chairs were draped with white linen tied with fat bows at the back, and sitting in them were all of the people she cared about . . . except for one.

Gabby looked over the field of spring wildflowers where she'd sprinkled her mother's ashes, wishing with all her heart that her mother could be with her right here, right now. Gabby looked at the bouquet she carried, picked in that field, and she smiled softly. The tables for the barn wedding were decorated with wildflowers in Mason jars with raffia bow accents just like the ones Gabby used to bring to her mama. Oh, how she ached for the presence of her mother in this shining moment that represented the beginning of her life with Reese. But she knew her mother would be so happy for her. She had found the right man.

Gabby looked at her husband-to-be, standing at the altar looking so very handsome in the suit that was a replica of the one he'd worn to the dance at Whisper's Edge. Reese caught her gaze and held it and when he smiled Gabby's eyes filled with tears. She remembered Joy sternly telling her not to cry and ruin her makeup and she blinked and sniffed in an effort to ward off the hot moisture threatening to spill down her cheeks. But when Gabby glanced at Joy, her maid of honor, she saw her friend brush at a tear.

Sara had gotten her brother, Jeff, a rising country star, to sing, and instead of the Wedding March, Gabby had chosen "From This Moment," the beautiful song for which Addison had named her bridal boutique.

Tony, the best man, also beamed at Gabby. She smiled back at him and then looked over at Trish, who gazed at Tony with adoring eyes. Although their banter never ended, Tony and Trish were officially a couple and Gabby wouldn't be surprised if they tied the knot someday down the road.

Tessa and Mike didn't sit together, but Gabby caught him looking her way and wondered if their love was strong enough to endure all of the heartache he'd caused. She hoped so. Although Gabby didn't have any blood relatives in attendance, her friends had become her family. She'd grown to love Tessa, who fussed over her like a mother hen and treated her like a daughter already.

Clyde approached her and offered his arm. "Are you ready, Gabby?"

Gabby nodded, so touched when Clyde had said he wanted give her away. She leaned in and whispered, "You look so dashing in your suit. Save me a dance at the reception, okay?"

"With pleasure," Clyde promised with a wide smile.

When Jeff started to sing, Gabby looked over to the field of wildflowers and inhaled a shaky breath, praying that her mother was watching over her wedding. She took Clyde's arm and just as they were stepping into the barn Gabby felt a featherlight sprinkling of rain from the heavens above. Squeezing Clyde's arm tightly, she paused and looked skyward but failed to see a cloud in the sky.

"Happy tears," Gabby whispered, feeling the presence of her mother like a warm embrace. She smiled and then took a step forward into the beautiful barn and her wildflower wedding.

Don't miss the next novel
in LuAnn McLane's charming
Cricket Creek series,

SWEET HARMONY

Available from Signet Eclipse
in October 2014.

1

Dust in the Wind

"RIGHT TURN IN FIVE-POINT-TWO MILES," THE FEMALE voice of Cat's GPS stated with staccato precision.

Although she was tired to the bone, Cat had to grin. "Is it my imagination or do you sound as road weary as me?" Cat glanced at the screen on her dashboard half expecting Rita, the name she'd given the voice, to answer. Earlier, Cat had accused Rita of being a bit tipsy when she sounded as if she were slurring her words.

Cat glanced at the map showing her SUV driving down the two-lane road and sighed with relief. "Yes! I'm almost there." After driving all day from her parents' home in Chicago, she was anxious to reach her destination near the city limits of Cricket Creek, Kentucky. Because Cat wanted solitude for songwriting, her friend Mia had handpicked the location of the log cabin nestled in the woods with a river view from the back deck. Cat knew the cabin was nicely decorated with rustic yet stylish furnishings because Mia had sent dozens of pictures. Cat was also aware that the fridge was fully stocked, including a chilled bottle of Cupcake Chardonnay because Mia had even sent pictures of the contents of the fridge. To say that Mia was excited about Cat's move to Cricket Creek was a vast understatement.

"It sure is pretty here, Rita." The sun was dipping lower in the sky, casting a soft golden glow over cornfields in the early-spring stages of growth. In the distance, tender green leaves made the woods appear fresh, and redbud trees added a splash of bright reddish purple to the landscape. When she passed cows lazily grazing in the grass, Cat waved and offered a tired "Moo."

Although Cat knew she would miss living in Nashville, her switch to small-town life already felt like the right choice. So did leaving Wayside, her big corporate record label, for independent My Way Records in Cricket Creek. But changes, even ones for the better, still held an element of fear that Cat couldn't completely shake.

"In one mile, turn right on Riverview Lane," Rita reminded her.

"It's not soon enough." When the sign appeared, Cat smiled, having been worried that the road out here in the countryside wouldn't be marked. She turned down the dusty gravel lane, and even as weary as she felt, her pulse kicked up a notch. This was going to be her home.

Cat had sold her sprawling home in Brentwood, Tennessee, completely furnished, except for music-industry awards and personal items. She'd donated most of her designer clothes to charity and sent dozens of shoes to Mia's Cricket Creek–based foundation called Heels for Meals. Cat wanted a fresh start, a new beginning—to go back to performing and writing songs for the love of music, not worrying as much about record sales and concert attendance.

A sudden stiff breeze caused dust to kick up, and the field of wildflowers on either side of her started dancing in the wind. I'm going to like living here, Cat thought, and she felt a sense of peace chase away her lingering fear. During the past year of legal entanglements with her record label, selling her home, and ending a toxic relationship, Cat had vowed to keep negativity out of her life. Through it all, her charity work had kept Cat grounded, bringing her some joy, along with the constant reminder that there were those in dire need, which made her own problems seem somehow trivial.

Luckily, Mia had done the legwork with the local Realtor and found the location on Riverview Lane. Not only did Cat trust her best friend's judgment, but the never-ending pictures already had her in love with the quaint cabin.

The fields of flowers gave way to woods, with only fingers of lingering sunlight able to reach down through the trees. Cat knew that there were a few other cabins nestled in the woods, but they were mostly for weekend use by tourists or fishermen putting their boats in Cricket Creek, which led to the Ohio River. So for the most part, Cat should have the solitude she'd been craving for the past year.

"Five Riverview Lane is located on the left. You have arrived."

"Thank goodness," Cat nearly shouted as she pulled up in front of the cabin. After killing the engine, she inhaled a deep breath and then blew out a sigh. Staying up late with her mother and father the previous night was catching up with her, but her parents were heading out of the country to do some charity work. She knew it would be a few weeks before she'd see them again, making her fatigue worth it.

"Oh . . . wow," Cat said when she spotted a doe walking up from the edge of the trees on the opposite side of the lane. Knowing she would frighten it away, Cat sat there for a moment and drank in the deer's quiet, gentle beauty. As she suspected, as soon as she opened her door, the deer bolted, doing a graceful jump back over the gulley, and then disappeared into the woods.

Cat walked around and opened the tailgate of her white SUV, now covered with a light sheen of golden brown dust. She leaned in to drag out her overstuffed suitcase, but the doggone thing barely budged. Thinking of the hearty snacks and chilled wine waiting inside, Cat tugged harder, grunting with the effort. "Apparently, I need to do some lifting at the gym," she grumbled, but then remembered it had taken both Cat and her father to heft the suitcase up into the SUV. With a quick intake of pine-scented air, she braced the heels of her boots into the gravel, grabbed the handle with both hands, and gave the suitcase her best tug.

It worked.

The suitcase slid across the slick tailgate much quicker than Cat had anticipated, making her backpedal, but not nearly fast enough. The painful impact of the heavy luggage smacking into Cat's legs sent her stumbling backward. Her butt hit the gravel with a bone-jarring thud. After a stunned grunt, she uttered a string of words that didn't even fit together, but she was so spitting mad that she continued saying them, adding a random curse word here and there. "Stupid, ye—*ouch*, oversized, damn piece of luggage. Dear God, that hurt. Oh, my shins. . . . Sent from holy hell . . ." She sat there breathing like she'd just run a marathon and then glared at the suitcase as if it were somehow to blame. "Wow, ohhh, that hurt like . . . ohhh. I hope your blasted wheels are broken, you lousy piece of ugly . . ." she whimpered, and then added weakly, "leather . . . *crap*."

Cat desperately wanted to dislodge the luggage from her legs, but all her brain could deal with was the pain shooting up her shins. Rocks bit into her denim-clad butt and both elbows stung. "Don't you know I bruise easily?" She intensified her glare, but then sudden tears welled up in her eyes, and with a little groan, she shoved hair, which had escaped from her ponytail, off of her forehead. Cat considered herself a tough cookie, but this past year had tested her mettle in more ways than one, and in that moment, she threatened to fall to pieces. "This is your new beginning! No damn negativity," she reminded herself, and swallowed hard. "Get a damn grip!"

Cat gritted her teeth, determined to shove the suitcase aside. "Get off me."

But just as she leaned forward, she heard the crunch of gravel and her heart rate increased. Could it be another wild animal from the woods? But this time, instead of a doe, could it be the kind with claws and big teeth?

Before she could turn around to face her fear, the suitcase was suddenly lifted from her legs as if it didn't contain piles of clothing, which had the lid bulging like a muffin top. From her sitting position, Cat looked at scuffed brown cowboy boots and jean-clad legs.

"Hey, are you okay?" His deep-voiced Southern drawl oozed with charm and a hint of concern.

Cat leaned back on her palms and tilted her head up. Wow, he was tall. And even through the pain throbbing in several places, she noted that he filled out his flannel shirt quite nicely. "Define *okay*." She meant it as a joke, but her voice had a slight hitch in it.

"*Okay* as in are you hurt?" The tall cowboy flashed Cat a slight grin, which caused two very cute dimples to appear in cheeks covered in dark stubble, which matched the dark hair clipped close to his head. He had a strong jaw and a straight nose, but it was a full mouth that suddenly captured her attention. "No, really, are you okay?"

"Sorry but I was distracted by . . . ah . . . your sudden appearance." She blinked at him. She wondered if he'd recognize her with her hair pulled back and not a trace of makeup; she hoped he wouldn't. Cat wanted to remain on the down low while she got her life together. "To answer your question . . . um . . . yes."

" '*Yes*', as in okay?"

" '*Yes*' as in hurt. Everywhere. In fact, I think I'm one giant bruise. Where did you come from, anyway?"

He jammed his thumb over his head. "I heard your . . . um . . . rather colorful shouts of distress and decided I needed to jog up here and investigate. So, just bruises?"

"And maybe broken bones." She frowned at her legs.

His grin disappeared and his blue eyes suddenly grew concerned. "Are you serious?"

"Why do people always ask me that? Yes . . . Well, kinda. Oddly enough, I've never had a broken bone, so I don't know, but it sure feels like my legs are crushed." Okay, she might be a teensy bit overdramatic, but she was a singer, an entertainer, and an only child. Drama was in her blood.

"Well, I've had a few broken bones, and believe me, you'd have a pretty good inkling."

"Come on, it was the attack of the killer suitcase. That thing is a monster on wheels. Do you really think I'm overreacting?" she asked with an arch of one eyebrow.

"A little." He gave her a slight grin. "Although that overstuffed monster does weigh a ton." He tilted his head in the direction of the suitcase. When he knelt down beside her, she got a subtle whiff of spicy aftershave, which made her want to lean closer. "So, do you think you can move?"

She made a show of wiggling her toes. "That's a good sign, right?"

He nodded. "Think you can stand up?"

"I'm sort of afraid to try," Cat admitted with a wince. "I think I'll just chill here for a few minutes. Or maybe overnight."

"Out here with coyotes and raccoons?"

Cat glanced toward the woods. "Okay, scratch that idea."

"Do you want me to carry you inside?"

His question made her eyes widen. "No!" Cat replied, but in truth his offer held more than a little bit of appeal.

He held up both hands in surrender. "Gotcha."

Although Cat could be a bit dramatic, she also thrived on being independent, so her unexpected, rather needy reaction to this perfect stranger felt confusing. She blamed it on fatigue. Or maybe low blood sugar. Or maybe she was damn tired of being strong and wanted to lean on a shoulder other than those of her parents, who didn't fully understand what was going on in her life and career. No, it wasn't that last one! Fatigue and hunger were the culprits. She glanced at those wide shoulders. Maybe.

"Well, then, at least let me help you up."

Cat gave him a quick nod, conveying more conviction than she felt, and then accepted his outstretched hands. His grip was warm and strong as he effortlessly tugged her to her feet. Cat was tall and had a solid build, but he suddenly made her feel feminine. He held on after Cat had stood up, presumably to make sure she remained steady on her feet, which she didn't. To her dismay, her legs hurt and her knees felt wobbly.

"The offer remains," he said with a hint of concern.

Cat inhaled a deep breath. "I'll be okay, really." She stiffened her spine. "I've just had a long day of driving, and I pushed too hard to get here. Low blood sugar," she added, but when she pulled her hands from his, she swayed slightly, and he immediately put an arm lightly about her waist.

"Are you sure about that?" His question still held concern, but with a slight hint of amusement.

"I'm fine," Cat insisted. In the cool air, his body felt warm, and she fought the urge to snuggle closer.

"Hey, just let me help you inside. Look, I know we're strangers, but not for long. I live in the cabin just around the bend in the road. My family owns this property, and it butts up to our farm. The local real estate company handles the rentals for us. I didn't realize you'd be moving in, or I would have come over to help earlier. That's the way we do things around here."

"Oh." Cat wondered why Mia hadn't mentioned that she would have a cute country-boy neighbor, but then maybe she didn't know.

"I'm just being a neighbor and a gentleman. I'll bring your suitcase to you once you're inside."

"Okay, thanks. But now that I'm standing, I'm feeling better," she lied. "It was just the initial shock of pain that threw me for a loop. I can make it on my own."

"My mother always told me to err on the side of caution."

"And do you?" She tilted her head up to see his face. There was something familiar about him that she couldn't put her finger on.

"No." Oh, there were those dimples again. "Dare me and I'll do it. It's kind of a country-boy thing."

He helped her up the three steps to the front porch, which Cat knew wrapped around back to overlook the river in the distance. She knew there was a grill, a swing, and a hot tub—all pictures sent from Mia. Unfortunately, her friend had had to head out of town to watch her husband play baseball, or she would have been there to greet Cat. "Oh, I forgot. There is supposed to be a packet with keys and instructions in the mailbox."

"Sit down here in the chair, and I'll go get it for you."

"Thank you." Cat eased into the big wooden rocking chair and watched her neighbor walk across the lawn. While she wanted the cabin in the woods for solitude, it was comforting to know she'd have what seemed to be a nice guy to rely upon nearby, if an emergency occurred. He certainly oozed small-town charm, and she suddenly wondered if he had a girlfriend but then quickly squashed that thought. She was on a mission to switch gears in her music career and didn't need any complications to get in the way.

And yet Cat looked at the flannel stretching across his shoulders and suppressed a sigh. Because she stood at five foot nine, Cat was always attracted to big, tall men. Throw a sexy Southern drawl into the mix, add arresting blue eyes, and he was quite a pleasant package. The dimples and crooked smile were just an added bonus.

Mia had to have known that Cat would find this guy attractive, and she wondered if the location of her rental had anything to do with it. Cat nibbled on the inside of her lip. Surely, her friend wasn't trying to do any matchmaking. Well, if so, Mia's efforts weren't going to work. Although Cat did have an unfortunate knack for ending up with jerks when it came to her boyfriends. Maybe a matchmaker wasn't such a bad idea after all.

Cat watched his long, lazy stride and realized she was staring. She cleared her throat and squared her shoulders. As he approached, she tried to act nonchalant.

"Here you go." He handed her the packet. "By the way, in all of the commotion I forgot to introduce myself. I'm Jeff Greenfield."

"Really?" Cat raised her eyebrows. So *that's* why he seemed so familiar. " 'Outta My Mind with Lovin' You'? I was singing along just a little while ago when it came on the radio. I love the lyrics. Did you write it?"

"I did." Jeff smiled. "Thanks."

"You're with My Way Records."

"Yes . . ." Jeff said, and then tilted his head sideways. "Oh boy, wait. You're Cat Carson." He shoved his fingers through his hair. "Wow, I'm sorry. I can't believe that I didn't recognize you. I guess I was so concerned with you being hurt. . . ."

Cat waved him off. "If you don't mind, I'd like my residence here to be kept under wraps. I'm planning on doing some songwriting, and I'd like some peace and quiet."

"Aren't you with Wayside Records?"

"Not anymore," Cat answered darkly.

"Wait. Did *you* sign with My Way Records?"

Cat paused. "Yes, but keep it quiet, please? Rick wants to make an official announcement after I get some songs written and a single ready to release. He's going to team me up with Maria Sully! I am so thrilled."

"But you just came off of a big year. I don't get why you'd want to switch to a small label when you were with the big dogs."

Cat shrugged. "It's simple. Rick Ruleman will let me take my music in the direction I want it to go."

"Which would be?"

"Less pop sounding and more traditional," Cat answered, and watched for his reaction. He tried to hide it, but she could feel Jeff's slight but sudden withdrawal. She understood. Jeff's music was traditional country, much like legendary George Strait's, and she bet he wasn't a fan of her songs. Old-school country artists often felt as if singers like her were simply jumping on the county bandwagon, and although popular with fans, they weren't taken seriously by the icons in the industry.

"That's . . . um . . . good," Jeff said but shoved his hands in his pockets and his gaze flicked away. "I mean, I do get it. I wanted complete control over my career too."

Cat arched an eyebrow. "So, I have to ask, do you switch the station when one of my songs comes on?"

"No," he answered a bit too quickly. "Why would I do that?"

"Oh, if I might be so bold to ask, do you have a favorite song of mine? Just curious." She gave him an innocent look and waited.

His mouth worked but nothing came out. "Um . . . 'Sail' . . . um . . . 'Moonlight' . . . um . . ."

"'It's a Sail-Away Summer'?" Just because she wanted to go in another direction now didn't mean she wasn't proud of her beach-themed songs, many of which she had written. Cat just didn't want to do them exclusively.

Jeff rocked back on his heels and nodded a bit too hard. "Yes, uh, that one."

"Or did you mean 'Moonlight Dance'?"

"Oh, I like them both."

Cat suspected he liked neither. "Thank you."

Jeff nodded but appeared a bit uncomfortable.

Cat gave him a smile that felt rather stiff. She'd certainly felt the backlash of having her star rise swiftly, making some artists feel as if she hadn't paid her dues. And because her music bridged the gap between pop and country, she had a wide following, much like Sheryl Crow, Kelly Clarkson, Taylor Swift, and Carrie Underwood. When she'd been named female vocalist of the year at the CMA's last year, Cat had felt the heat in more ways than one. That's when she started to reexamine where her life and her career were headed and found the need to make changes.

"You have a huge fan base," Jeff added, as if that would make up for his obvious lack of interest or knowledge of her music.

"I'm lucky to have such loyal listeners." Cat adored her fans and loved her songs, but she was tired of doing the same themes, which were starting to blend together and feel stale. "I don't want to disappoint them, but I'm going to explore more traditional country with a splash of bluegrass," she explained, thinking that admission might change the expression that he was politely trying to hide. Although she'd moved to Nashville three years ago, most people thought she was a city girl from Chicago, where her parents still lived, but she'd spent her childhood in South Carolina. "And get back to my Southern roots."

He only nodded.

"Let me guess." Cat gripped the arms of the chair. "You don't take me seriously."

"I didn't say that."

"You didn't have to."

"Wow." Jeff tilted his head to the side. "So you can read minds?"

"It's written all over your face."

"Really?" Jeff leaned back against the railing. "And maybe you are making assumptions that you shouldn't."

And maybe she was suddenly tired and sore and grumpy. "Right. Listen, I can get things from here."

"Don't be stu—silly. I'll get your suitcase. You'll have a tough time getting it up the steps."

"Watch me," Cat boasted, knowing she sounded stubborn and childish. "Thanks for your help," she added but didn't sound all that thankful. What was wrong with her?

"No way. I won't allow it," Jeff insisted, and turned on his heel.

"'Won't allow it'? Are you kidding me? Did you really just say that?" Cat stood up, but when the blood rushed down her legs, she sucked in a sharp breath. She was going to be so sore tomorrow. She knew she was overreacting, but she'd been pushed around enough for the past year, and she wasn't about to be told what she couldn't do any longer.

Jeff turned around and gave her a concerned frown. Well, she was standing now, so she was invested. Gritting her teeth, she took a tentative step forward. Not too bad. Apparently, she was just going to have massive bruising—not that bruises were anything new. Cat had a knack for running into things. Being tall and gangly all of her life had something to do with it. Her choreography onstage remained minimal for that reason. With a bracing intake of breath, she moved forward, brushing past Jeff, but had to grab onto the handrail for dear life.

"What exactly are you trying to prove?"

More things than she could begin to count. "That I don't need your help." Petulance wasn't in her nature, but she just couldn't stop.

"This sudden burst of anger is all because I don't know your songs?"

Are you that vain? remained unspoken, but Cat felt it when Jeff glanced over at her. She was used to having people make assumptions about her family, her music, and her life in general, when the reality of her daily existence was nothing remotely close to the rumors or gossip. Cat also tended to be outspoken about issues that she believed in and that also sometimes landed her in hot water. She usually had fairly thick skin, but for some reason, Jeff's apparent judgment put her on the defensive.

When he folded his arms across his chest and looked at her expectantly, she refused to dignify his question with an answer.

"Thanks again for your help, but you can leave now. I've got this." Cat felt his eyes on her as she walked stiffly across the lawn to the suitcase. Her legs did hurt in an achy kind of way, but she did her best to ignore the discomfort. Carly Simon's song "Haven't Got Time for the

Pain" filtered into her head, and Cat had to smile. Her mind continually revolved around lyrics, sometimes making her feel as if she were living in her own personal musical. Her brain was a Wikipedia of songs, and she could give anybody a run for the money with music trivia. There was so much more to her than catchy beach tunes, and she longed to prove that she had more depth and talent than people were giving her credit for.

Grabbing the suitcase's handle, she raised it upward and rolled the heavy thing awkwardly across the lawn, hoping Jeff would get bored with the embarrassing situation and decide to leave her to her own devices.

Of course she was wrong. With his arms still folded across his chest, he leaned against the railing looking all smug. And hot. No! Scratch the hot part. Cat paused at the first step, gathering her waning strength. This was silly. She should allow him to help, and yet she couldn't bring herself to give in and ask for it.

After taking a deep breath, Cat muttered a silent prayer, but before she could even begin to try to lift the suitcase, Jeff swiftly descended the steps and grabbed the handle from her.

"Hey!" Cat protested but was secretly so very glad for his help. "I could have managed," she added, trying not to admire his nice butt in his Wrangler jeans.

"I have no doubt." Jeff positioned the suitcase close to the front door and then turned around to face her. "But my mother taught me to be a gentleman. Put some ice on those bruises." He waited until she nodded. "My number is listed in the contacts in the packet. If you need ice packs or anything, please don't hesitate to call, okay?"

"Sure." Cat nodded, but she wasn't about to call him.

He hesitated and then said, "It wasn't my intention to insult you. I'm really not like that."

"And it isn't in my nature to be so stubborn."

"Really?"

"Maybe a teensy bit." She held up her finger and thumb to demonstrate.

His slight grin and the appearance of the damn dimples got to her in ways she couldn't begin to understand. Cat pressed her lips together, suddenly feeling oddly vulnerable, needing a hug so badly that she took a quick step backward and knocked the suitcase over. When it landed with a loud thud, she yelped and then felt supersilly yet again. Cat closed her eyes and sighed. "Look, it's all good," she assured him, but when she attempted a smile, to her horror, it wobbled a bit. She hoped he didn't notice. "It's just been a long day." She faked a yawn. And a long year.

Jeff's expression softened even more, and when he stepped forward, Cat thought for a heart-pounding second that he was going to give her the hug she so sorely needed. But he moved past her and righted the suitcase. Cat swallowed hard and tamped down her disappointment.

"Can I help you get the suitcase or anything else inside?" he asked.

"No, I can manage. Well, from here, anyway. My clumsiness knows no bounds."

"You don't look clumsy."

"Trust me, I can trip over my own shadow. But I've got this from here."

He looked as if were about to protest but then nodded. "Welcome to Cricket Creek, Cat."

"Thank you, Jeff," Cat said, and watched him walk away. She inhaled a deep breath. "Well, that was an interesting little welcome wagon," she whispered, and then reached inside the packet to retrieve her keys and open the door to her new life.

Also available from

LuAnn McLane

MOONLIGHT KISS

The Cricket Creek Series

Investment consultant Reid Greenfield wants to stop his sister from turning their family farm in small-town Kentucky into a wedding reception venue, and he's sure that bridal boutique owner Addison Monroe will be an ally in changing his sister's mind. But having the two of them gang up on him wasn't the plan—especially when he starts falling for Addison...

"No one does Southern love like LuAnn McLane."
—The Romance Dish

Also in the Cricket Creek series

Whisper's Edge
Pitch Perfect
Catch of a Lifetime
Playing for Keeps